In Rhewar of the seven thrones,
The greatest king, of dust and bones,
Has left an empty winter crown:
 With blood one shall find it,
 With honor shall bind it;
Signs of the Seven he must win
Before the Fates will set him in
 The Highest Throne.

A MagicQuest Book

Mont Cant Gold
PAUL R. FISHER

TEMPO BOOKS, NEW YORK

MagicQuest Books by Paul R. Fisher

Mont Cant Gold

The Ash Staff Trilogy
The Ash Staff
The Hawks of Fellheath
The Princess and the Thorn

This Tempo Book contains the complete
text of the original hardcover edition.
It has been completely reset in a typeface
designed for easy reading, and was printed
from new film.

MONT CANT GOLD

A Tempo Book/published by arrangement with
Atheneum Publishers

PRINTING HISTORY
Atheneum edition published 1981
Tempo edition/February 1985

ISBN: 0-441-53602-6

"MagicQuest" and the stylized "MagicQuest" logo are trademarks
belonging to The Berkley Publishing Group.

Tempo Books are published by The Berkley Publishing Group,
200 Madison Avenue, New York, New York 10016.
Tempo Books are registered in the United States Patent Office.
PRINTED IN THE UNITED STATES OF AMERICA

Ynysandra
and the Ynysandra Cycle

This story takes place on Ynysandra, a distant, ocean-coated world dotted with a few medium-sized islands. Each of these is so far from its nearest neighbor that it is almost a world in itself, though a few Ynysandran ships pass from one land to another, carrying legends from island to island.

But Ynysandra's history in some way reflects ours. The island of Rhewar, in the wild western seas, looks almost like certain islands on our planet. But at the same time Rhewar is peculiar: it has seven guardian Fates and a family whose fame has spread through all of Ynysandra, as far as Cavansea and Haersea—a royal House called Mont Cant.

Prologue

On his way to the feast, Rhian Mont Cant stopped. Catching sight of himself in a wall of mirrors, he halted. He intended first only to rescue his medallion from beneath his heavy brown beard, but when he had done so, he did not move on. Twilight-gold mountains, framed in arches along the other side of the vault, took his breath. He had seen such a color of gold before. Many years before.

"Autumn First," he muttered, fingering the medallion. "The mountains go gold."

He raised his head. Shafts of sunlight lit stone arches above the mirrors, where seven cuttings, seven pairs of concentric circles, framed glittering designs. The signs. The signs of the Fates of the West, the seven great guardians of the island of Rhewar. Most brightly lit was the sun of Canrhion, the First Fate. As it should be, for Autumn First was Canrhion's day.

"Cruel Canrhion," Rhian whispered, "cruel, cruel Canrhion." That he should call her such surprised him. She had given him much. But she had taken much away. "Canrhion," he said again.

> *"Canrhion, of the sun a Fate,*
> *We watch thee as the hour grows late:*
> *Gently fall into Erda's arms."*

He finished the verse before he knew he was speaking. The same words, he knew, were being spoken now all over Rhewar. He had himself led candle-bearing throngs to mountaintops to say the words, and the words of the prophecy that followed:

1

> *"In Rhewar of the seven thrones,*
> *The greatest king, of dust and bones,*
> *Has left an empty winter crown:*
> *With blood one shall find it,*
> *With honor shall bind it;*
> *Signs of the Seven he must win*
> *Before the Fates will set him in*
> *The Highest Throne."*

His voice sounded louder in the vault than it had from the mountaintop. But the Fates would not hear it. The Fates, he knew, did not hear words. They heard only deeds. "Cruel," he said again, looking at the other signs. All of them were cruel, as hard and silent as the stones into which their signs had been cut. *They hear only deeds,* he thought again. But his mind spoke with a voice that was not his, a soft voice that spoke as if its owner stood beside him again: "You must not mistake the Fates. They do not love us as well as some say they do. They are passionless and demanding, each one of them. Canrhion offers power, but only after power has been extended in her service. Bran the moon is kind, but only after she has milked the last drop of mercy from us. Serron gives wisdom freely—to those who have bled her dear price for it. Fing, Fate of love, is easy to delight, but her true fire is as hard to find as a lightning-lit blaze in a downpour. Armadon the sea Fate works miraculous change, but only after the change is half-wrought already. Erd sees only his creation, the earth, and is convinced only by the sweat and blood he sees fall on it. And Enrhion. Ah, Enrhion—he of all the Fates is most ruthless, for he demands death and sorrow and gives in return only his dark mark. All of the Fates have been bargaining longer than we have, so their exchanges are often shrewd and bitter." Rhian remembered why he dreaded Autumn First. And especially this Autumn First.

"Father?"

"Ianwy," Rhian said, looking away from the signs. The boy, finely dressed for the feast, had come halfway down the colonnade without Rhian's noticing. He quickly closed the remaining gap between them.

"Father," he said, silver eyes touching Rhian's face. "Are you feeling well?"

Rhian took a deep breath. "Very well."

"You're coming to the feast, then?"

"Of course I am coming to the feast."

"Mother had begun to wonder," Ianwy said, looking at the floor. "She said you might not want to hear Uncle Pinwy's Great Poem."

"Of course I want to hear Pinwy's poem," Rhian said. "He has been working on it for years. The least I can do is spend a night listening to it."

"You don't seem eager," Ianwy said.

They started walking. The light on the mountains was burning away to brown. "I have never been much for poetry, Ianwy."

"That isn't true!" Ianwy said, almost fiercely. "That isn't why you would rather not hear the Great Poem. I know there is another reason. I wish you would tell me what it is."

"It's Autumn First," Rhian returned, "and that should be enough. I have seen far more Autumn Firsts than you have, Ianwy; some I will always remember and some I would as soon forget. But I would much rather have a quiet evening to think about—perhaps the Autumn First after my father died, the first time I climbed Mont Cant, the highest peak in the kingdom of Canys, to say the rites of Canrhion—"

"But that is how Pinwy's poem begins, Father. He read the first part of it to me. It tells how Fach-ne-Canys looked, all surrounded by fog, how it seemed deserted when everyone went to the mountain, how looms were left half-threaded, how cauldrons lay empty in ashes—"

"And how, sweeping up from those moors, Mont Cant went up, seeming to rise from the very doorstep of Fach-ne-Canys itself," Rhian said, looking at the windows again. "The path, shiny with rain, wound up through the forest, up toward the peak." He patted Ianwy's shoulder. "Yes, I have read Pinwy's poem, too. Almost all of it, in fact. And most of it moments after he wrote it. You can't forget that I lived the whole tale he has now put on gold-margined scrolls." Rhian sighed and glanced toward the mountains. "I led the mountain climb for the first time that day. I was a very new king. I was only two or three years older than you are now. It was raining. It always rained in Canys on Autumn First—"

"But you left the clouds behind with the trees," Ianwy said, his eyes flickering up. "The summit of the mountain was clear. It flamed with sunlight and thrust out from the clouds like the hilt of a sword—"

"That was Pinwy's observation," Rhian said. "I simply thought it was windy."

"Was it?"

"Very. It took your breath away."

"According to Pinwy's poem," Ianwy said, "so did your performance of the rites."

"Pinwy overstates things sometimes," Rhian said.

"I wish I could overstate things as well," Ianwy said, staring at him. "That's one reason I wanted to find you before the feast. Pinwy says he will teach me poetry if you say he can. I would like that very much. If I could write verses like Pinwy's—"

"If you could write poetry as well as Pinwy," Rhian said, frowning, "you would have gone through all Pinwy has gone through. He wrote his first poem the night our mother died, and after our father died, he would scarcely come out of his room. I suppose I was envious of the link, through poetry, he still had with our parents. I blamed him for spending so much time at it. I blamed him for other things, too. Ianwyn tried to explain him to me, but I didn't listen. Talwy listened even less, and he gave Pinwy a horrible time about his poems. In fact, it was a fight between them that made me lose my temper with Talwy, a few weeks before Autumn First. He stole a horse from the stables that very night and rode away—"

"To Mont Enrhi?"

"To Mont Enrhi," Rhian said, "though we didn't know that at the time." He sighed. "But that is all part of the Great Poem, and if you and I are to hear it tonight, we should not spoil it for ourselves." Rhian looked away from Ianwy, into the twilight dimness of the corridor. "The Great Poem," he muttered. He fancied memories stirring in the dimness, lifting familiar faces, speaking in familiar voices; familiar shapes brushed past him and touched his mind. He smelled rain again, and the musty odor of sycamore leaves made him see Fach-ne-Canys. It was almost as if it were all beginning again.

I

Canrhion

Mont Enrhi loomed over her sister mountains. No stars broke the night sky, and no sound but wind against stone betrayed itself to the black-robed man who crouched beside his horse.

Talwy glowered as he rose from his haunches. "Blast the Fates!" he growled. His eyes flashed from his hood as he peered down the length of the ancient road, following it southward toward the stark rises of Mont Enrhi, the Black Mountain. He laughed. "I have lost the Canys men—my brother sent fools to track me!" He rubbed his blistered hands against his flanks then touched a scab on his wrist. He laughed again; his laughter fled into the ravines on either side of the road. "They thought," he said, "that they could keep me from my goal. Fools! All of them are fools. Even the Fates are fools when they try to hinder me!"

His face twisting, he seized the horse's reins. "Fates of the West!" he shouted, raising his fist to the sky, "I am Talwy, Magic-son, the mightiest king of Canys! I do not fear you! You cannot touch me, not for all your power." No answer came from the sky, no more than a flicker of lightning, far away and faint, in the north.

He mounted. His horse side-stepped under him, whickering; but he dug his heels into its flanks and forced it into a trot. Mont Enrhi, lit now by occasional lightning, rose ahead.

Then a stab of nearer lightning revealed Talwy and his horse for a split second. His eyes widened with fear; he grimaced to himself, spat on the stones. He began to suck his wrist, prying the scab free with his teeth.

The horse continued to climb, faltering periodically on broken stones. The few trees—most of them winter-splintered alders—fell behind; the soil of Mont Enrhi was soot-colored and rocky. As darkness settled in, the horse's hooves were more unsure; Talwy's eyes, however, seemed to pierce the darkness. They glowed with a faint, dust-colored light.

At length a single star pricked the gloom. It glittered in the southern sky just above the mountain. Talwy cursed it under his breath and concentrated on the warm blood flowing from his wound onto his tongue.

"Blood is strength," he muttered.

Strength. The mountain would give him its power, too. The great journey from Canys was behind him. And he had earned the silent respect of this country through his persistence.

Yet the star mocked him still. It reminded him of things he would rather not remember. Then lightning came again, running through the sky, brilliant light in flood. Thunder followed far behind; he guessed the lightning fell in Bellain Vale. That was good. The Oerth men could pay for hindering him. He hoped tides of fire would burn across their land.

Burning. He felt it in his mind, flaming as it had for now uncounted years. Its spark had been cool and silver at first. Harmless. He had fed it faithfully, though. It had grown slowly to begin with, but it had extended threads of flame into his deepest reaches. Then it had begun to leap up and crackle as he heaped on fuel, until now it blazed with the heat of a smith's forge. It seared through his veins into his fingers, his lips, and finally his eyes until the darkness was no longer a barrier. It let him see Mont Enrhi in all its detail: every wind-gnawed rock, every twisted crevice, every broken ledge of the mountain glowed for him. And he saw at the summit a blood-colored light that took his mind from the star in the south.

The Dark Mountain swallowed the sky as the mare struggled upward. Sheer rises and fingerlike boulders rose to bar his way, but cursing, he urged the horse around them, upward on the ever-steepening slopes.

When the horse halted and resisted his spurs, he dismounted. His feet met rubble with a crunch. As he turned to the mare, she trembled, gasping wearily for air.

He sneered. "At last we part, stupid beast. How glad I will be to be rid of you!" He drew his sword, snatched up the mare's bridle, and with a sudden lunge drove the blade between her forelegs. The mare screamed and reared. He threw himself against her, twisting the sword inward with all his strength, ducking to keep from her hooves. Blood gushed over his arms. The mare faltered backward. She sank to her haunches, then pitched onto her side. Twice her forelegs twitched. Then she lay still.

Talwy withdrew the sword and sheathed it without wiping it clean. He smiled at the body of the horse. Then he started up the mountain again.

Soon he saw nothing but the red light. He could almost hear it; it sounded like a bell tolling a long way off. He could taste it, warm and salty on his tongue. He could sense its throbbing strength, its unending, fateful power. Around it the whole world seemed to revolve.

When the pinprick had become the glare of a hundred high windows, he knew he had at last finished his journey.

He halted and called out, "Sorcerer!"

Darkness answered him with silence. "Enrhi the Dark!" he shouted. "Sorcerer! I, Talwy Mont Cant, have come!" With a creak, the great door opened, spilling fire onto the peak of the mountain.

A voice thundered, "Welcome!" But before Talwy Mont Cant passed the door, he saw the star again, and at the moment of his greatest triumph, a face in his memory tore victory from his grasp, a face framed with red-brown hair, whose clear grey eyes searched for his. He bent nearly double with pain.

He must not feel love before Enrhi the Dark.

2

"Pinwy. May I come in?"

Prince Pinwy, sitting on his bed, did not answer at first. But the voice persisted, so at last he said, "Come in, Ianwyn."

She opened the door, and he felt her grey gaze on him. "Hello," she said. "I'm surprised to find you here. I thought you would be at the feast. Are you feeling well? You seem a little pale."

"I'm always pale," Pinwy said without looking up. He heartily wished his sister would leave him in peace. The gnawing unhappiness that had built in him all day was just dying down to numbness, and he knew Ianwyn would mention Rhian and start the pain all over again. "Ianwyn," he said, "I'm all right. I'm just feeling a little glum, that's all."

"Glum? Why?"

She sat down beside him. He felt her curl her arm around his back, and he peered at her. Her lips drew across her teeth in a way that reminded him of their mother. He blinked and looked at the floor again. The unhappiness—a sharp, senseless kind of unhappiness—was beginning again already. It made him want to run away.

"You don't have to worry, Ianwyn," he said. "You must have a thousand things to do. You don't have to stay. I don't much feel like talking, anyway."

"When you least feel like talking, you need it most," she said.

He stared away at the night fog rolling beyond his window. Sensing her eyes on his neck, he straightened his collar and concentrated on his writing table and its stacks of parchment, tub of ink, and two books, a well-worn thick one and a smaller one bound in leather—a book of poems his father had given him for his birthday. He swallowed an urge to pull away from Ianwyn.

She touched his arm. "I'll bring you an apple from the pantry. An apple won't spoil your appetite for the feast."

"I won't be going to the feast," Pinwy said. "I don't feel like it." He put his elbows on his knees and sank his head into his hands. He thought of running again.

"You aren't going? But the Feast of Autumn First is the best meal you are likely to get at Fach-ne-Canys until spring. Why don't you want to go?"

"It doesn't matter, Ianwyn. Please . . ."

"It does matter. I want to know."

"I wouldn't mind knowing myself," Pinwy snapped, lifting his eyes. "Oh, Ianwyn, it's no use. You know it isn't. Rhian still blames me for Talwy's running away. He still thinks I said something—"

"He thinks no such thing," Ianwyn said.

"He does. He said so on the way up the mountain this afternoon."

Ianwyn shook her head. "Even if he said so, do you think he meant it?"

"How am I to know whether he meant it or not? The climb, in fact," Pinwy said in a lower voice, "is one reason I am glum. It seemed so futile to climb that mountain in the rain, just to chant nonsense!"

"Don't tempt the Fates," Ianwyn cautioned.

"All right, then. It wasn't *nonsense*. It's traditional to go to the top of the mountain every Autumn First to give praise to the First Fate—"

"Canrhlon is the patron Fate of Canys!"

Pinwy threw up his hands. "Yes, all that! But it was so cold and miserable and boring and time-consuming, I didn't even begin a poem today."

Ianwyn patted his knee. "You can always write a poem tomorrow," she pointed out. "Nothing is happening tomorrow. Besides, with the fog, it's cold in here. The King's Hall is much warmer."

"Under Rhian's gaze, perhaps."

"If Rhian's gaze is warm," Ianwyn said, "it's warm with affection."

Pinwy threw back his head and laughed. "Then Talwy was a loving brother."

"Pinwy!" Ianwyn said. "Please!"

"Very well," Pinwy said, standing up. "But don't ignore the truth, Ianwyn. Rhian's truth is a different sort of thing from mine lately; you ought to know that better than anyone else. And the reason I will not go to the feast is that no one will notice me if I am *not* there."

Ianwyn looked at the fog. "I will."

"Of course, *you* will. But you don't count."

"And how am I to feel about that?" Ianwyn said.

"Oh, Ianwyn, you know what I mean. You're different from anyone else I know. You aren't like Rhian, hard and stern and fierce—"

"I would hardly call him fierce," Ianwyn said.

"Because you never see his fierce side," Pinwy returned. "And I don't think you've seen his cold side, either. His cold side is a new invention, specially designed for Pinwy, ever since Pinwy had the pluck to cross Talwy. He's turned his cold side toward me for so long he's forgotten I live in the castle. When I don't come to dinner, *you* scold me. But Rhian doesn't say anything about it. Not anything at all."

"What you must remember," Ianwyn said, "is that Rhian is

king of Canys now. Do you remember how, all summer and even after the autumn rains began, Rhian traveled all over the kingdom, meeting village lords, inspecting royal properties, and giving advice to farmers and herders? Why, you know he spent more than a week just on the Bran frontier, helping gather the Mont Encant sheep after marauders had scattered them—"

"But Rhian isn't chasing sheep now—"

"But he is fully as busy," Ianwyn broke in. "Even if there wasn't this uproar about Talwy's disappearance, which he's been trying to keep quiet, he would have his hands full managing his alliance with the king of Bran and his peace with the king of Serhaur—"

"Admirable," Pinwy muttered, "but chasing sheep and courting kings will get him Canrhion's badge, not mine!"

Ianwyn's eyes flickered. "I don't understand what you mean."

"Besides being patron Fate of Canys, Canrhion is the Fate of kingship. You know that. Rhian may be fulfilling Canrhion's law by sheep-herding and mountain-climbing, but he certainly seems to have forgotten about everything else. You and I, for instance."

"He hasn't forgotten us," Ianwyn said.

"But does he remember us?" Pinwy stared at her. "He perhaps pays more attention to you than he does to me, but he harps on Talwy more than either of us. I have begun to wonder if running off is the only way to have Rhian notice me."

Ianwyn closed her hands together and stood up. "You must try to see Rhian's side of this," she said. "And you really should go to the feast. It should be marvelous." She turned to the door, then glanced back. "Besides," she said, "I will miss you very much if you don't."

He heard her footsteps pause at the door before it closed behind her. For a long time he sat on his bed; then he stood up and went to the window. Outside, fog brushed against the sill and touched the glass like feathers. He saw it twine around stems and tug at needles in the thickets. It lifted and billowed among the hemlocks at the bottom of the hill. For a moment he imagined himself astride a horse, at full gallop away from the castle, into its depths.

He dropped to a seat, snatched up his quill, bit its point, then sank it into his inkpot. Hurriedly he scrawled on a blank parchment:

Riding on the night, fog is my companion

The poem, however, proceeded no further, for he could not think of anything that rhymed with *companion* and had the least thing to do with fog. "Blast!" he exclaimed. He shoved the parchment into a stack of paper between the two books. The would-be verse fell in with the thick ranks of Pinwy's incomplete poems, his First Liners.

He lay down his pen and rocked back in his chair. He imagined the whisper of mist rising against his window and the drip of rainwater from the roof. He had always loved silence, silence like foggy evenings, silence like sleep, silence like faraway, forested countries that might be reached on horseback. More distant sounds soon replaced the nearer, however— the clank of cauldrons in the kitchens, the thump of feet, the trickle of conversation punctuated by laughter. His eyes began to sting.

"He won't win my friendship by being a great king," Pinwy said to himself. But he saw Ianwyn's smile in his memory and heard her say again that she would miss him at the feast.

"All right, then," he said, stopping his inkpot. "The feast it is."

3

When Princess Ianwyn emerged into the courtyard, she found it wet and cold; fog oozed between the bars of the gate and seethed under its footing. It wound down the roofs in pale rivers, eddying around the chimneys, dropping into the arms of the sycamores in the courtyard. Beneath them someone waited, his form blurred in the fog.

She saw it was a village boy, a messenger, still in the cloak he had worn for the mountain climb. He went wide-eyed when he recognized her. Glancing sidelong through the gate, he clutched against his chest something she could not see. "I have a message from travelers for the king," he said.

Ianwyn smiled. "King Rhian is at the feast. If you like, I

will take your letter to him. Your own dinner must be waiting for you."

The boy brightened. "Yes," he said. He took a parchment roll from his jacket, turned it in his hands as if he expected the seal to be broken, then handed it to Ianwyn. "You are very kind, Princess," he said. He turned for the gate but hesitated. "You are quite sure the king will get the message?"

"Quite sure," Ianwyn said.

The boy bowed before starting for the gate. Ianwyn, wishing she were recognized as Ianwyn more often than as a Mont Cant, started for the King's Hall. But something made her hesitate, then turn away. Few messages would come for the king on a feast night, she knew. Few but important messages. And she knew of only one important message Rhian expected.

By the time she reached her tower door, she had fumbled the seal from the parchment. She knew she should not read Rhian's message, so she averted her eyes as she climbed the stairs. But moonlight fell through windows to make milky patches on the stairs, and every time it struck the parchment, she picked up a word or two of the bold hand of the note. So by the time she reached her tower room, she had a fair idea of what the parchment said. As she had expected, it was not pleasant news. Not, at least, for Autumn First.

She groped for a candle, lit it, then moved into her room. Light played on the undersides of the wooden ceiling and on the circular stone walls. Light sprinkled across her bed onto her oak chest. Beside it an old white cat stretched on a braided rug. Above, inside a makeshift cage, a starling, one wing bound, chirruped and fluttered against the bars. While she lit a second candle, a spider descended from the rafters, suspended on a gleaming thread. But she simply moved out of its way, sat down on her bed, and spread the parchment into the candlelight. The cat, after shaking sleep from its legs, mounted the bed and nudged against her arm. She scratched its chin as she reread the message.

"Ianwyn," she whispered to herself, "this is Rhian's business, not yours!" The cat, purring hoarsely, plumed its tail in her face. Taking him into her arms, she knelt on the rug and opened the chest. She pinched some grain from a cup inside and sprinkled it into the starling's cage. "Rhin," she said to the cat as she allowed the starling to peck off the grain that had stuck to her finger, "do you suppose I should..."

The cat did not seem to suppose at all, and Ianwyn placed him on the bed.

"Do you suppose," she said again, "that I could take care of this myself?" She glanced out a circular window at the fog. "After all, Rhian is busy at the feast, and I don't think the treasury has more than a gold piece left in it. That could be embarrassing for Rhian." Ianwyn realized then that she was thinking aloud, a habit she wanted to break. She had, however, made her decision.

She dropped to her knees beside the chest. In it glistened all the oddments she had saved over the years: buttons, thread, poems Pinwy had given her, thimbles, rose petals, her mother's ring, and, buried in a corner, a stack of shimmering gold pieces. She had gotten one every birthday for as long as she could remember. Each of them reminded her of a particular day. But she snatched them up.

The cat, yawning cavernously, curled around her ankles. "I'll bring you something from the feast," she promised, starting to the door. But the cat was asleep before she blew out the candles and stepped onto the stairs.

She saw the gold pieces gleaming heavily in her hand; they felt warm against her fingers. She understood why people loved gold. Though she felt no such desire herself.

She realized on reaching the courtyard that her father had given her the top coin under these very sycamores the year before his death. The weight in her hands was far more than gold.

From the courtyard she could tell the feast was already underway. She heard shouts followed by laughter, and she smelled roasting beef and mutton. She thought of Rhian and hoped he was doing well; he had been worried about his first performance of the rites of Canrhion.

When she came to the gate, the skirt of her gown caught on the gate latch. The rip widened as she worked the skirt from the iron. She shuddered at the rent the snag had made, but she gripped the coins and started down the road toward the lights of the village.

Wind started out of the west, tugging at the swirls of fog and making the hillside thickets rattle. The smell of the sea came in the wind; she sensed it in the sharpness of the air.

Soon the lights of the village fell among the branches of hemlocks, and as the road turned seaward, the lights vanished altogether.

The note, she reflected, had not said how far out on the Armad Road the men would be. She suspected, though, they would wait near the old ruins just beyond the village bridge. There Rhian had first met them. She wished suddenly she had not come alone; the men had made her nervous even when Rhian was with her, and the ruins—she shuddered to think of the great heaps of molding stone, the remnant of some barbarian fortress destroyed in the Winter Wars.

Crossing the plank bridge, she found she was right. Two men, obscured by darkness, waited at the turn of the road. Both men, flanked by horses, were bigger than she remembered them to be. She bit her lip and halted.

"Ho there," the taller of the men shouted, to his companion rather than Ianwyn. "What sort of wench has come to meet us?"

Ianwyn could read neither of their faces in the gloom. "I have come in the place of King Rhian," she said, pinching her voice to keep it from wavering. "I have come to pay for your services."

The second man laughed; his eyes glinted, and he moved nearer. Ianwyn stood her ground. "And what should we think of King Rhian? What kind of king sends his house-wench to pay his men? Get back to your hearth, girl."

"If you want to be paid," Ianwyn said, "you will tell your news to me."

The taller man swore. The other said, "Get back to your fire!"

"To begin with," Ianwyn said, "I don't have a fire. And to end it you won't get your pay unless you give me your message. The King of Canys is at feast, performing the autumn rites."

"Take us to him, then."

Imagining these men breaking in on the feast, Ianwyn grimaced. "The king will not see you," she said.

"More likely the king doesn't want to see us," the taller man growled. "He doesn't want the fancy nobles of his court to know he hired men like us to track his brother halfway across Rhewar. Well, he doesn't thank us by not meeting with us. We have the news he agreed to pay for."

"What the king of Canys does is his own affair," Ianwyn

said. "By the First Fate, you will not disturb his feast. Give me your news, and I will give you your pay. If you go to the King's Hall, you may be paid only with angry words."

The ruffians looked at one another. In spite of the darkness Ianwyn could tell both had just come from the wild; both smelled of sweat, earth, and horses. They spoke with the accent of Oerth, and again she regretted that Rhian had been forced to hire outlanders to follow Talwy. But he had wanted no rumors of the mystery surrounding Talwy's disappearance spreading through Canys.

"Each of you must be enjoying the fog as little as I am. The king is busy, so if you want to speak and be remembered, do so to me. What have you found?"

She sensed their reluctance, like a wall, in the darkness. The taller man cleared his throat then said, "We didn't see any sign of the king's brother beyond the borders of Oerth. He is as cunning as a fox and harder to follow than a crow."

"Talwy was always clever," Ianwyn said under her breath, then out loud, "Then he left Canys?"

"Yes," the second man said. "But we never *saw* him after that. We saw only the trail of rumors and destruction he left behind. People all along the old roads in Oerth had seen a black rider go by. The river farmers were missing food from their pantries. And folk slowed him down just outside Bellonbain. Blood was spilled there."

Steadying herself, Ianwyn asked, "And where from there?"

"We never came near enough to know. No one lives in the Monte Bellain on the edge of Enrhimonte, so we had no news of him, and he left no trail in those black rocks."

"Enrhimonte?" Ianwyn said. She squeezed the gold in her hand. "What could Talwy want in the Black Land? There is sorcery there, or so I have heard. I don't blame you for not following him further."

The men stared at Ianwyn, suddenly silent. One of them touched his beard.

"Where in Enrhimonte did you lose his trail?" she asked.

"Near Mont Enrhi, the dreaded mountain," the first man said, adding with a glint in his eye, "my lady."

"Enrhi," Ianwyn mused. The word was thick on her tongue, out of place like a raven fallen on new snow. A grim understanding set in, but she faced the hireling. "For your pay," she said, "will six gold pieces be enough?"

The man seemed surprised, but he smiled. "More than enough."

"Six gold pieces then," Ianwyn said.

Both edged nearer but with seeming reluctance. "You are most generous, my lady," the second man said.

Ianwyn pressed the coins into his palm. "I am not generous," she said, watching the gold disappear into a bag at the man's belt. "You have the generosity of King Rhian of Canys."

Before she turned to go, Ianwyn saw the first ruffian bow his head. Perhaps he was not as wilderness-hardened and ruthless as he imagined himself. "We will spread the good name of King Rhian of Canys," he said.

4

Mist whirled against the doors of the King's Hall, and inside a fog of seasoned smoke hung among the beams of the ceiling. The clank of crockery, the drum of conversation, and the cadence of laughter filled the room.

The King's Hall, like the rest of the castle, was built of drab stone and fitted with many fireplaces and a few narrow windows. With the perpetual damp cold of the moors, the design was not unpleasant, particularly when the hall was warmly lit. Broad gold tapestries, embroidered with the sun of Canrhion, filled the walls between the fireplaces. Above the dais, above the congested door to the kitchens, was a golden bas-relief of the sun, hung beneath with brown and gold cloth— the colors and the symbol of the House Mont Cant, the ancient and present rulers of Canys.

Rhian, king of Canys, leaned toward Oenan, his chief counselor. "You would think that for the Autumn First feast," he said, "more Mont Cants would be present." He nodded at the two empty chairs on his right and frowned.

Oenan gulped ale from an oak flagon. "Princess Ianwyn will be here," he said. "In fact, I'm surprised she isn't here already. By the Fates, perhaps your sister is helping the kitchen maids with the cooking again."

"That wouldn't surprise me," Rhian said, grinning. But he

frowned and began to thump his fingers on the table. "But it isn't Ianwyn I worry about. It's Pinwy! The way he slinks about! I have to threaten him with his life even to get him to leave his room." But Rhian had told Pinwy how important this feast was, to make an impression on the nobles of the kingdom. Pinwy should understand that much.

Oenan reached a fork to a neighboring platter and brought back a slice of mutton. "Ianwyn says he writes good poetry," he said, "which is more than we might say for the Court Minstrel."

The Court Minstrel, fortunately, was out of hearing.

"Poetry," Rhian said, rolling his eyes. Could Pinwy think of nothing else? He pushed himself back in his chair. Not quite a throne, the seat was carved in a motif of suns. Rhian watched his guests with gray eyes, silver eyes that were as much a sign of the House Mont Cant as the sun of Canrhion. Catching his reflection in an empty platter, he thought he looked far older than seventeen; stubble of a dark blond beard pricked from his chin, half-trimmed. For as it grew, he could never decide whether to let it grow or shave it off; a king should have a beard, but Ianwyn was forever telling him to shave. He envied Oenan at his side, who, bearded and barrel-chested, had more the dimensions of the former king, Rhian's father, than Rhian had.

"Congratulations, sire," Oenan said at length.

"For the success of the feast, you mean?" Rhian said. "I can't take credit for it. Ianwyn arranged it."

"This feast is the best one ever held at Fach-ne-Canys," Oenan said. "But that isn't what I meant."

"What did you mean?"

"The mountain, sire! The rites of Canrhion. After all, your father, King Elevorne (may the Fates preserve his memory) has been gone less than a year. That was your first time leading the trek up the mountain to chant the rites of Canrhion. In my estimation, you did well."

"Did I?"

"Would I flatter you, sire?"

"Would you?"

"Never," Oenan said after a gulp of ale. "You *did* do well. Everyone agrees. Even Toran, I think."

Toran, seated at Oenan's left, looked up. He turned a wrinkled face to Rhian. After studying Rhian's face with small black eyes, he croaked, "Fair enough."

From Toran, that was a compliment. Shaking off Toran's stare, Rhian helped himself to another slice of beef, then dribbled ale into his flagon.

A tap on his shoulder brought his eyes to Ianwyn, who with a tray balanced on one arm, stood beside him. "Come sit down," he said, catching her free arm. "Waiting on the guests is a task for the king's servants, not for the king's sister."

"As usual," Ianwyn said, "you're right. But the servants were all so busy in the kitchen, I had to help them. I'll be back in a minute."

She vanished into the crowd. Rhian wished, suddenly, he had asked her where Pinwy was. He might not see her again soon, perhaps not for the whole evening. "Blast Pinwy," he said to Oenan. "Where in Rhewar—" He stopped himself, for his brother was standing by the doors at the back of the hall.

"At last," Rhian said. "What on earth kept him so long?"

Pinwy, Rhian noted, even now seemed to be in no hurry. He came, head bowed and shoulders slumped, weaving among tables, taking a roundabout route to the dais. His posture straightened momentarily when he saw Ianwyn, but he scowled before taking a seat a chair away from Rhian.

"By the Fates, Pinwy," Rhian said, "you look more like a wounded dog than a prince! Don't just sit there. Eat something. And if it isn't too much trouble, smile a little; this is the greatest feast of the year—we must seem happy! What will the visiting nobles think?"

"Blast what they think," Pinwy said. "Blast your nobles, and blast your kingdom, too!" Turning his head away, he placed his arms on the table.

Rhian pressed his eyes closed and shuddered; he stared at Oenan, who scratched his beard and looked uncomfortable for a long time. "This ale," Oenan said at last, sipping at a newly filled cup, "is the best Canys has ever seen."

"It isn't bad," Rhian said. "But the lamb this year is far better."

"That, too," Oenan said. "For that matter, the beef and pork as well. People are saying this year's harvest will rival the best of legendary years, and not just in wheat—Canys has horses and timber besides pigs and cattle and grain. Your first year as king has been good to us all. You have pleased Canrhion, Fate of mastery and power; our neighbor realms no longer see us as the smallest country in Rhewar—"

"They see our growing power," Toran interrupted, "but mark my words; our fortune will only plague us with spies."

Rhian laughed. "Spies? Here?"

"Here," Toran said. "Perhaps in this very room. You cannot see what I see, Mont Cant. You see only good. But I am old enough to see evil. Boast of your harvests if you will, but know that there are some in Fach-ne-Canys who wish Rhian Mont Cant no good."

Rhian's mind swept over the people of his kingdom he had met in the last few months, but not even in the roughest farmer's face did he read treachery. "Who?" he demanded.

"Your brother was one."

"Talwy is gone," Rhian said, suppressing a spark of fear.

"Gone, Mont Cant, but not forgotten. And not gone forever." Toran smiled slightly. "And there are others."

"Others? Who?"

Toran drew his collar to his throat. "Others," he repeated, "others. Perhaps the new page you hired from the village. His father lost a smithy in Fach-ne-Armad through an order from your father. Bitterness glitters in his eyes, even if you are blind to it."

"He was cordial enough with me," Rhian said.

"With lips, perhaps. But do not read lips. Read eyes."

Oenan, who in the meantime had moved his chair and was looking from Rhian to Toran, stood up. "Men of Canys!" he shouted, thumping his flagon to the table. "Men of Canys, hear me!" The roar of conversation crested, receded, then washed into silence. Ianwyn slipped to a seat between her brothers.

"Men of Canys," Oenan said again. "The watches are rapidly passing toward dawn, and if you have eaten half as much as I have, you will have to roll yourselves home."

A stuffed but contented silence followed.

"Because some of you want to sleep before morning, I stand to propose a last salute to our king." The crowd, Ianwyn, Toran, and even Pinwy, stood up. Rhian's cheeks burned as he sat back in his chair, feeling eyes turn toward him.

Then, under Oenan's leadership, the cheers began. "Hail King Rhian, Lord of Canys! Three shouts for the King of Canys and the House Mont Cant! Seven shouts for the Seven Fates, and may they keep our lord ever strong!" The cheers, the applause, the shouts joined with squeals and whistles from the younger members of the crowd and from those who agreed with Oenan's view of Canys ale. In spite of himself, Rhian felt his cheeks flushing.

"Thank you," he said when the shouting had died down. "Thank you all. May the Fates preserve you, too. May the Fates preserve all of us, and our worthy kingdom."

At this point, Rhian noticed that those who had been fidgeting in front of empty plates quietly rose and slipped out the doors. As the hall began to empty, those lingering in hope of another helping began to leave as well. Soon only the people on the dais remained.

Rhian took a deep breath, then sighed. "I'm glad *that's* over. I thought the feast might last forever."

"Over?" Ianwyn said, standing up. "Finished? What about the mess? What about the dishes?" She vanished into the kitchens.

"If I may say so, sire," Oenan began, "I don't think it's proper to have your sister doing dishes and sweeping up with the servants."

"Of course, it isn't," Rhian said. "But have *you* tried to stop her?"

"She *is* strong-willed when she wants to be."

"Strong-willed?" Rhian said. *"Impossible* is the word I would use. But nicely impossible, don't you think?"

Oenan nodded. Toran, clutching the back of his chair with a crooked hand, pushed himself to his feet.

"By the Fates!" Rhian exclaimed. "Where has Pinwy gone? He was there just a moment ago."

"It seems," Oenan broke in, "that both of your siblings are impossible. But then again, you are rather impossible yourself. Nicely impossible, to borrow your own words." He picked up his cup, turned it in his hands, then went on, "In fact, with fewer ears open nearby, I would venture to say, after the job you did today, that you may be the greatest king the House Mont Cant has seen since Dorhan the Golden."

Rhian blinked hopefully, but burst into laughter. "You do flatter me."

"I am quite serious, Your Majesty." Oenan's lips hardened beneath his beard. "Your father, King Elevorne, once told me, when you were still very young, that if any king was to sit in the great throne and rule Rhewar, you would be he. He may be right."

"You have had too much ale," Rhian said. But he hoped Oenan would go on.

"True. But I mean quite soberly that you could become the Great King of all Rhewar."

"That's impossible."

"I said just now that *you* were impossible," Oenan said. "You and the great throne would get along well, I think."

"But there has been no king of this island for five hundred years," Rhian said. Oenan had gone a step too far.

"Seven kingdoms have been too long under their own kings to accept a great king," Toran said, his eyes dull like lead. "This island will not be whole again unless the Fates intervene. Mont Cant, you heard the words you said on the mountain. No human power will create the great king when his day comes. Only the power of the Fates can set him in the highest throne." The words of the prophecy returned to Rhian as Toran spoke them:

> *"In Rhewar of the seven thrones,*
> *The greatest king, of dust and bones,*
> *Has left an empty winter crown:*
> *With blood one shall find it,*
> *With honor shall bind it;*
> *Signs of the Seven he must win*
> *Before the Fates will set him in*
> *The Highest Throne."*

"Superstitions," Oenan said under his breath.

Toran's eyes flamed. "May the Fates forgive you, Oenan-ne-Fach, for those are their words. When a man earns their approval, when he through deeds and sacrifices earns their seven signs, and only then, will a new great king rise in Rhewar. And when that time comes, that man will need no cattle or harvests or flattery or swords. The Fates will fight his battles for him."

"In other words, you think that no man will come to the throne," Oenan said. "No man has earned even one of these 'signs,' none, at least, that I know of. Certainly no one has earned seven."

"Then you take my meaning," Toran said. He straightened himself, threw a glance at Rhian, then hobbled away.

"Serpent," Oenan muttered after him.

"A wise snake," Rhian said. "I will not take anything he says too lightly. You know as well as I do, Oenan, that your talk about the great throne was farfetched."

Oenan sighed. "But I meant every word of it."

"It was a pleasant notion," Rhian said. "I appreciate your confidence in me, but I have a hard time ruling Canys without having to worry about all of Rhewar." He remembered riding through his kingdom earlier that autumn, how vast it had all seemed, how long it had taken him to reach the remote villages. Canys was indeed challenge enough to rule.

Ianwyn emerged from the kitchens, her arms ringed with suds. "As long as you two are sitting here," she said, pushing her hair back, "maybe you'd like to help me clean the cookpots. The conversation is just as good, and the room is warmer."

"As I was saying," Oenan told Rhian, "I can hardly keep my eyes open. I'll see both of you in the morning."

Ianwyn smiled. "Good night, Oenan. May the ale you've drunk be kind to you."

When Oenan had gone, Ianwyn turned to Rhian. "Well? Are you going to help us or not? Naturally you don't have to. But we haven't even begun to clear the tables. The servants will be working till noon tomorrow."

Rhian pushed his chair back, stood up, and glared at Ianwyn. He caught her hand when she reached to load a tray with empty goblets. "You, Ianwyn, are going to bed. I have decided you shouldn't be doing dishes."

"And why not?"

"Because I say so," Rhian said. "You're not going to sneak back and help, either. I'm going to walk you back to your tower."

Ianwyn opened her mouth but closed it again. She peeled off her apron, then followed Rhian toward the door. But after only a few steps, she darted back and took an apple and a lamb chop from the apron pocket. The chop was for her cat, Rhian knew, and the apple—it could be for almost anyone. Since the apple harvest, Ianwyn had given away so many apples she had earned the nickname Appletree. She had always found the name amusing.

They stepped through the door into soft night shadows. While Rhian fixed the bolt, Ianwyn stood watching the gate and beyond, the faint, flushed rumor of dawn that had touched the sky with gold.

"I have something to tell you," Ianwyn said. "Something about the trackers you sent after our brother."

"You mean after Talwy."

"He is still our brother," she said. "Rhian, he is your twin."

Rhian looked away.

"I met the trackers," Ianwyn said. "I met them because I received their message to you. I'm sorry, but I didn't want them to disturb the feast. They told me . . . they said they followed Talwy through Oerth and into the heartland of Enrhimonte. They lost his trail in the mountains—"

"That is just as well. He can't do mischief in that empty country." Rhian swallowed. "I have decided, with some difficulty, we should forget about him as much as possible. If we forget, maybe we can forgive."

"But Enrhimonte isn't empty. Rhian, there are powers there that have survived the five hundred years since the last king sat in the great throne. One of the trackers mentioned Mont Enrhi itself."

Rhian laughed. "Don't tell me you believe in the Dark Wizard of Mont Enrhi. You don't think Talwy would bring dark magic against us, even if such a thing existed. Certainly, he was bitter—he had a dark heart—but *sorcery?* Even Talwy wouldn't resort to whatever tatters of power remain at Mont Enrhi."

"Then you don't know Talwy as well as you pretend," Ianwyn said. "You called Talwy bitter. Indeed he was. But he was far more than that. Talwy was, and continues to be, evil."

"Not all evil, certainly."

"Oh, not completely. No one is completely evil. But in the months before Talwy left, I saw him maim his good self until his good side no longer had say in what he did. Even before you became suspicious of him, Rhian, he hated you enough to kill you. I cannot hate him, even now, but I fear him. And I dread what he can do."

Rhian did not answer.

She searched his face. "I'm sorry," she said. "I should keep to dishes."

"Oh no," Rhian said, "you shouldn't. The dishes don't deserve you. And perhaps," he added, "neither do I. You're quite right. Toran said the same thing. I have not lived long enough to see evil in people, as Toran does, and I have lived too long to see only the good—when evil is overt. And you, Ianwyn;

you are two years younger than I am, but without your wisdom I would have perished in my first week of being king."

"Those times were hard for us all," Ianwyn said. "And knowing your weakness, doesn't that make you stronger? That is one of Canrhion's laws, isn't it?"

Looking at her, Rhian decided she was beautiful. He had always loved her, from the very moment her face first peered from his mother's lap. And he could remember others of her faces: a face freckled with sun and dimpled with laughter, and an odd face, a mere glimpse of it, pale and streaked with tears, from the night their mother Queen Amnewyn had died. But the face Ianwyn wore now was serene and beautiful.

"You have pleased both Fates and men today," she said. "Pinwy says you please Canrhion because you are a good king."

He did not answer. Early morning sounds—the barking of dogs, the distant squeaking of beds—began to drift into the courtyard.

"You *are* a good king," she said.

"I am Canys," Rhian said simply. "I am nothing more. I am good only when Canys is good. But I am a lucky king. Lucky enough to have you as my sister."

"That isn't luck."

"But you bring luck, Ianwyn. The trackers I hired, for example. They could have demanded as much as four gold pieces for following Talwy, and since we collected no taxes from the sea villages because of the tempest, the treasury is empty. I could never have paid those trackers. But they seem to have disappeared . . ."

"Luck, indeed," Ianwyn said.

"Also," Rhian went on, trying to sound indifferent, "the harvest this year has been good. Oenan said that with such luck I might someday become king of all Rhewar—" He had meant to mention cows and ale rather than the high throne. He cut himself short.

"All you need," she said, "are signs from the Seven in the West. If luck is real, it comes from the Fates."

"Please," Rhian said, closing his eyes. "Forget what I said. I have been too proud to be king of Canys today. I have begun to imagine things. I trust, though," he added, patting her arm, "that you will do no more dishes tonight."

Ianwyn nodded. She turned toward the tower. But suddenly she stopped, froze, then pointed toward the gate, her eyes widening. At first Rhian saw nothing but the rim of the sun through the gate. Streaking amber across the sky, it rose into a circular frame formed by the curve of the hills and the arch of the gate.

Seizing Rhian's arm, Ianwyn whispered, "Rhian, it's a sign! Look, Rhian! Canrhion gives her sign! The sun in a circle. The First Fate shows her sign!"

Like the suns stamped on the Mont Cant coat of arms, the sun blazed from its dark circle as if it had been branded on the sky.

II
Bran

The next day was almost warm. In the vigorous sun, gray leaves blushed back to green, and flocks of starlings clouded from thickets and warbled from walls and trees. There seemed to be no one in Fach-ne-Canys or in the village who did not step out to sample the air and squint at the clear sky. And, except for Pinwy and Ianwyn's caged starling, everyone at the castle found excuses to be out.

The uncommon warmth, it seemed, came from the east wind, the wind Rhian and his kingdom loved best. Looking over the dry expanse of moors toward the sea, Rhian stood on the meadow in front of the gate, wondering whether people in the windows of the castle were watching him put on his breastplate.

"By the Fates, Ander, that hurts!"

"I almost have it buckled," the War Lord said. "Steady now."

The grass, strewn with armor and weapons, gave Rhian no real foothold; it was slick with dew in spite of the east wind. "I would almost rather be stabbed than put this nonsense on," Rhian said, glaring at the War Lord. "I feel silly enough dressing in a tunic and robe for feasts, but this is worse." The breastplate was heavy and hot.

"This armor was your father's and his father's before that. You don't have a choice whether you wear it or not. It's traditional. And as long as you are King Mont Cant, you had better get used to fighting with it on."

By this time the regalia was nearly complete: Rhian wore a bronze plate on his chest and one on each of his knees. All were stamped with the sun of Canrhion. A gold battle cape brushed the ground behind him, and a helm, meant to be close-fitting, wobbled on his head. "Beastly stuff," he brooded. "How I hate it. Talwy loved it, you know. He always wanted to put it on. I wish he had stolen it."

The War Lord, in his own armor, stepped back and frowned. "I will admit you looked better at the feast."

"Feasting is always better than fighting."

"A good king must do both," the War Lord said. "And you need practice."

Rhian smiled sourly. "Sticks first?" He pointed to a pair of oak rods lying on the grass.

"I don't want to lose an arm just because you aren't warmed up. Yes, sticks first, of course." The War Lord seized a rod from the grass and batted it against Rhian's breastplate, which rang dully.

"That isn't fair," Rhian said. "You didn't say we were starting. Besides, I can't bend down to pick up a stick."

The War Lord scooped up the other stick, tossed it to Rhian, then sprang back. "In a real battle," he said, "are you going to tell your enemy you weren't ready?"

"In a real battle," Rhian returned, "would I be buckling on my armor with an enemy standing beside me?"

For an answer, the War Lord prodded Rhian with his stick.

But this time Rhian leaped forward and pushed his stick under the War Lord's guard. The War Lord jumped back, and the fray began, each of them taking turns striking, blocking, parrying, swiping at legs, and stabbing at breastplates. Sounds of wood against wood and occasionally of wood against metal fled across the field toward the castle.

From the outset Rhian knew the War Lord had the advantage. Ander was older and more experienced. He anticipated every strike; no blow passed his guard. Rhian, however, had some pride in his ability to fight—he was after all king, and if he wanted to defend his kingdom, he had to be, to some degree, a warrior. He soon brought his height to bear; he hovered above the War Lord, aiming each stroke at the man's helmet or shoulders.

The War Lord, breathing hard, finally called a halt. He thrust his stick into the soft earth and crumpled over it. Puffing, Rhian threw down his stick and doffed his helmet to let the wind dry his hair.

"You aren't bad," the War Lord wheezed at length, "especially considering you are a Mont Cant. I would have an easier time serving almost any other royal house in Rhewar. I am sometimes tempted to shift my loyalty. A louty bunch of warriors your family has always been."

"Unwarlike," Rhian said.

The War Lord only muttered something about not being as young as he once was. Then he sat down on the grass.

When Rhian saw that a crowd had gathered at the gate, he felt satisfaction at having been the one left standing. He hoped Ianwyn had been watching. He had told her he was going to practice swordplay, and he knew she would be impressed by his victory.

He did not see Ianwyn, but he saw Oenan, who strode across the meadow. Oenan wore a comfortable-looking homespun outfit, threadbare at the elbows. The wind fluffed his beard and pushed his hair back from his eyes. "A fine day for fencing," he said. He acknowledged the War Lord with a nod.

"Fine, indeed," the War Lord said. "I wish I were fencing in Serhaur, where they make real warriors."

Rhian faced Oenan. "It is hot in this armor. How can I enjoy the weather when I am caged in bronze? But Oenan—you didn't come here to comment on the weather."

"No, I didn't," Oenan said. "But the matter is not worth interrupting your match."

"I interrupted my own match," Rhian said. "Now what is it?"

Oenan grinned. "I have news from Bran, sire."

Bran? For a moment Rhian was confused. Bran was the name for both the moon and for the Second Fate, Fate of the moon and kindness. But Bran's third meaning—the country to the north of Canys—was undoubtedly what Oenan meant. Word from Bran, in fact, was quite common. Over the centuries the House Mont Cant had both quarreled and allied itself with the House Branmawr, with equally disastrous results. Rhian's own great-grandfather, Canhawr Mont Cant, had lost the island of Cae Tal to Bran through one of these arrangements. At present Bran and Canys were at peace, for Rhian, since he was only months old, had been betrothed to the Bran princess.

"The princess?" Rhian said. He did not often think about his future marriage; like breathing, it was not something he kept in his mind.

"Political arrangements," the War Lord snarled. "Treachery!"

"Would you rather have the Winter Wars all over again?" Oenan said. "Or do you *want* war with Bran?"

"Blast wars," Rhian broke in. "What is the news?"

"A messenger came a few minutes ago," Oenan said. "He brought a letter from Princess Sereniel asking if she may come to Fach-ne-Canys." Oenan handed Rhian a parchment scroll. "She would like to meet you this autumn, before your wedding at Branfach next spring."

Rhian read a few lines of a thin, graceful script. He suppressed an odd tingling in his stomach. "We hardly need to meet," he said. "But if she wants to come, the winter may be more interesting. We can have a feast—"

"Feasts cost too much," the War Lord said. "Our treasury is short on plunder."

Rhian ignored him. "Does the letter say when the princess will come?"

"Read for yourself," Oenan said.

Rhian read swiftly, then handed the scroll back to Oenan. "A fortnight is not much time to arrange for her stay."

"We will need to have a welcome at the village gate," Oenan said.

"We must prepare our warriors for review," the War Lord said. "And don't forget," he added sourly, "to give her presents."

"Since when are you interested in such arrangements?" Oenan said.

The War Lord bared his teeth. "I don't care whether the princess is comfortable or not, if that is what you mean. I only know that if she marries the king, Canys and Bran will be joined into one kingdom. And King Caldwy Branmawr's Crescent Knights (not to mention his ships, when his death makes his daughter his heir) will be under my—er, under King Rhian's command. Then the other kingdoms will fear us. Even Armei might think twice about attacking us!"

"That," a voice from behind Rhian said, "is why spies from Armei and other kingdoms are already among us." Turning, Rhian saw Toran, who was wrapped in his black robe. His eyes glinted in the shadow of his hood. "Armei will do anything to prevent the marriage of Rhian Mont Cant and Sereniel Branmawr."

"You think too much of spies, old man," the War Lord growled.

"And you too little."

The War Lord threw up his hands. "Save me from the Mont Cants and their hearthside counselors. I have heard enough of betrothals and spies. Listen to me, all of you. If we want the power of Canys to grow, we must fight. Raid Serhaur. Harry the borders of Oerth. Plunder our neighbors. Do any of you know how many years have gone by since even one of our warbands crossed the border?"

"Yes," Rhian said.

The War Lord glared at him. "Rhian Mont Cant, you want to become a great king. I feel it. I see it in your face. Behind those quiet, gray Mont Cant eyes, you want to be great. You want to be more than another name linking the first Mont Cant to the future Mont Cants. Conquest is the way, Rhian Mont Cant. Conquest! You have not raided the hill-folk of Bran— they grow rich! A king who does not go to the summer wars will soon lose his kingdom. Or, forget summer campaigns. Now the weather is good. You can call up a warband today and cross into the breadlands of Oerth before winter."

Chill silence swallowed the War Lord's last word.

Oenan spoke with worn grimness. "My lord, do you want another two hundred years of the Winter Wars? Do you want to see blood spilled in oceans, men fall like autumn leaves? Be careful what you say!"

"I will," the War Lord said, "when I speak to cowards and fools. I have served the House Mont Cant for many years. I have been faithful. But I will be silent no longer; as War Lord I demand to be heard. I demand to do battle—for the king. Keep me too long out of my profession, and I will have to find work elsewhere—perhaps against the king."

"No more talk of battle," Rhian said, glaring at him. "I, too, do not want war, winter or otherwise. For right now, I would rather finish my sword practice so I can take this armor off and see Ianwyn about arrangements for the princess of Bran's visit. You three, with your talk of plunder and spies and alliances, are enough to make even the east wind feel cold." Rhian glared at each of them in turn, but less severely at Oenan.

"Mark my words, Mont Cant," Toran said, "Armei will have spies thick within our walls for the arrival of Princess Sereniel. A wise king will sharpen his eyes."

"And his wits," the War Lord murmured.

Long after Toran had made his way to the gate, Rhian turned to Oenan. "And what do *you* think about spies?" he asked.

"Today is too fine a day to worry about them. If I were you, sire, I would pay no attention to Toran."

"If you aren't going to heed any of our counsel," the War Lord said huskily, "the least you can do is ready yourself for battle, in case, by providence, the Fates take us to war." The War Lord unsheathed his sword.

"Blast," Rhian said. "I must not have been awake when I went to the armory this morning." He pointed to the grass. The sun caught the gem-crusted hilt of a huge broadsword.

"The Sword of Dorhan!" Oenan exclaimed.

"Hardly a sword to use in practice," Rhian said. "I was looking for the sword I used last summer, but the armory was dark . . ." Rhian frowned; the Sword of Dorhan was the ancient weapon the Mont Cants for generations had been presented with at coronations and had worn only in battle. The second king of the House Mont Cant, Dorhan the Golden, had worn the sword in the closing battles of the Winter Wars.

"I will find another sword," he said.

"Whatever for?" the War Lord said. "The sword is as good for practice as any. Unless Your Majesty is trying to avoid practicing . . ."

"But I'm not used to the sword," Rhian objected. "And it's so . . . bulky. And no Mont Cant has ever used it in *practice*."

"Then it is time one did," the War Lord said. "Save me from the Mont Cants and their cursed logic! May I remind you—"

Oenan broke in, "I will be happy to bring Rhian another sword. You don't have to go to the armory in all your trappings. You are right; the sword is for battles, not for practice." Oenan reached for the sword, but the War Lord shook his head at him, so Oenan started back toward the castle without it.

"I won't wait until he comes back with the other sword," the War Lord said. "We will never practice if we wait. Pick up the sword, Your Majesty, and let's begin."

Rhian hesitated, but when the War Lord glared at him, he stooped and took the Sword of Dorhan from its sheath. As he raised it toward the sun, it wobbled in his hand as though someone had welded lead to its tip. He could not steady the sword even when the War Lord struck the first blow. The sword seemed too heavy to wield easily.

The War Lord charged before Rhian was ready. Rhian parried, but his arm buckled, and with a wooden-sounding smack, the War Lord knocked him backwards. His boot caught on a tussock, and he landed on the grass.

"Get up, get up!" the War Lord yelled. "Don't just sit there!"

"But the sword!" Rhian said. "I can't—"

The battle, however, began again after the War Lord pulled Rhian to his feet. Rhian struck forward, but the War Lord met his attack; the din attracted a crowd at the castle gate. Between strokes Rhian saw Oenan running toward them, yelling something.

But Rhian had no time to listen. Neither he nor the War Lord held back now, and each crash of their swords rang more loudly. Then, the sword clanged dully, shuddered, then shattered. Rhian pitched backwards. The War Lord's sword crashed against his breastplate. The hilt of the sword whirled from his hand.

Blackness closed in. Pain sprang in Rhian's shoulder then in his wrist. The sun blurred. Shouting drummed in his ears. He staggered, dropped to one knee, then fell into the grass. He saw distorted shapes of men gathering around him, shouting to him. Ianwyn swung into view, her face pale. She fell to his side and began worrying at the bindings of his armor. In the murmur of the gathering crowd, he heard two voices.

"But I tell you, it shouldn't have broken!" The War Lord.

"It should not have been used at all." Oenan's voice, with an unusual touch of scorn and fear. "The king may be hurt."

"Listen to me. I know about swords. I am the War Lord! And that blade was forged of the finest Fingonlain steel. It shouldn't have broken!"

A lull in the argument followed, during which the sound of the crowd grew to a roar. With his mind reeling from heat and pain, Rhian saw only Ianwyn biting her lip as she watched something he could not see. The last word Rhian heard before his mind darkened was a single, almost incomprehensible syllable: "Lead!"

2

A lantern lit most of the King's Hall; it shone from among half a dozen men hunched around the dais table. Ianwyn thought the group would be more appropriate to a council of war; not one of the men smiled. She felt her own cheeks tighten as she looked at her brother, at his golden tunic drawn aside to show a cumbersome bandage beneath it.

"Let's get on with it," the War Lord said. "It won't do us any good to sit here and brood over what has happened. We have to act. Somebody—and we have to find out who—reforged the king's sword, intending, of course, for it to break in the next battle the king fought. Someone," he said, "wanted the king to die."

"Certainly you don't believe anyone remade the sword intending King Rhian any harm—"

"Oenan is right," Rhian said. "It's unfortunate that the sword shattered, but I can't believe anyone would want me to die. I have no enemies, no *real* enemies. I'm too young to have made any. Who would want to kill me?"

"There are those who hate Rhian," the War Lord said. "But there are more who hate *King* Rhian, or Rhian Mont Cant—" His eyes glinted.

"Your House has made many enemies," Toran said from the shadows. "The Mont Cants may not often have been warlike, but they earned the hatred of many even so." He spat. "Your own father, Elevorne (may the Fates keep him in their clutches), had a hundred slain, a hundred outlaws, traitors, assassins, thieves, and murderers; all of them have relatives with long memories. And there are spies. Remember the spies, Mont Cant. Every land in Rhewar has a spy here in Canys. Perhaps even at this table."

"What you say is mad, old man," the War Lord said. "You imagine too much—as all Mont Cant counselors do!"

"Enough!" Rhian said. His eyes flashed into a rage that reminded Ianwyn of her father. "There is no one in my kingdom whom I count as my enemy. Why should anyone quarrel with me? I can't help what my ancestors did or didn't do."

Ianwyn nodded in solemn agreement.

But the War Lord's eyes glittered. "Your Majesty is very young, and such words show it. Whether you know it or not, King Rhian, there are those who would love to see you fall on the battlefield. And had that sword not broken this afternoon, had you been slain on a campaign on the moors, we might never have known what happened. Whoever reforged the sword was quite clever."

"He may elude us easily," Oenan said.

"Who has the keys to the armory, Lord Oenan?" Toran asked.

Oenan only shrugged. "I will swear by the Fates I have given them to no one but the pages—"

Toran laughed. "I think," he said, "we have found our villain already." Toran turned to Rhian. "The newest page, Mont Cant! I warned you about him. Your father made enemies of his family."

"But he is so young," Rhian said. "He can't be more than twelve."

"Other minds directed his treachery," Toran said.

"And other fingers." The War Lord landed a thick fist on the table. "I have examined the sword—it was first broken by a hammer, then welded together again with lead. Only the strongest smith and the hottest forge could do that."

"Then today's deviltry must have been made a long time ago, for only I have keys to the forges," Oenan said. "Sire, I think we should forget what happened. The page could not have done this, no matter how his parents might hate the House Mont Cant. If indeed there is a plot, it is a very old one and dead one."

The War Lord pushed back his chair. Uneasiness began to collect around the lantern. Ianwyn saw that Toran was watching her from across the table.

"Wait," he said. "Not all the shadows have been searched. I have read treason in the page's eyes before now. Tell us something, Princess Ianwyn. What does the boy's father do in the village?"

"He is the village blacksmith—" Ianwyn began, but she cut herself short.

All of them looked at her. "We have our traitor," Toran said.

The War Lord nodded. "One of them," he grunted. He glared at Rhian.

Rhian looked at Oenan, but he offered no objection; he only muttered something under his breath. Rhian hesitated.

"The penalty for such a deed is death," the War Lord said. "Not only for the page but for his father as well."

Ianwyn felt a twinge of pain. She did not know the page well; he was a small boy, tightly built and darkly featured. She had given him an apple once, but he had never smiled. She somehow felt responsible for his condemnation. Lest she show her feelings, when Rhian looked at her, she made her face blank.

All of them looked at Rhian. Though Ianwyn sensed his thoughts, she could not guess what he would say. He touched his bandaged shoulder before speaking, slowly and deliberately. "Have the page and his father put in the dungeon."

"The lower cells?" the War Lord asked.

"The upper," Rhian answered. "When Talwy and I were children, we spent an afternoon in the lower dungeon—Talwy had locked himself in, and I tried to get him out. No, no, Lord Ander, put them in the upper cells. And see they are well fed and cared for."

"A gallows for the morning?"

"No gallows."

The War Lord's face twisted. "Don't be a fool, Your Majesty. Mercy is a quality that runs too thick in Mont Cant veins. If you keep them even a day, there is a chance they may escape. They may have powerful friends—"

"If they are spies, Mont Cant, they have deadly friends."

Rhian stood up. "I am king here," he said. "Will any of you deny that the king of Canys has the right to decide this matter? I won't condemn a man, much less a boy, with such evidence as this. I will speak with the boy and his father and decide the case myself." Rhian stopped murmurs with a movement of his hand. His fingers grazed the lantern; it shook, and because of its swaying light, Ianwyn fancied the room trembled. "I am king of Canys!" Rhian went on, "and if any of you interfere to harm the prisoners, you will account to me."

The War Lord flinched, but his scowl turned into a snarl.

Even Ianwyn drew back, for Rhian reminded her all too much of her father, perhaps a little even of Talwy, and for a frightening moment she imagined he was not Rhian at all, but Talwy himself.

3

"I have been expecting you ever since that day on the moors. When my raven friends first spotted you, you had passed the Rock of Stars. I expected you to be here much sooner."

"I was delayed. In Oerth. The cursed farmers near Bellonbain. They thought they could waylay me, as they might an ordinary man. But I am not an ordinary man. I am Talwy Mont Cant, king of Canys."

"When I last saw you, Magic-son, you were prince of Canys. The *second* prince of Canys."

The room was small, clotted with darkness; a purplish fire burned on the hearth. The light exaggerated the features of both the boy and the man; the boy's hair in sunlight might have been golden, but here it seemed stained and brown. Beneath his lips the beginnings of a beard stood out, and above his nose his gray eyes glittered with a fever.

Talwy scrutinized the sorcerer. "I have not been crowned king of Canys, but I will be."

Enrhi the Dark shut the door and returned to a carved chair by the fire, his robes rattling on the flagstones. He smiled slowly. "You are your brother's younger twin," he said. "That must mean the Fates decreed that Rhian should be king."

"May the Fates perish," Talwy said.

"Be careful of which Fates you curse, Magic-son. Six of the Fates are nothing to me. But the Last Fate, the Seventh, Enrhion, Lord of All Darkness, is my master. All my power— that power I know you crave—comes from Him."

Talwy's eyes widened. Certainly this sorcerer could give him power. But he narrowed them again, for the sorcerer's smile mocked him.

"You know why I have come," he said.

Enrhi the Dark gathered his robe around his knees. He settled back in his chair and began stroking his short black beard. "I do. You have a long memory, Magic-son."

"Three years is not long to remember. Scarcely three years ago my father's warriors caught you in the foothills of Mont Cant and you, Seer of Darkness, Priest of the Seventh Fate, cowered before them." Talwy laughed. "They would have killed you, and it would have made little difference to me. But when I called them off, when I set you free, you swore an oath that for my service to you, you would grant me one wish. I have come to ask my wish."

"Ask it then," Enrhi said, his eyes glittering.

But Talwy only glanced away and pursed his lips. The sorcerer's tower, he noted, had none of the symbols of magic he had expected. He saw no familiars, no tomes bound in dragon skin, no skulls, only a pair of stone goblets and a robe draped over a stool.

Then he said, quietly, "I want to use your power, Dark One, to make me live forever."

"Then you are a fool," the sorcerer said. "Why do you want to prolong your life when you hate each moment of it?"

Talwy's jaw tightened. "I have told you my wish," he said.

"But it is a dangerous wish. Suppose, for instance, your brother captured you. Suppose he chained you and tortured you so you could not endure the pain. If you could not even escape by giving up your life, what then?"

"Then you will make it so that only *I* may choose to accept death," Talwy said, leaning forward. "Don't tell me you cannot grant my wish, sorcerer, because I know you can. You yourself are the sole keeper of your life."

Enrhi stood up and loomed over Talwy, eclipsing the firelight. "You are a fool, Magic-son. But a clever one."

"Then you will grant my wish."

"The mastery of your own life I can give you," the sorcerer said. "But you will not win it so easily. If I give you the gift, you will feel pain you have never even imagined. You will freeze in your own hatred as the power of Enrhion closes over you. For you it will be worse than it was for me, because you are not as evil as you might like to think. I, I feel love toward nothing. But you—you are weak. I saw regret in you when you came to my door. I saw love!"

"I love no one!" Talwy said. "You lie!"

"Do I, Magic-son? No! I tell the truth—you love your sister!"

"It is a lie!"

"It is a flaw, a costly weakness," the sorcerer said. "But I will not argue with a fool—indeed, you will see just how much love you have when the hands of Enrhion twine around you." Enrhi wrapped his cloak more tightly around him as he sat down on the stool beside Talwy. "Your wish will take many days to bring about. You are a reckless fool, Talwy Mont Cant. You threw yourself on my doorstep blindly, seeking only the wish I promised you on the moors." Enrhi leaned nearer, and his voice sank to a murmur. "But I am Enrhi the Dark, most powerful sorcerer in Rhewar. I can bring you the throne of Canys, if you will let me."

Talwy drew away. "I will take Canys myself." But he said, tentatively, "What would *you* gain from helping me overthrow my brother? What does the little land of Canys matter to you?"

"I am a priest of the Fates. I read their intentions in the fabric of the skies. The constellations show great things arising in the north, perhaps in Canys." Enrhi's eyes flickered, and he added quickly. "I ask nothing more than to be your counselor. I have a plan—"

"I don't need a plan. I know my brother and his weaknesses."

"His greatest," the sorcerer said, "is that though you have scorned him and become loathsome to him, he still does not hate you. Love is a great weakness—ah, do I read surprise on your face? You did not know, perhaps, that your brother Rhian hates you much less than you hate him. You do not know your brother as well as you suppose—"

"Rhian is weak," Talwy said. "I am strong. That is all I need to know. I should be king of Canys."

"You are weak," the sorcerer said. "But I will make you king of Canys."

4

Within two weeks of Autumn First, the good weather failed, and the familiar clouds crossed Mont Serhaur and hid Mont Cant in a sheet of rain. Rhian, however, had other concerns the day he climbed the stairs to Ianwyn's room. His mind, like the sky he glimpsed from the windows, brimmed with storm.

"Come in!" Ianwyn shouted when he knocked. He pushed open the door and stepped into the room. Except for Ianwyn, kneeling next to a box, and Rhin, her cat, the room was empty. Ianwyn was fitting a blanket into the box.

"By the Fates," Rhian said. "Are you moving out?"

"Naturally," she said. "And it has not been easy. It is surprising how many useless but dear things I have accumulated over the years. But I have moved them all—all except this box and Rhin—to the servants' quarters."

"The servants' quarters? Ianwyn—"

"Aren't the servants' quarters better than the warriors' quarters?"

"I suppose. But Ianwyn, why are you moving out at all?"

Her face went blank. "Oh," she said. "You don't know." She smiled sheepishly. "I'm sorry, Rhian—I have a habit of taking things into my own hands."

"I know," Rhian said.

"You asked me to find a place for the princess to stay," Ianwyn said. "And because this is the nicest room in the castle—"

"But the princess won't be here long. I don't think you need to move out. We could have put the princess—"

"Where?"

Rhian swallowed, then shrugged.

Ianwyn chuckled. "It isn't your fault, Rhian. This castle is hundreds of years old. The Mont Cant who built it liked battlements and dungeons better than guest rooms. Now if you had built Fach-ne-Canys, Rhian, you would have thought of everything."

"If I had built Fach-ne-Canys," Rhian said, "I would have forgotten even the warriors' quarters." But seeing Ianwyn's eyes fixed on him, he added in a louder voice, "Ianwyn, I want to talk to you about something."

"If it is about helping the servants with the dishes every night," Ianwyn said, "I know it isn't courtly, but I can't bear to see them working in those hot suds all night. And besides, the servants are letting me stay with them while Princess Sereniel is here."

Rhian threw up his hands and laughed. "It isn't that."

Ianwyn glanced at the cat, who leaped to the windowsill and rubbed his flank against the glass. "If you are worried about arrangements for Princess Sereniel," she said, "I have taken care of everything. There was enough in the treasury for a feast, now that the autumn taxes have been collected, and I have had tailors start on two gowns for gifts. I have even persuaded Pinwy to read one of his poems at the feast—"

"Pinwy? At the feast? What next?"

"His poems are very good."

"If you say so," Rhian said. "But I already knew you were taking charge of everything for the princess—in fact, I was counting on that. By the Fates, Ianwyn. What would I do without you?"

"The same thing you do with me, I suppose." She guided Rhian to the window, where she sat down. Rhian sat down stiffly, for though his shoulder had shed its bandage days before, he could not put too much weight on his arm without bringing back dull pain. "Now," Ianwyn said. "Tell me what's on your mind."

Rhian looked out the window. "How long have I been king?" he asked.

"Almost eleven months," Ianwyn said.

"It seems like eleven years," he said. "Already, in spite of all I have done to be a good king, I have had a wound and a run-in with the War Lord. My brother ran away, and someone tried to kill me—at least, everyone says the blacksmith and his son broke and leaded the Sword of Dorhan, and I still have to go to the dungeons to question them. I think I'm afraid they're guilty. I don't want to kill anyone, Ianwyn. But if I don't, I can't say what the War Lord will do. He has been threatening to leave my service if I don't stop 'acting like a milk-blooded Mont Cant.' And Toran—"

"Are you afraid of Ander or Toran?" Ianwyn said. "I know you aren't. And I know things aren't as bad as you paint them. Remember to look on the bright side. What about the success of the feast, of the rites of Canrhion? What about the good harvest and the low taxes? And what about Talwy? It's a good thing he left, as painful as all of it was. We don't need any more bitterness at Fach-ne-Canys than we already have." Ianwyn straightened her sleeves before continuing. "Don't let your counselors bother you, Rhian. If you don't like what they say, dismiss them. Let the War Lord leave your service. If you don't want to hang the smith and his son, don't. You are the king—"

"I sometimes wish," Rhian said, "I were still a prince."

"You were meant to be king," Ianwyn said. "And I think you already are a better king than Father was, though he ruled well. I'm not the only one who feels that way. So does Canrhion."

The memory of Canrhion's sign returned; Rhian shivered. "I want your advice, Ianwyn," he said.

"I give it often enough without being asked. Ask whatever you like."

Rhian grinned. "Are you really only fifteen, Ianwyn?"

"Everyone tells me so," she said. "Was that your question?"

"No," Rhian said. "It's about . . . the princess of Bran." He shifted and pushed an imagined picture of Princess Sereniel from his mind. "There is such a troublesome lack of women—ladies, I mean—around this castle. I don't know what to expect." He struggled for words. "I want to make a good impression on the princess, but I'm not sure how to do it."

"You can begin by calling the princess by her name, not by the name of her country," Ianwyn said gently.

"That is just what I mean," Rhian said. "How should I address the princess of Bran—Sereniel, I mean. Do I act as if she's a visiting noble, or a dignitary, or—"

"Treat her as you would any other person you like very much."

Rhian looked blank. "What do you mean?"

"People like to be themselves," Ianwyn said. "Do you like being known as a Mont Cant or the king of Canys all the time?" Rhian nodded, but Ianwyn did not see him. "I'm sure Sereniel feels the same way."

While Rhian considered, the cat yawned and stretched; he leaped heavily into Ianwyn's lap. She scratched his chin and began to pet him. "I don't claim to know all the answers," Ianwyn went on, "but I *am* a girl, and I know that the more naturally you act, the more I would like you if I were Sereniel. Simply be yourself."

"But which self? Ianwyn, there is Rhian Mont Cant the King, there is Rhian Mont Cant the Judge, and there are Rhian Mont Cant the Fool and Rhian Mont Cant the Child. Which one should I be?"

Ianwyn smiled. "Try Rhian Mont Cant the Man," she said.

5

The night before Princess Sereniel's arrival, Rhian was plagued by dreams. Some of them might be expected before such an event—glimpses of odd faces his mind supposed to be Sereniel.

But one dream seemed to have nothing to do with any of the others, and Rhian found it disquieting.

He dreamed he was a child again, sitting in a stable, learning lessons from a tall, pale woman. She was asking him about the Fates, particularly about the Second Fate, Bran. But few of her questions made sense, and when he could not answer them, she shook a stick at him. "What is the Second Fate?" she asked him. He answered that Bran was the Fate of the moon and of kindness. But as if she had not heard, she asked the question twice more. Rhian answered the same thing, but before he finished the last time, he saw a child peering at him through the bars of one of the horse stall gates. The child, a grubby creature with tangled hair and big, black eyes, seemed trapped. She stared at him. "What is the Second Fate?" the pale woman demanded again. He did not answer but went to the horse stall and tried to open the gate. The woman told him to leave the gate alone and struck him with her stick. But he drew the gate open until the child wriggled out, and when he turned around to answer the woman's question, she was gone. He found himself alone in the barn, with only the moon glimmering in a high window.

He awoke before dawn with the memory of the dream thick in his mouth. The moon, masked by clouds, had just edged into his window. He shivered and drew his blankets around him. The next day would be cold.

6

Though he had just put wood on the fire, Pinwy shivered. Fear was part of it, but the weather complicated his mood: it had rained all day, and its soft drumming, which Pinwy usually found helpful to the rhythm of his poetry, had become monotonous. The rain had ruined more spirits than his own—it had spoiled the welcome for Sereniel Branmawr, and everyone was out of sorts. The damp mood had changed even Ianwyn. She had been in his room only a few moments before to ask if his poem was ready, but when he offered to recite it to her, she had only rushed away.

All this, when Pinwy had begun to wonder whether he wanted to read his poetry in front of everybody or not. As much as he wanted the rest of the castle, and especially Rhian, to hear his poetry, it would be hard to stand up and recite it.

He had fretted all day over which of his poems he would read. He had been so busy leafing through parchments, he had forgotten about the welcome for the princess at the front gate.

At first he thought he would read a poem about the sun, which he had compared to a white bird in a slow glide across the sky. But that one would not do. With the bad weather, it would hardly be appropriate. Besides, the sun being the emblem of the House Mont Cant and of Canys, its slow death at the end of the poem might be taken wrong. Next he had tried to write a poem especially for the occasion. He had forced out two lines before he realized he didn't know what the princess looked like. It would be embarrassing to praise her for her beauty if she was repulsive, or to talk of embraces and love at first sight if Rhian and Sereniel obviously disliked each other.

Thus, as the rain beat against his window and as the fire burned low, he still looked for the right verse to read. It began to get dark, so he chose a verse he liked only slightly, a poem about the sparrow and the moon, a retelling of an old legend. The moon was after all the symbol of the land of Bran.

He practiced the poem until the damp imprints of his fingers stood out on both sides of the parchment. Soon he could say it by heart without a slip—to himself. What might happen in front of the courts of Canys and Bran he dared not think. And he had spent so much time choosing and going over his poem, he was sure the feast had already started. He had not even dressed.

He put on a yellow tunic, but as he left his room, he felt his hair beginning to stick up already. An unusual quietness filled the halls, a hollowness accentuated by the distant thump of rain and hiss of wind. "I'm late," he kept telling himself. "I'm late." He walked faster.

Almost running, he hardly heard the sound in the patter of the rain. But just before he came to the courtyard, he stopped, and in spite of his hurry, listened. Voices conversed softly nearby.

The odd thing about the voices was their tone; it was hushed, like the voice Rhian used when he talked about Talwy. Pinwy drew back in the corridor and listened.

"It isn't right to eavesdrop," he remembered Ianwyn saying, but for once he chose to ignore her advice. Who would have a conversation in the rain? He crept forward, pressed himself against the door, then peered around the edge of it.

Two men stood near the gate. He had seen neither of them before. Both wore long blue capes pinned with silver moon brooches. Beneath their cloaks were hints of gear less courtly, shapes of longswords and belt-daggers, the glint of finely crafted chain mail. Pinwy at first thought them to be the princess's guards, but he soon realized otherwise. One of them wore a golden circlet, and the other, an older man, had scars running into his beard. Pinwy withdrew behind the door and waited, his breath suddenly short.

"But when, Lord Oergant, when?" one of the voices said. By its thickness Pinwy guessed it belonged to the older man. *"When* is the question! You are in love, and you forget the greatest weapon of a warrior—patience. You simply can't ride off with the princess. Things are not that simple. We are in the land of Canys—there are political considerations—"

"Blast political considerations! I want Sereniel *now*. I knew I wouldn't like seeing that boy king kiss her hand and escort her—"

"Listen to me! And listen well. You may be second only to the king in Bran; you may be of the House Oergant; but you are as foolish as any other man in love. Don't forget that Sereniel and that 'boy king' are betrothed. If you sweep the princess back to Branfach, her father will have your head."

A pause followed.

Pinwy, hugging the carved suns of the door, bit his lip. He had not heard of Doran Oergant before, but obviously the man was enough in love with Princess Sereniel to threaten kidnapping her. But what about Sereniel herself? Was she a willing part of the scheme? Pinwy had a brief vision of the princess chatting and laughing with Rhian but her eyes alive with hatred.

"After the feast," the thick voice said. "That would be the best time, Lord Oergant. Let the king slip just once in his protocol, miss one shred of etiquette, and we have our excuse to end Sereniel's visit—and her betrothal."

Pinwy inched back from the doorway. He decided to wait in the shadows until the two of them went into the feast. Then he would warn Rhian—

But the wind gusted in the doorway, and on the slick doorstep, he stumbled. He sprawled into the courtyard. For a moment he saw nothing but pellets of rain, but soon two shapes blocked his view of the sky. He winced.

The older man pointed to Pinwy's brooch. "The prince of Canys," he told Doran Oergant. Then he spoke to Pinwy. "Has Your Majesty forgotten the way to the feast? Has Your Highness paused at the door to remember it? Now, we would be most pleased if you thought further—long enough to miss the feast altogether."

Powerful arms lifted Pinwy to his feet. Both men grinned at him. "But I will be missed," Pinwy said in an unsteady voice. "I am reading a poem for the princess." He managed to bring the parchment from his pocket; he shoved it as proof toward the nearest man.

The men looked at each other. "You will give your poem," Doran Oergant said. "But you will say no word more, no word less than what is written here, if you value your life. And," he added, "Lord Espan and I will take you to the feast. You will sit between us."

7

Now that speeches were finished, everything seemed to be going well. Ianwyn had had frightening moments throughout the day, such as when the minstrels came dressed in gold and green instead of gold and blue, or when the War Lord took a look at a special tapestry featuring the moon of Bran and the sun of Canys and began to complain about the cost of Armein silk. Fortunately, Ianwyn had been able to hide the minstrels among the trees, and she had silenced the War Lord by promising to talk to Rhian about a campaign when the good weather returned.

But the feast was going well, and Rhian, the Princess Sereniel on his right, Oenan, Toran, and Sereniel's nobles all seemed pleased. It was fortunate, she decided, that Pinwy had found a seat in the back, among the nobles of Bran, for there wasn't really room on the dais.

"I hope his poem will go well," she thought. She bit her

lip when she saw him watching her from across the hall. His face seemed gaunter than usual, and he was rubbing his hands together.

She gave him a smile, then turned to pour ale for Rhian. He hardly noticed her; his eyes were fixed on the princess.

And no wonder, Ianwyn thought. Sereniel's face, above the white ruff of her collar, had an elfin look: she had a thin nose, high cheeks, and large, earth-colored eyes. This combined with her thin, mobile eyebrows made Sereniel seem mischievous to Ianwyn, possibly temperamental. But her full lips and thick brown hair reminded Ianwyn of her own mother, Queen Amnewyn.

Sereniel began speaking to a lady across the table, oblivious of Rhian's preoccupation with her. When he glanced at Ianwyn and sighed, she could give him not more than a smile for encouragement. Sereniel had seemed aloof from the first. And though as she had made the rounds of the castle she had had a ready smile, something remained wrong in her eyes—something like a wall that made them seem shallow.

Rhian himself was certainly at his best. He wore a yellow tunic, with a sunburst embroidered on the breast, and a thin golden circlet. His face shone with excitement, and his words to Sereniel had been gentle and well-formulated. He had kissed her hand, helped her into her seat, and introduced her at the feast magnificently.

And still . . .

"Are you enjoying the feast, Sereniel?" Rhian asked.

"Oh, it's delightful," she said. But her interest, Ianwyn noted, lighted on Rhian only an instant before skimming away. "We don't have such beef in Bran. It's too cold to raise cattle. And your drapes and carvings are exquisite—wherever did your sister find them? I especially like the *clever* eclipse of the moon and the sun—" Sereniel paused long enough to smile at someone in the crowd before continuing. "And I must compliment your cooks. You must remind me to get some recipes from them before I start for Branfach again. Just a moment, Your Majesty. What was that, dear?"

As quickly as she had been engaged, Sereniel was distracted by one of her ladies. They began discussing the needlework of the tablecloth, and Rhian, with a shrug, turned to Oenan, who sat across the table.

"*One* glass of ale?" he said. "*One* slice of beef? Come,

Oenan, eat! A barrel-bodied man like you ought to empty that platter, and more."

Oenan smiled, but he toyed with his mug. "I am not really hungry," he said. "You will have to eat my share, sire."

Rhian squinted at him as if trying to read his face. But a commotion from the back of the hall distracted him.

"They are getting ready for the poetry," Ianwyn said. "Pinwy will be first. Oh, Rhian, you will like his poetry . . ."

Rhian touched Sereniel's hand. "My brother, Prince Pinwy, is a self-styled poet. His poetry is basically sound, but it lacks emotion." Ianwyn did not think this was fair, for Rhian had never heard Pinwy's verse. But she chose not to bring the matter up in front of Princess Sereniel.

"I'm sure he's very good," Sereniel said, watching Pinwy get up. But her eyes did not follow him to the center of the room.

By the time Pinwy reached the dais, his eyes were burning. Ianwyn smiled at him, but he was not looking at her but instead at Rhian. Rhian, however, watched Sereniel, who in turn stared at something at the back of the hall.

Pinwy opened his mouth, but no sound came out. Finally he said, his teeth gritted, "The Sparrow and the Moon."

Ianwyn bit her finger. Yet still Pinwy looked at Rhian. Though his voice wavered as he began, it grew firmer after the first few lines.

> *"The sparrow lived in misty lands*
> *Where sunshine, gray and watered, shone,*
> *And fog reached with its ermine hands*
> *Upon the cliffs of stone."*

Rhian still watched Sereniel. Pinwy strained to force words between his teeth, and sweat dotted his forehead.

> *"The lonely sparrow loved the moon,*
> *Her grace that lit the stormy night.*
> *And hoped he that at one day soon*
> *He'd meet her in his flight."*

Suddenly Ianwyn knew something was wrong. Something more than Pinwy's nervousness. He had never stressed such odd words before, never so deliberately stumbled on simple

phrases. Over the next few stanzas, he drew out seemingly
unimportant words and nearly choked on others. Only at the
last line did Ianwyn understand.

> *"The moon so bright and framed by star*
> *Would leave before the break of day."*

Polite clapping lasted until Pinwy returned to his seat, but
in it there was murmuring. Ianwyn saw Pinwy sit down between
the two lords of Bran, his eyes still fixed on Rhian.

"Not a bad verse," Rhian said, "but it was poorly given."

"Rhian," Ianwyn said, stiffening. "You are wrong. You are
dead wrong."

8

"I demand to know," Princess Sereniel said, glaring at Rhian,
"where we are going. I don't appreciate being taken from the
feast with no warning and no word of explanation."

"I'm sorry," Rhian said. "I wouldn't interrupt the feast unless it was important." He glanced at Ianwyn.

The three of them hurried along the corridor to the hiss of
torches, the drone of the rain on the roof, and the swish of the
skirts of both princesses.

Treachery? Rhian wondered again. Ianwyn had whispered
to him something about that. Maybe she had been listening to
Toran too much.

He halted, fished a set of keys from his pocket, then opened
a low door. He strode into a dark room—a storage room, by
the smell of it—he had not chosen it for any particular reason.
The room was cold, but he ignored that as he brought a candle
from the corridor and lighted two torches beside the door. Once
they sputtered to life, they revealed the room, cluttered, as
Rhian had expected, with boxes and crates and kegs.

"Sit down, both of you," Rhian said.

Ianwyn did so wordlessly. But Sereniel glowered. "Just who
do you think you are, Rhian Mont Cant? I have kept my temper
until now, but I'm on the verge of losing it. Taking me out of
the feast was one thing, but bringing me to your beer cellar

and ordering me to sit down is quite another."

"I have a good reason," Rhian said.

Sereniel sniffed, but Rhian thought fear along with indignation sparkled in her eyes. "I don't care about your reasons, Rhian Mont Cant! You are brash and uncouth. As soon as I go back to Branfach, I will tell my father what you've done."

"I am the king of Canys," Rhian said. "And you are in Canys, Sereniel Branmawr, not in Bran. I am not trying to disgrace you. I only want to talk to you. Please sit down."

Sereniel descended to a seat on a nearby keg. "Very well, King of Canys," she replied in a defiant half-whisper, "talk to me. But I warn you, when I return to Branfach—"

"My concern is that you might return too soon."

"And how did you get an idea like that?"

"Don't think we are blind," Ianwyn said. "And don't think we are deaf. The young Bran lord, the one you were watching at the feast, was keeping a close eye on my brother. He tried to tell us something through his poem, though I'm not sure what. I think he discovered something about that Bran lord—something that involves you as well."

"Rhian," Sereniel said, "your sister is mad—"

"Really, Ianwyn," Rhian said, his grimness breaking. "Aren't you stretching things a little?"

Ianwyn folded her arms. "I know Pinwy," she said. "And I think I know Princess Sereniel," she added, "at least enough to know that she and the Bran lord are in love."

"That isn't true!" Sereniel exclaimed. "Lord Doran and I—" Sereniel stopped short, then said, "I mean, I'm not in love with any lord of Bran. I don't know what you mean."

Rhian glanced at Ianwyn, then turned to Sereniel. "I think you do," he said.

"Supposing I did love Lord Doran," Sereniel said, looking down. "What business would that be of yours?"

"I am to be your husband."

Touching her hands to her cheeks, Sereniel kept her eyes low. "Doran told me the Mont Cants would be like this," she said. "The Mont Cants aren't like any other royal House. They aren't warlike or despotic or treacherous or cruel or masterful, he said, but they are dangerous—they have a magic, an enchantment that has kept them in power for hundreds of years without wars or reigns of terror. A Mont Cant can see through a lie in an instant, and some of them reach into you and play on your heart as if it were a harp, until you sing out your deepest secrets." Sereniel's eyes met Rhian's. "That is what Doran warned me. And he was right. You are an enchanter, Rhian Mont Cant."

"I am not an enchanter," he said. "But still, I want to know the truth. Tell me, Sereniel Branmawr."

Her lip began to tremble. "First of all, I don't love you."

Rhian flinched, but the stinging inside him was reflected only in Ianwyn, who seemed to blink back tears.

"That wasn't easy to say," Sereniel said. "You see, Doran and I have loved one another for more than a year now."

Rhian looked at his hands. He hardly knew Sereniel—the pain he felt was unaccountable. But it remained inside him, sharpening as Sereniel went on.

"Doran becomes jealous so easily. He didn't want me to come to Fach-ne-Canys at all, and he tried to keep me from leaving Branfach. But I had to come here. I had to meet you. I had to understand a little more about my future. I thought my visit would be harmless, to you and to me. But once Doran saw you, he decided we should leave at once. He told me before the feast he would make plans with our War Lord to break up the betrothal and carry me back to Branfach before morning."

"Tell me, Sereniel," Rhian said, laboring to speak. "Do you want to be carried off? Do you want our betrothal broken?"

Her face remained unreadable. "For all Doran's jealousy and impatience," she said, "I love him. I will never love you as much." Her eyes glittered as she looked at him. "The answer is yes."

"I am . . . pleased with your honesty," Rhian said, aware that Ianwyn was watching him. "But you ought to realize, Sereniel, that no matter how your lover arranged to break our betrothal, your father would hang Doran and send you back to me as a prisoner in the spring. Your father has made a pact he won't dare break—"

"Still," Sereniel said, "I love Doran, and if he wants to take me to Branfach, I will go with him. We both will suffer what we must."

Rhian felt twisted inside. Looking now at Sereniel, even knowing her feelings, he thought he loved her. His betrothal to her had been so automatic; the fact they were to be wed in the spring had been as inevitable as the season itself. That they might not love one another, that Sereniel might love someone else, had hardly occurred to him. Suddenly Rhian yearned for

counsel. But Toran and Oenan were still at the feast; and Ianwyn, doggedly silent, would not look at him.

"Sereniel," he said. "I hate to say what I have to say."

Sereniel went pale, and Ianwyn tensed.

Rhian gritted his teeth. "Your flight to Bran is out of the
question. It wouldn't do any good for you or Lord Doran. You
will stay at Fach-ne-Canys until your appointed time of departure. I will lock Lord Doran up, if he is hot-blooded enough
to defy me."

Sereniel turned her head away.

"When you leave for Branfach," Rhian went on, "I will
send with you"—Rhian swallowed hard—"a letter to your father
that I consider our betrothal dissolved."

Sereniel looked at him, uncomprehending. Then her face
flamed with a smile, and with a gasp, she threw her arms
around him. Standing up, she asked if he was serious, and
when he nodded, she kissed him. She began to laugh.

"Please," Rhian said. "I hate to think what Lord Doran might
do if he saw you acting like this. I am in no mood," he added,
"to take him on in a duel because of your gratitude. In fact,
go back to the feast and explain to him my offer. I don't want
him looking for me with a drawn sword."

Sereniel smiled again and started toward the door. But she
paused and looked at him. "Aren't you coming back to the
feast, Rhian?"

"Yes. In a moment."

Sereniel hesitated. "I won't forget you, Rhian Mont Cant,"
she said softly. "I know that breaking our betrothal won't do
much for Canys. And nothing for your personal reputation.
But if it makes you feel any better, I won't forget you. Rhian,"
she added, in a sudden whisper, "Rhian, I think I love you
after all." Then she was gone.

Rhian collapsed onto a keg and put his head into his hands.
Already he heard Toran and Oenan and the War Lord shouting
at him; only now did he realize the price of his favor to Princess
Sereniel. He snatched the gold circlet from his head and cast
it to the floor.

Ianwyn sat down beside him. "That was a hard thing to do,"
she said. "I didn't want to say anything—the price was too
high—but I somehow knew you would do what you did."

"I am too soft-hearted to be a king," Rhian said.

"Kindness is Bran's virtue," Ianwyn said.

"But I am a king, Ianwyn! Kings are supposed to have wills

of iron. They are supposed to be ruthless. Talwy would have been a better king. He always liked making people do things they didn't want to—"

"Talwy would have ruined Canys," Ianwyn said. "Evil dominates, but it never builds or strengthens. Didn't you hear what Sereniel said? We Mont Cants have kept the throne of Canys for hundreds of years without any tyrants. And we will keep it for another few hundred years."

Rhian said nothing. Instead he listened to the rattle of the torches and the howl of the wind.

Ianwyn stood up and placed her hand on his shoulder. But her grip went tight. "Look, Rhian," she said. "Look. The window!"

Rhian raised his head. "Yes," he said. "Someone ought to put shutters on it. The wind is cold—"

"No, Rhian, look!" Ianwyn persisted. "Look at the moon!"

The clouds that had hidden the sky had thinned enough that the sickle of the moon stood out, a silver crescent behind woolen clouds. By some combination of wind, rain, and high fog, a bright aura encircled it, framing its blue beauty.

"Bran," Ianwyn said. "Rhian, haven't you seen that symbol before? It's the sickle moon, the same as on the brooches of the Bran nobles! The sign of the Second Fate! Bran is giving you her sign, Rhian, for the kindness you showed Princess Sereniel!"

Rhian stared, unbelieving, the cold hollowness in his stomach warming suddenly to fear and awe. Already the silver ring faded, as fingers of drab cloud extended over the moon.

"A fair trade," he said dolefully, thinking of Sereniel's face again. "I lose the promise of the land of Bran and its princess and gain the favor of its patron Fate!"

"Don't jest," Ianwyn said, frowning. "Don't tempt the Fates. They have given you a kinder bargain than you suppose, for they are often more cruel. You must not mistake the Fates. They do not love us as well as some say they do. They are passionless and demanding, each one of them. Canrhion offers power, but only after power has been extended in her service. Bran the moon is kind, but only after she has milked the last drop of mercy from us. Serron gives wisdom freely—to those who have bled her dear price for it. Fing, Fate of love, is easy to delight, but her true fire is as hard to find as a lightning-lit blaze in a downpour. Armadon the sea Fate works miraculous change, but only after the change is half-wrought already. Erd sees only his creation, the earth, and is convinced only by the sweat and blood he sees fall on it. And Enrhion. Ah, Enrhion— he of all the Fates is most ruthless, for he demands death and sorrow and gives in return only his dark mark. All of the Fates have been bargaining longer than we have, so their exchanges are often shrewd and bitter. Your trade with Bran may have been painful, but it was a fair trade. A very fair trade, indeed."

"I only hope," Rhian said, "that the War Lord will feel the same way."

III
Serron

The storm came as rain at first, clicking on the roof, leaving dampness in the air, but soon small flakes scrambled under doors and shutters. A deep cold set in and snaked, bearing snow, down the chimneys to quench the flames of hearth fires and to douse the last embers and coals.

Waking with chattering teeth before dawn, Ianwyn went with the servants to start the cooking fires. She was determined that the snow would not keep her from her day's errands. Indeed, she could scarcely afford even time for breakfast. During Princess Sereniel's stay, Ianwyn had been too busy entertaining or arranging feasts to carry on her usual work—she was days behind. She had told the servants to take her belongings to the tower room, but because they were so busy themselves, she did so herself. She then hunted in the pantries for a bit of meat for Rhin before bundling up and wading through the snow to the village, to bring a basket of food to the wife and younger children of the imprisoned smith. Once back at the castle, she paused just long enough to shake the ice from her cloak before preparing another basket to take to the upper dungeon, to the smith and his son themselves. Though she realized they may have wanted Rhian dead, she could not help feeling sorry for them. She was sure the dungeon would not be warm, so she added one of her own blankets to her package.

On her way to the dungeon she met Pinwy. As she passed his door, it burst open then slammed shut.

"Good morning," she said, gently opening the door again.

"I'm afraid it isn't," he said. "Thanks to Rhian."

"Rhian?"

"Of course, Rhian."

"Pinwy, you haven't been quarreling with him again, have you?"

"Ianwyn, it has gone far beyond that." Pinwy paused, bristling. "I asked him this morning how he liked the poem I read at the first feast. He said it was fairly well done. *Fairly* well done. When I nearly burst myself trying to warn him about Sereniel's plot without changing the words of the poem? By Canrhion! He didn't even thank me for warning you about Lord Doran. He didn't give one word of thanks. Not one word. In fact, he talked to me about being late to the very same feast!"

"I'm sure he means well," Ianwyn said quickly.

"He means ill," Pinwy contradicted. "Or he means nothing at all. I wonder why I even bother to talk to him, Ianwyn. I don't want to sound like a martyr, but I'm beginning to think he wouldn't notice if I was walled up in the dungeon, kidnapped by spies, or if I ran away, as Talwy did. And the man simply has no ear for poetry—"

"*I* like your poetry, if it's any consolation," Ianwyn said. "Have you written anything new?"

"A couple of verses," Pinwy said, distracted. "This morning I started a ballad about a prince who runs away from his cruel surroundings and makes a journey to Cavancaer and the other Far Islands of Ynysandra. I call the poem 'Minarets of the Sun.' I have it right here if you would like to read what I have finished."

"Maybe later, Pinwy. Tonight?"

She told herself she had been cruel. But a moment later he was only a flicker of thought in her mind. For she was trying to remember the names of the new servants she had met. "Ienan," she whispered. "Sounds like 'Oenan' but not quite. The big, broad groom with a mole on his cheek." She murmured a few more names, with descriptions of their owners: Rhan, Enfath, Eriel, Merta. "Miriel," she said, finishing the list. "The one who looks somewhat foreign, with those wide blue eyes." Miriel, Ianwyn reflected, did not seem a servant girl at all. "Lady Miriel," she said, to help herself remember the name.

Soon Ianwyn reached the stairs to the dungeon. She hurried down a staircase, then turned aside. Her errand now was not only to the dungeon but to the armory also, where she hoped to find an old shield marked with Canrhion's sun for decoration

in the King's Hall. She dug in her apron pocket for the key
Rhian had lent her, but she found the door already open.

Orange light blazed on the threshold. After the cold castle
passages, the air in the doorway was warm; it smelled of coal
and hot iron. Though the door absorbed much of the sound, a
steady tapping came from within, and the growl of a fire punctuated by the squeak of bellows. Someone was at work in the
forge.

She stopped in mid step. No one should be in the smithy.
The only smith at Fach-ne-Canys was in prison. The clanking
paused, then began anew. Tensing, she tiptoed to the door.

She peered around, and a blast of air and a flash of reddish
light made her squint, but soon she saw clearly again; someone
was indeed hunched over the forge, at work on something small
and silver. Surrounded by swords and armor, dressed in a
homespun shift, he was no one Ianwyn recognized immedi-
ately. And he did not turn around but kept tapping at the bit
of silver metal. Then it struck her what the thing was.

"My ring," she thought. The wink of the sapphire made it
unmistakable. She drew back from the door. She had given
the ring to someone to have the setting fixed. Someone was
going to send it to Armad to be repaired. But who had it been?
Whoever had volunteered to take her ring to Armad was himself
a smith, but he did not seem to want anyone to know that.
Whoever was in the armory was skilled enough to work precious metals and had access to the armory. Whoever was in
the smithy could have been the one who had broken the Sword
of Dorhan. The traitor to Rhian might be in the armory, not
in the dungeon.

She moved away from the door, wishing she was wrong.
But she could not be, for from the forge now came Oenan's
unmistakable whistle.

2

Hunched over his writing table, Pinwy glared at the blot of ink
that ended the second line of a furiously scrawled poem. It
blurred as he blinked back tears. Writing was no use, he told

himself bitterly. Not any more. Who would read his poem?
Who would care? Not Rhian. He had not even acknowledged
that Pinwy's poem at the first feast had unmasked Princess
Sereniel's conspiracy. And not Ianwyn. She was too busy.

A knock at the door made him start. He moved to the door
and opened it. Rhian stood beyond, and for a split second,
hope shot through Pinwy. Perhaps Rhian had come to thank
him for what he had done, now that the princess was gone.

But Rhian was frowning, a tight, preoccupied kind of frown.
He brushed past Pinwy without looking at him and said, "Do
you have a moment?"

"Yes," Pinwy said. He sat down on his bed. "What is it?"

"I am concerned about you," Rhian said, narrowing his eyes
at Pinwy's writing table. "You spent entirely too much time
in your room all the while Princess Sereniel was here. We
hardly saw you—"

"Did you expect me to chat with the Bran lords after what
they tried to do to me?" Pinwy said, glaring at him. "Did you?"

"Oh, come, Pinwy. They didn't mean any harm. Besides,"
Rhian added, "it is quite rude to leave dinner early when guests
are present. And you did that several times. Even when I
warned you—"

"I couldn't stay," Pinwy stammered. "Not with those lords
whispering about me and you glaring at me!"

"Glaring at you? I never glared at you!"

"You're glaring now. And you're shouting!"

"Only because you aren't listening," Rhian snapped, turning
red. "Honestly, Pinwy, I don't know why you have to argue
every time I try to talk to you. I'm only concerned about you,
and about the reputation of Canys, which you haven't helped!"

Pinwy faced the wall and folded his arms. "The reputation
of Canys!" he burst out. "Is that all you care about? Your
precious kingdom? Your blasted reputation? I don't matter in
your scheme of things, do I? I don't even matter when I saved
your hanged reputation and your bloody kingdom!"

"Watch your tongue."

Pinwy spun to face him. But fury stopped his throat, and
wordless with rage, he stared at Rhian, eyes glittering. Rhian's
neck was tight, and his eyes flamed in return. By the time
Pinwy found words, they were low and hissed. "You are a
monster, Rhian! You are, no matter what Ianwyn says. I have
been right about you all along, but foolish enough to think that

maybe, under it all, you really did care for Ianwyn and for me. But you don't, do you? We don't matter to you any more than Talwy did; we just don't cross you as often. I have had enough. Enough of your blindness and coldness and criticism! Enough of your blasted kingdom! Since you want it more than anything else, you can have it!"

He bolted for the door, but Rhian caught his arms and shook him. "You little beast! Is that what you spend your time doing? Feeling sorry for yourself? Feeling unloved? Making lists of things I do wrong? I have a list of my own, then, for you—"

"I won't hear it!" Pinwy said, pulling himself free. "I won't hear any more from you. Get out! Get out of my room! You may rule all of Canys, but this room is mine! Get out!"

Rhian backed through the doorway, his cheeks twitching. "I may just take away your room. Maybe sleeping with the servants would sober you."

But before Rhian could say more, Pinwy slammed the door and threw the bolt down. He fell against the door with his fists, but he hardly felt the sting.

3

Rhian's unexpected confrontation with Pinwy soured the rest of the morning. He meant to arrange for Pinwy to sleep with the grooms, as the reward of insolence. But because he felt he ought to consult Ianwyn about Pinwy, and since she was not to be found, he spent the afternoon in his study.

It was not his study entirely—the tomes of accounts, the chronicles of Canys, the histories, the volumes of verse, and the other books in the room were used more often by Ianwyn, Oenan, and Pinwy than he. Poetry and history did not interest him, genealogies bored him, and the records of the treasury depressed him. Especially since Princess Sereniel's visit.

He came to his study, instead, to ease his frustration with Pinwy and to warm up. The castle had been cold all day, and the study was the warmest room outside of the King's Hall. Small and low, it was heavily draped and carpeted with gold, and it had a big hearth crowned with Serron's symbol of knowledge. Better still, it had a comfortable chair where Rhian slouched, rubbing his hands over the fire.

Always while he warmed his hands he read the inscription beneath the sign of Serron over the mantel. The saying had been a favorite of his father's. It was his own, too, for it summed up his feeling about the tomes stacked around him. WISDOM LIVES IN MOUNTAINS, NOT IN BOOKS, it said. He did not understand its meaning completely—it was one of the many maxims floating around the tradition of the Third Fate—but he had always liked quoting it to Oenan all the same.

"Come in!" he said when a knock brought him from his thoughts. He looked over his shoulder, almost expecting a contrite Pinwy, but he was disappointed. "Hello, Oenan."

"Good afternoon, sire."

A little drowsy from the heat of the fire, Rhian took his time standing up. Oenan closed the door but remained near it.

"You *can* come in," Rhian said. "I was just warming myself and wondering what to do with Prince Pinwy. Sit down, please. There is enough fire for both of us."

Oenan walked to the fire and held his hands toward it. But he did not bring a chair or take off his cloak. His boots gleamed in the firelight. "I can't stay," he said. "I meant to leave this morning, but I had a job to finish—"

"Off on errands?" Rhian surmised. He yawned. "You don't need to hurry, Oenan, not with the storm drifting snow under the doors. Where are you going now? To the village to visit the council? Or to Fach-ne-Armad?"

"Neither, sire. I am leaving . . . for good." Oenan turned to Rhian, his eyes lowered.

"For good?"

"I am afraid so. I have made up my mind, and by the Fates I will leave Fach-ne-Canys today."

"Oenan! By the Fates, you won't. You promised my father to serve as an advisor to me. I don't know why you're talking about leaving. What would I do without you? You must not be serious—"

"I am completely serious."

Rhian shook his head. "Come, you must not be. Where would I find another counselor? Good men are hard to find."

Oenan forced a bitter smile. "They are indeed," he said.

"You will stay, then."

"No. I'm sorry, sire, but—"

"But what?"

"But I can't stay."

"By the Fates, why not?"

"You ask difficult questions," Oenan said, looking at the fire again. His face hardened. "When I tell you why, I think you will agree that I should go."

"Tell me, then."

Oenan swallowed, then said, "Sire, it was I who reforged the Sword of Dorhan."

"You?" Rhian said. A tentative smile flickered, then died on his face. "You can't be serious."

"I wish I weren't," Oenan said. "But I, not the smith and his son you are holding in your dungeon, reforged the sword. Listen to me. Listen! If you believe I am guilty, believe also my reason for being so. I did not want to harm you, Rhian Mont Cant. I am your cousin, Rhian, but you are a brother to me. I never dreamed that what I did would endanger your life."

Rhian frowned. "Then why did you reforge the sword?"

Oenan clenched his hands into fists, then said, "Talwy."

"Talwy?"

"Year after year, before King Elevorne (Fates rest him) died, I saw how your brother hated you and took advantage of you, how he hurt Ianwyn and scorned Pinwy, how he profaned your mother." Oenan's face contorted. "Hatred is an awful thing to feel, and because I hated Talwy, I think I began to be, in one respect, very much like him. I would have killed him openly, but I realized that if I did so, I would only hurt the rest of you more. Instead I observed how Talwy watched over the Sword of Dorhan, how he desired it. I was sure he would take it for himself one way or another. So, almost a year ago, before he left, I reforged the sword. I forgot what I had done until the day you . . ."

Rhian sat down. "Oenan," he said. "Oenan."

"Do with me what you will," he said.

"Talwy is my brother," Rhian said, with difficulty. "And though I have felt the same hatred you talked about, Talwy is tied to me by blood, and I think a corner of me still remembers him from our childhood and still loves him."

"Sire—"

"What cuts me most," Rhian went on, "is that you didn't explain this to me earlier. I was within windbreath of having the smith hanged, and I have kept him and his son in my dungeon for weeks."

"I could not speak, sire! I kept stalling by telling myself it was better to wait until the matter lost its fury, until Princess Sereniel had gone—the House Mont Cant did not need such a scandal to explain to the House Branmawr. Believe me, sire, if you had moved to hang the smith, I would have spoken."

Rhian kept his eyes from Oenan's. He knew he could not let his personal feelings cloud his judgment.

"Oenan," he said after a time, "you have served me and the House Mont Cant well, and you are perhaps not as corrupt as you think. You have my best wishes." He paused, then added, "And my leave to go."

Oenan slowly nodded. "One more thing, Your Majesty." Out of the corner of his eye, Rhian saw Oenan dig into his breast pocket, pinch something glittering between his fingers, and place it on the mantel. "Princess Ianwyn's ring," he said. "Will you give it to her, sire? I can't bear the thought of saying good-bye to her."

"I will give it to her."

"Farewell, then," Oenan said. "But do not think I will break my Fate-tied oath to your father. Although I am leaving Canys, I will not stop serving the House Mont Cant."

Rhian pressed his eyes closed when he heard the door close. After a moment he took Ianwyn's ring from the mantel. It was still warm.

The fire flickered on the walls and the drapes. As Rhian sat in silence before such fire, he began to notice how alone he was. He closed the ring in his hand.

4

"Rhian! Rhian!" Catching sight of him down a passageway, Ianwyn ran to him and caught his arm. "I have been looking for you. Someone said you had gone to the village, then someone said you had gone to the stables. And as I was going through the scullery, Miriel spilled a jug of milk, so naturally I had to stop to help her mop it up. But I am glad I found you.

I have something I must tell you." She forced herself to speak more slowly. "I don't want to bear ill tidings, but I am afraid I must."

"Ill tidings?" Rhian said. "I have already had bad news today."

Ianwyn stopped herself, noticing that Rhian seemed troubled. She took his arm as they started toward the center of the castle. "Your face is awfully red," she said, touching his cheek. "Have you been out in the storm?"

"No," he answered. "I have been in the dungeon, though. I released the smith and his son and saw them out the front gate. I can see now how Father made so many enemies, even without being cruel. I offered them gold in return for keeping them unjustly. But they refused it. Hate was in their eyes, if there was none before. I don't want to be hated, Ianwyn."

"Nonetheless it's good you let them free now," Ianwyn said, a little puzzled. "They weren't guilty of trying to kill you, Rhian."

"I know," he said. "No one tried to kill me." He brought the ring from his pocket and handed it to Ianwyn. She took it grudgingly.

"Then all of it is true?" she blurted out. "I had hoped I was wrong, that I was mistaken. Please, Rhian, whatever you do to Oenan, don't hang him. I don't think he wanted to kill you. And he has helped you through some hard times—"

"I won't hang him. I won't even imprison him. He was more loyal to me than I can know. If he has a fault, it is foolishness. And the Fates know I am foolish, too. If he has done wrong, he has paid for it enough. And he is gone."

"Gone?" Ianwyn said. "But—"

"I think it is for the best, Ianwyn," Rhian said gently. "I will drop the matter of the sword altogether. Let me explain," he said, "and then you will understand why it must be our secret."

5

When Rhian and Ianwyn came to the King's Hall, they had talked for several hours. Their talk had made Rhian hungry, and from the dimness in the King's Hall, he feared they had missed dinner altogether.

"We aren't really late," Ianwyn said, looking at the empty tables. "You would think they would have had the decency to wait—"

"But it doesn't look as if anyone has eaten at all. Look at the settings—they're all clean, and the ale flasks haven't been opened. Nor has the wax on the cheese been broken."

"It is awfully quiet," Ianwyn said. The only sounds were remote and dreamlike: wind, the sifting of snow, the creak of the rafters, the crackle of dying fires, the flutter of conversation from the servants in the kitchen. The King's Hall felt hollow.

"But where *is* everybody?" Rhian said.

"Oenan won't be here," Ianwyn said.

"But still we ought to have the War Lord and Pinwy and the Minstrel and his lot—"

"The Minstrel is in the village this evening," Ianwyn said.

"There is Toran," Rhian persisted.

"I don't think he is feeling well. He mentioned something to me this morning about not coming to meals."

They paused. "At any rate," Rhian said, "it's late. Pinwy ought to be here—unless he's trying to make me angry after the fight we had this morning. Blast the boy! He would be much better off without his poetry."

"His poetry is his life," Ianwyn said. "Sooner or later you will have to realize that and accept it. He isn't always late for supper. I'm surprised he isn't here now."

"I'm not. Sulking in his room, no doubt. Since we seem to have nobody else to eat with, why don't you find him and bring him here? Tell him I order him to come."

Ianwyn hurried from the hall. "Blast Pinwy," Rhian said to himself, and sat down.

It might be some time before Ianwyn and Pinwy came, so he made himself comfortable. He leaned back in his chair. Tapping his fingers on the table, he drew a deep breath of smoke-scented air. His chest swelled and his shoulders rose until he caught a glimpse of one of his gold buttons without lowering his chin. I am king, he thought suddenly, looking over the hall. His hall. I am king of Canys.

But the moment passed, and the air hissed from his lungs. He looked around him, suddenly sheepish, wondering if anyone had seen him. But the tables between the flickering hearths were silent, and the growl of the wind against the roof seemed to tell him he was alone. He reached for a piece of bread, but he froze.

Someone stood at his left, watching him. He reddened.

"I beg your pardon," the person said. "I didn't mean to startle you. But I came from the kitchens to see if you need anything else for your meal." The person, a girl Rhian had never seen before, smiled, and Rhian knew she had seen his mock-nobility.

"We have all the food we need," he said quickly. "We lack only people to eat it."

The girl laughed; she had a long, golden laugh that put Rhian at ease. "Maybe," she said, "your nobles don't want to leave warm rooms even for dinner. Or perhaps they don't trust the new cook." Rhian did not even know there was a new cook. That sort of thing had always been under Ianwyn's supervision. But he laughed back all the same.

He tried not to stare, but he could not help looking at her. Though she could not be more than sixteen, her smile and carriage made her seem older. Though clad in a plain cambric shift, her thick black hair, which fell well beyond her shoulders, dark eyebrows and sparkling blue eyes made her seem more like a lady than a servant. "My name is Miriel," she said. "I am one of the new servants from Armad."

"Miriel." Rhian tried the name and found it pleasant, like the girl herself. "I suppose I don't need to introduce myself. Not after my king-like pose."

Miriel laughed. "Canys is prospering, and the House Mont Cant has very noble blood." Her eyes (he decided they were the color of a stormy spring sky) studied Rhian with bright intent. "If I were you, I would be proud of what I had. Including myself."

Rhian blinked, then smiled. "Miriel," he said, "you are refreshing. Where are you eating tonight?"

"In the scullery with the others," she said with a shrug. Her eyes, however, fixed on Rhian.

"As I said before," Rhian interrupted, "we are short on nobles this evening. Could you eat with us?"

"You are the king," Miriel said.

Rhian took a swift breath. He pulled back a chair on his left, but before he could ask Miriel to sit down, the doors of the hall flew open, and Ianwyn burst in. "Rhian!" she shouted.

"Rhian! It's Pinwy. He's gone! I looked in his room and in the hallways, and even in the armory. He's gone!"

"Come now," Rhian said, irked at being interrupted. "Pinwy is always disappearing. Where could he go, anyway?"

"He was upset," she said, coming around the table. "You had a fight with him. What sort of fight was it? What did you say to him? If he's done something drastic, both of us are at fault!"

"Ianwyn!" Rhian repeated. "Where could he go?"

"I don't know," she said. "But he's nowhere in the castle, and I have a feeling he's run away. Rhian, stop smirking! He could be out in the storm!"

"If he is," Rhian said, "he deserves what he gets. That boy is too moody, and he has no respect for authority! Ianwyn, it isn't hard to find out if he's left the castle. Miriel, go to the stable and see how many horses are there."

"How many horses," she said. She started across the room.

"He's bound to be all right," Rhian told Ianwyn. It bothered him to see her tears. "Don't worry. At least not yet. Pinwy will turn up, sulking in the moonlight or something."

Ianwyn had taken the chair next to him. "Your attitude scares me," she said, without looking at him. "Did you say something to him? He was pretty broken down when I talked to him. He was on the brink, and if you've done something to push him over . . ."

Rhian coughed, but said nothing; Pinwy's face appeared briefly in his mind. Ianwyn, however, continued to speak. She told him of her encounter with Pinwy that morning, of how upset he had seemed. Then she demanded the details of his fight with Pinwy. As he told her what had happened, her eyes went narrow. "Rhian!" she said. "How could you threaten to take his room!" She blinked back tears. "And how could I have refused to listen to him? This is my fault!"

"From what you told me," Rhian said coolly, "Pinwy is angry with me, not with you. And there's nothing unusual about that. Pinwy is almost as stubborn as Talwy—that's his main fault—and he does get carried away by his moods." He squinted at the doors of the hall, where Miriel had just appeared.

"Five horses," she said. "Two roan mares, a black colt, and two stallions."

"The gray mare!" Ianwyn exclaimed. "She's missing."

Rhian gripped the edge of the table. "Let's not jump to a

conclusion. After all, the War Lord isn't here; I haven't seen him all day. He generally rides the gray mare when he goes to the village."

"The War Lord didn't take the mare," Miriel said. She glanced at Rhian, then at Ianwyn, then placed before them a scrap of parchment marked with crisp penscript.

"I found this in the stable," she said.

Suppressing a chill, Rhian took the note and muttered the words:

> *Ianwyn,*
>
> *The stars are more hidden*
> *By mind than by mount;*
> *If they are forgotten,*
> *They no longer count.*
>
> *Don't try to follow me.*
> *Pinwy Mont Cant*

Then in smaller letters, hastily added:

> *Good-bye, Ianwyn. I hope you will forgive me.*
> *Maybe Rhian will appreciate you more, having*
> *lost me. The servants can have my room.*

Ianwyn and Rhian stared at each other. Rhian stood up. "Go to the stable again," he told Miriel. "Tell the grooms to saddle my stallion."

6

Sunrise found Pinwy high in the mountains. Though the morning was mercilessly cold, though ice sparkled on his cape, Pinwy was not unhappy. He had left unhappiness behind. Morning found him lumbering from sleep over the neck of his horse, warm enough in his wrappings and secure in the thought that he was free.

He had often thought that liberty might be like this, a spot of warmth in a chaos of cold, and that striking into the wild like this would be glorious. If he regretted having left Fach-ne-Canys, it was only because he had escaped too easily, because Rhian or Ianwyn had not tried to stop him.

But from the time he had crept, laden with his poems, from the kitchens to the stable, he had seen no one. And no one had watched him pass into the snow.

His journey so far had been easy. Though the snow had come down the whole day before his departure, it had stopped long enough for him to ride from Fach-ne-Canys. It had resumed only an hour later to fill the hoofprints of his horse. A wedge of cheese and an apple had been his meal that night; it had been filling and warming, and Pinwy calculated the food he had brought would far outlast his ride over the Monte Serhaur into Serhaur.

The choice to go to Serhaur had been simple for Pinwy; after all, that land of forest and river was famous for its minstrels and poets. Besides, Serhaur was the perfect place for a runaway Prince Mont Cant to find refuge. The House Esteran, the rulers of Serhaur, had been enemies of the House Mont Cant for as long as anyone could remember, and a prince gone rebel against the Mont Cant king would be welcome there. This thought was both promising and frightening to him. His best reason for going to Serhaur, however, was that it was the only place he could go. After what had happened with Doran Oergant, he did not want to go to Bran. Oerth, Armei, and Fingonlain were closed in his mind because Talwy had gone in that direction. He cared about his reputation at Fach-ne-Canys enough not to want people to say he had followed Talwy. And there was always the horrifying possibility, if he went south, of actually meeting him.

But Pinwy no longer plotted. He no longer even fed his anger with Rhian. The mare struggled through drifts in a willow grove, and seeing the blue ice of the river farther down, Pinwy decided to write some poetry. He had little else to do, for he had scarcely guided his horse since leaving the castle. He did not know how to find the pass into Serhaur, but the horse had often been taken to Fach-ne-Rhoanith, where the War Lord had relatives.

> *"With jeweled voices ice may call*
> *From underneath the winter's pall*
> *On mountains where the snowflakes fall—"*

Pinwy muttered several more lines, describing the way the ice spoke in crackling voices as it lidded pools and patterned tree trunks. The verse was just reaching its climax when he stopped short. He realized he could not remember a word of the previous part of the poem. When he tried to start over again, the words became muddled and transposed. None of them fit as nicely as before, and he kept wondering what bits he was leaving out.

"Bother," he said. What good was inspiration if he could not remember the poetry he made up? He had packed a pot of ink, a quill, and some parchment along with his poems, but the ink was probably frozen, and writing done on horseback would be unreadable. Besides, poetry for the time being reminded him of Fach-ne-Canys and made him think of Ianwyn and Rhian.

He occupied himself watching the scenery. He had seen two mule deer, four rabbits, twelve snowed-under beaver ponds by the time it began to snow.

When the first flakes came, he hardly noticed them. But a sudden flurry of fat flakes struck him on the cheeks, and a moment later flakes dropped the size of goose feathers, and the wind began to hiss in the pines.

He kept to the fringes of the wood, where the drifts were shallower and the flakes less fierce. Still, even out of the wind, he began for the first time to worry.

The storm seemed serious, and he had no idea of where he was or how, in an emergency, he would find his way either to Serhaur or back to Fach-ne-Canys. Furthermore, the shelter of the pine forest was fast thinning. He was coming near the peaks of the mountains, the timberline, and the treacherous passes of the Serhaur summit.

His legs ached from riding. His toes throbbed with cold. His stomach growled with hunger. He felt a blister on his nose that might be frostbite. Worse, he sensed the weight of what he had done in leaving the castle in the middle of a storm. Travelers' yarns came back to him, tales of wolves and sorcerers, of avalanches and deaths beneath high, lonely cliffs.

"Home," he muttered. He could scarcely move his lips. But home was not Fach-ne-Canys any longer. He tried to remember his list of grudges against Rhian, which he had calmly written out and included with his poems. But he could remember surprisingly few. They seemed less outrageous than they had before. But still, Rhian had wronged him. Not just once. His true life lay ahead of him, in Serhaur.

7

"Are you sure he went that way?" Rhian yelled against the storm.

"Of course I'm sure." The War Lord's reply was almost lost in the wind. "I know what I know, and I don't appreciate your lack of confidence in me. *I* didn't want to search for your foolish brother! This is the only pass through the mountains. And if your brother has even slight sense, he will find it, or that mare will lead him to it."

"But there aren't any tracks!" Rhian bellowed. "Knowing Pinwy, he could be anywhere in these hills!"

"By Serron! The wind could have drifted snow over his tracks. It's covering ours already. Blast this wind!"

The two riders and their horses were almost lost to each other in the storm, for they had left behind the last trees and the snow and wind had full sweep. The searchers found themselves, at the dimming of the day, at the crest of a cliff, squinting toward the highest peaks. A glacier spread from a peak on their right, and to their left a torn line of cliffs extended westward. Up along the shoulders of the rock faces the trail wound, broken here and there by drifts. To Rhian the route seemed not only treacherous but also impassable.

As he steadied his horse, he looked at the path and found it hard to think Pinwy had gone that way. Pinwy might be stubborn, but he was not a fool, not fool enough, at least, to attempt such a dangerous crossing.

"I don't think he went this way," Rhian called out.

"I tell you he did! There is no other way."

"If you're wrong, I'll have your skin!"

"I didn't ask to come!" the War Lord snarled. "It was your sister who persuaded me. So, if you can't trust me, you can bloody well hunt up your idiot brother by yourself!"

"You've threatened me enough! Go, if you want to. But

don't expect to be welcomed again at Fach-ne-Canys!" Rhian
snapped the rein, urging his horse ahead toward the cliffs. His
anger burned inside him and kept his gaze fixed ahead. He did
not bother to see if the War Lord was following him. "The
only way across the mountains, indeed," he muttered to himself. But he realized his own ignorance about these hills.

In fact, he decided as the wind cooled his fury, he did not
know the first thing about tracking someone in the wilderness;
only by the War Lord's direction had he come this far without
mishap. Maybe the War Lord, in spite of his insolence, was
right.

He reined his horse. "All right!" he shouted back. "You
win. He must have come through this pass." He twisted in his
saddle. But he found himself alone.

"Ander!" he cried out. "Ander!" No answer came. "I suppose he's taking his time catching up," Rhian said to himself.
He stared at the snow behind him, searching for the shape of
the War Lord's horse.

The snow swept past unbroken. He saw nothing, nothing
but the storm in the bent trees below. The feet of the mountains,
as well as Canys itself, remained hidden in the storm. He was
alone on the mountain.

"Canrhion's rise!" he cursed. "I should have known not to
push that man so far!" The War Lord, apparently, had been
angry enough to take Rhian seriously. A picture shot through
his mind of the War Lord warming himself in front of a fire
at Branfach or Bellonbain.

Then came shock. No matter how ill-mannered the War
Lord was, he had brought Rhian this far into the mountains.
And only he could bring Rhian safely out again. Only the War
Lord could make further searching for Pinwy profitable. As
Rhian realized this, he realized also that the War Lord had
known it. Blast him!

But, oddly enough, he did not think more about the War
Lord's treachery. Instead he began to think about Pinwy, to
wonder if he really had come through the pass. For all Rhian
knew, Pinwy might be just out of sight, freezing to death.

Grimacing, Rhian urged his horse on. Pinwy was his brother.
And, Rhian realized, Pinwy had always been hard to fathom,
but he had never been cruel like Talwy. Picturing Pinwy, Rhian
wished he had been more willing to listen to him. Maybe Pinwy
had been right about Rhian's concern only for his kingdom.

Ianwyn said Pinwy was wise. And Rhian felt suddenly that he
needed nothing so much as wisdom.

8

Once the path left the pass and came back into the trees, the
snow began to slacken. A spot of light appeared in the clouds
to the east, heralding dawn. Pinwy, his mind still drugged by
sleep, slowed the tired mare in the first trees and slid from her
back. His feet crunched in the snow.

He patted the horse and straightened stiff knees. Memories
of the night—an awful mixture of nightmare and reality—
returned: the biting snow, the hideous darkness, the howl of
the wind, the distant cry of wolves. How he had survived he
would never know. He suspected, however, that the experience
and sense of the mare had kept him from dropping off a cliff
or being buried in an avalanche. More than once she had swerved
to miss the fall of a wind-thrown boulder; more than once she
had leaped over a crevasse, jolting her half-awake rider. Pinwy
rubbed her neck as she searched the snow for grass. She had
at least earned the right, he thought, to look for breakfast. What
she really needed was a rest.

But he knew that something beside the mare had protected
him. He shivered as he thought of what that might be. For,
during the night, when the storm almost took him from the
saddle, he had cried out in fear the name of Canrhion, the First
Fate. In fact, in his terror he had muttered every chant he knew,
whether it applied or not. It had struck him, however, that
Canrhion might not want to save him. Canrhion was after all
the patron Fate of the Mont Cants and of Canys, and Pinwy
was running away from both. He was bound for Serhaur, the
country of the Third Fate, the Fate of the stars and knowledge.

"Serron!" he remembered crying out. His appeal had been
brief, but still, once the wind had taken his cry, the storm had
seemed to calm itself, and he had seen (or imagined) a few
stars in the roof of cloud. They had lighted his way across the
mountains.

Moving away from the mare, Pinwy pushed through the

pines toward the sun. Soon he emerged onto an outcropping of stone overlooking the mountain forests beneath.

"Serhaur," Pinwy said in realization. "I am in Serhaur."

Below him cliffs fell away in wind-cut rock faces, and further on, pine-clad hills rippled down toward the lowland. Beyond lay land that seemed more or less flat but also thickly forested. This woodland stretched until it formed a black-green line on the shores of the distant sea.

"Land of forest, star, and tree," Pinwy said. A snatch from an old poem about Serhaur. "Bordered by both mount and sea." He knew his destination, Fach-ne-Rhoanith, lay northeastward across the forest on the edge of the sea. But in that direction, the sea was too far away to be seen. It would be a long ride.

Even so, he was not eager to continue his journey. He followed the rugged outlines of the mountains with his eyes. Something Rhian had once said came back to him, something about how all the royal houses of Rhewar seemed to match the landscapes of their respective kingdoms, how the Mont Cants had eyes the color of winter heather, a nature like summer dawn over the moors, and a temper like a winter hurricane. Pinwy knew this principle held true with the Branmawrs, who came from the cold north—he had met Sereniel, who had been cool at best. So what might the Esterans be like, ruling this vast land of wild forest, mountain, and river?

Pinwy crept back toward his horse. It might not be prudent to hurry to Fach-ne-Rhoanith without first learning more about the Esterans. It might pay to talk to woodcutters or crofters about them before appearing at their gates and demanding refuge.

As he mounted his horse, he told himself he was being silly. He urged the mare to the cliffs in search of a way down them.

He reached the edge of the flatland by noon; the mare found a path that led through a deep combe between rises of more formidable country. He met no trouble, but his ride, nonetheless, was not peaceful. The forest struck him as mysterious, veiled as it was with mist and light snow. Pinwy often mistook an old stump for an Esteran warrior. And whenever swallows flocked the wood, he ducked, imagining them arrows from an unseen archer.

At noon he ate his last wedge of cheese. It occurred to him that the War Lord of Canys was related to the House Esteran— the War Lord was one person Pinwy heartily hated. Compared with the imagined faces of dreadful Esterans, even Rhian began to seem less cold, less tyrannical, and less wrapped up in the kingdom than Pinwy had thought.

"Rhian may be thick-headed when it comes to poetry," Pinwy said aloud, "but he's not such a bad person, now and again." Without meaning to, he began to remember the times he had gone riding with Rhian, the Spring First Rhian had given him an ostrich quill and a phial of red ink, and the times Rhian had saved him from Talwy's anger. But Rhian himself had blamed Pinwy for sparking Talwy's anger the day Talwy had run away. And even when Ianwyn convinced him it was not true, he had not apologized. Nor had he thanked Pinwy for the warning about Doran Oergant. Nor did Rhian respect Pinwy's love for poetry. "Rhian heartily deserves whatever he gets," Pinwy said.

And yet, Pinwy no longer wanted to go to Fach-ne-Rhoanith. Not right away. This forest, on the other hand, pleased him. Tall, stately trees, unencumbered by low branches and bushes, let him see a good distance in every direction. Very little sunlight and even less snow penetrated the forest roof, so riding beneath the trees was almost like being indoors, in a hall with many pillars.

Maybe, he thought, he should not go to Fach-ne-Rhoanith at all. What would be wrong with staying in this forest? Certainly there were berries, roots, and fish in the streams, and better, the wood would be a perfect setting for writing poetry. Scanning the quiet trees, he imagined building a lean-to of logs and digging a fire pit in front. With the abundance of good wood and stone, he might after some years build a real home.

His house, he determined, would have plenty of rooms but not enough to bother him with cleaning and upkeep. He would have a kitchen and a pantry, with several fireplaces, and cupboards to hold all his earthen jars of berries and the cheese, apples, and beef he would get by trading with the nearest woodcutters' settlement. He would have several rooms with soft beds and big hearths, and his own room on an upper floor would have a balcony for looking out on snowy mornings. He would make time to write poetry, until he had a library-sized collection, then he would build another room in which to keep all the books of his works. This room, of course, would be in an accessible part of the house should he want to reread his work or perform it for visitors. He would have a feasting hall; it would have huge fireplaces, tables, and thick rugs on the floor. Pinwy would invite Ianwyn and Rhian and others to visit him, and they would marvel at the comfort of his existence.

Even Pinwy knew this could take place only in his imagination. But the idea was appealing. Thus wrapped in his fancy, he kept an eye out for a promising place to camp for the night.

He sensed he was approaching the right spot. The trees thinned and varied in kind; some he thought were wild apple and pear. Here also the stream was swifter, unfrozen and flanked by willows. The perfect place, he thought, might be just beyond the firs, next to the creek. He leaned forward to see if the site would fit his hopes.

He found to his surprise that at the very spot where he might have dismounted and built a fire was a house.

He reined the mare. The house, in fact, looked much like the one in his imagination. Built of gray stone, roofed with pine logs, it had at least a dozen chimneys, two floors, and at one side a window with a balcony.

He blinked then rubbed his eyes. But the house remained. He first thought to ride on and pretend he had not seen it. But he dismounted, fastened the mare's harness to a tree, and started for the door.

Stone steps rose to a heavy portal. Part of Pinwy made him knock and hoped someone would answer, but another part of him kept him ready to back away should the door open. It soon did, soundlessly. Pinwy stood his ground.

"Good afternoon, Pinwy Mont Cant," a voice said. "I have been expecting you."

Pinwy found himself facing an old man in a loose white robe belted with silver links. The man's beard was the color of the snow on the pines; Pinwy guessed the man was old. But he stood upright, and his shoulders were broad, and his eyes sparkled, clear green. His face, unless it was only the contrast with his beard, was brown. He seemed to be smiling, though his whiskers made it hard to tell.

"How do you know me?" Pinwy said. "I don't know you."

"Naturally we haven't met *before*," the man said, motioning for Pinwy to come in. "If we had met *before*, you would know me. I know you because we have met *after*."

"After?" Pinwy said. This was nonsense. The man must be mad. "You surely don't mean that you live backwards?"

"No," the man said, bringing Pinwy through the door. "Living backwards would be twice as troublesome as living forwards, which is difficult enough. No, I live *selectively*. If you know what I mean. An advantage of being a wizard. We enchanters don't live longer than anyone else, we simply move around in time enough to live all the most exciting moments of history."

Pinwy felt sure the man could not be sane. Still, the word *wizard* intrigued him, so he followed the man into the next room, a hall with a high roof and broad green tapestries.

"So you are a wizard," Pinwy said. "Do you mean a sorcerer?"

"A sorcerer?" the man said. He coughed. "That is not the right word. Neither is wizard, actually. In proper terms," he said, "I am a Priest of Six Fates—that term is deceptive, though, because I am the priest of only one Fate at a time. That is why I prefer to call myself an enchanter. What it comes to is that I am a practitioner of magic. Perhaps you know me as well as I know you. My name is Rhi."

"Not Rhi the Bright?" Pinwy said. "Not the enchanter who appears in all the old stories?"

"As far as I know," Rhi answered, smiling, "there is no other Rhi. And yes, I have managed to work my way into the old poems."

"But some of those poems are hundreds—thousands—of years old!"

"I told you already I move around in time," Rhi said. Then he blinked. "Or did I tell you that last time you will be here?"

As Pinwy tried to work that one out, Rhi guided him to a seat by the fire. Rhi tossed branches on the blaze then took a chair across the table from Pinwy. Near the fire it was almost too hot, so Pinwy took off his cloak. The name Rhi the Bright had awakened his interest, but he doubted if this man was the person he claimed to be.

"Would you like something to eat?"

"Yes, please," Pinwy said. He wondered if he should expect poison, but somehow this man, even if he were mad, did not seem evil.

"I hope white ale and new bread will be all right," Rhi said. He indicated with his hand a flask of ale and a plate of fresh buns that Pinwy had somehow overlooked.

"My favorite," Pinwy said. He narrowed his eyes. "How did you know?"

"Remember, I have met you *after,*" Rhi said. "The day you come up from Enfach Fawr to visit me, you will eat so many biscuits that my larder will not recover since."

Pinwy ate two buns before he noted the wizard was watching him. "Tell me," Pinwy said, uneasy again, "if you are really an enchanter who can shift in time, what are you doing in this empty forest. Why were you expecting *me?*"

"First," Rhi said, scratching his beard, "it is not an *empty* forest. You can see that. I am here catching my breath between adventures. I just finished cloak-and-dagger work for Talanwyn Esteran, the King of Serhaur—"

"Talanwyn?" Pinwy interrupted. "I thought Marmadan was king of Serhaur."

"He is," Rhi said. "Marmadan is Talanwyn's remote descendent. Talanwyn has been dead for three hundred years. I wouldn't think of serving the House Esteran these days. They do entirely too much beheading. Rather I am getting ready for my next task, which has to do with you."

"Me?" Pinwy said.

"Yes. And your brother, Rhian."

Pinwy looked at his hands. "I might have known Rhian would be involved with this."

"I hope you expected as much," Rhi said. "Because if you didn't, you are blind to what is happening to your brother. Perhaps you have been writing more poetry than is good for you." Pinwy folded his arms in defiance, but Rhi did not seem to notice. "Forces are gathering around Rhian," Rhi said, leaning forward. "There are wizards, myself and my brother, who have decided to come to this part of time. If you could only *begin* to realize what is at stake, you would soon forget your quarrel with Rhian. Two Fates have given him their signs, but those two Fates have given signs to kings before, and nothing came of it, because Serron, the Third Fate, is slower to recognize in anyone her quality for leadership, wisdom. Serron's fickle nature may cost us, because we have so little time. There are forces that want to keep Rhian from getting the third sign. Not to mention the other kingdoms that are afraid of the new power in Canys and may act drastically to curb it—"

"Do wizards always talk in riddles?" Pinwy interrupted. "I haven't understood a word you have said."

"I thought I was being very clear," Rhi said, lowering his eyebrows. "You poets are the hard ones to understand. Talk in riddles? Rather I think you are *listening* in riddles."

Pinwy only pressed his lips.

"Perhaps," Rhi said, "I can make it a little simpler. Forgive me, but the last time I talked to you, you will be much older and wiser. How old are you now?"

"Fourteen," Pinwy said. He reached for some ale.

"Let me put it this way, then. Your brother may be something more than just king of Canys. I have met him both in the future and the past (though in different guises from Rhi the Bright), and although he is far from perfect, he can take the power the Fates can give him. If you know old prophecies, you know what I am talking about. At any rate, I am interested in winning for Rhian the approval of the next Fate, Serron."

Pinwy sipped ale, still glaring at Rhi. "Why bring me into all of this?"

"That," Rhi said, "I can best explain through a spell." He stood up, his eyes bright, his lips tight together. He began to speak in a low, moaning voice:

> "Serron, Fate of stars and light,
> We watch the evening skies grow bright,
> Gently rise over Erda's breast.
>
> Ever stand the West,
> Bless the West,
> Sing the Seven Fates."

The wizard's hall sank to blackness; the fire, the patches of afternoon light from the shutters, the glow of candles on nearby tables vanished. The darkness made Pinwy's heart beat faster. He gripped the arms of the chair. "One moment," the wizard whispered, "wait one moment."

The blackness pressed in. But soon above him, beyond where the ceiling should have been, faint pricks of light appeared. Barely more than gray dots at first, they grew in number and intensity until the whole darkness above was ablaze with them. Pinwy realized only slowly that they might be stars.

They did not remain distant, twinkling stars, however; they grew and brightened, as if Pinwy was drawn in among them. Soon stars fell and splashed around him in crimson and indigo and lavender, like fireworks. Bursts of flame seemed to form dozens of unrelated scenes; looking at them, Pinwy suddenly knew why moths were fond of flame, why moonlight made good poetry, why the northern lights shone. It was something like reading a fascinating poem.

Then Pinwy found himself sitting in ordinary firelight, with Rhi staring at him. He stiffened and glared at the wizard.

"I still don't understand," he said.

"The Third Fate," Rhi said with a smile, "has a way with light. Of all the Fates, I find myself turning to Serron most often; I think she is the most pleasant of them all. Perhaps she is one of the most powerful." Rhi paused. "But I did not conjure up that spell to entertain you, Pinwy. People, as well as wizards, choose what Fate they will follow. And because of your poetry and because of your call to her on the pass, Serron has—adopted you, shall we say. Otherwise you could not have seen anything a moment ago."

Pinwy swallowed. A glimmer of understanding, possibly left over from Serron's spell, lighted his thoughts. "Because you and I are servants of Serron, we must persuade her to give her sign to Rhian."

"*You* must persuade her," Rhi said. "The Third Fate will approve Rhian only when you approve Rhian."

"Why?" Pinwy said.

The wizard's voice grew grim. "Because you will approve Rhian only after both of you have become a little wiser. And wisdom—a less spectacular kind of wisdom than the kind in books—is what both of you need desperately. The kind of simple wisdom that will lead you to understand one another or at least listen to one another. After all, how can Serron expect Rhian to understand anyone else if he cannot understand you, his brother? When he reaches to you, and you to him, Serron will give him her sign."

Pinwy looked at his lap for a long time before raising his head. "I think," he said in a small voice, "that I approve of Rhian right now. I can't be sure, but I think I have learned something. Rhian *has* given me the bad end of things. But maybe that's because he has had the bad end of things, too. Anyway, I am not angry with him now."

"What you have said makes a good start," Rhi said, "but you can't expect Serron to give Rhian her sign just because of something you say. The Fates do not hear words. The Fates hear deeds."

"You mean," Pinwy said, "I ought to go back to Canys and apologize to Rhian."

"Yes, you should. To begin with."

"To begin with?"

"The Fates are great beings. They overlook petty things and easy things. They concentrate on more noble and painful things."

"I don't know what you are trying to say. But I ought to start back now."

"You ought to indeed."

Throwing his cloak over his shoulder, Pinwy started toward the door. But he stopped and looked over his shoulder. "I almost thought," he said, "you might come back with me—"

Rhi laughed. "I would, but I am not well suited for traveling—in the way you do it. No, you must return to Fach-ne-Canys by yourself. But we will meet again, Pinwy Mont Cant; farewell for now."

"Farewell," Pinwy said.

9

The snow only increased in fury as the day went on. Blurs rose, fell, and loomed—shapes of rocks and cliffs. Rhian would have dismounted to lead his horse, but the trail was so narrow and the wind so strong he feared he would fall if he tried to climb from the saddle. So he gripped the bridle and concentrated on the turns in the trail. Used to the wind, he no longer felt the cold. Already his cheeks were bright crimson, his cloak heavy with ice, and his hair feathered with frost. The cold, in a sense, had become bearable. At least the aches in his cheeks and toes were muted by more severe pain at the tips of his fingers and ears. Still, there was something in the storm worse than the cold—fear.

The wind seemed to echo familiar voices. He thought of Ianwyn and Oenan, but mostly he thought about Pinwy. He wondered if Pinwy might be freezing to death or lying broken on the rocks somewhere below. "Pinwy!" Rhian shouted into the wind. "Pinwy, where are you?"

But growing with his concern for Pinwy was fear for his own safety. Although the storm seemed to be dying away, night was coming. Soon Rhian would find himself in a chaos of dark flying flakes; he and his horse could drop into some snowy pit. But he dared not stop, for he knew the cold might kill him if he spent the night without shelter. And because the trail was so narrow, he could not turn the horse for home. Besides, he had to find Pinwy.

The horse seemed nervous as well. He whickered and shivered, and Rhian felt his flanks quivering. "Drat the War Lord," Rhian growled, teeth still closed. "By Canrhion, if I catch him in Canys again, I will lock him in the deepest dungeon."

Lightning split the sky, and thunder rumbled on its tail. For a moment the whole mountain blazed up in white; the stallion's eyes rolled. He reared, with a twist that pitched Rhian back in the saddle. The stallion screamed, and the reins ripped from Rhian's hands.

He toppled backward. He felt his boots ripping from the stirrups. His back arched into nothingness. His arms splayed behind him, and he landed. For a few moments he heard the stallion bleating far above him. He smelled blood and felt pain in his leg. Then he dropped into nothingness.

10

Awakening slowly, Rhian became aware of his predicament bit by bit. First he noticed he was lying down, but not on a level—his legs were lower than the rest of his body, and one arm was higher. He saw nothing but the bright sky and the snow-crusted hem of his hood. He was cold, but because his cloak had wrapped itself around him as he fell, he had not frozen. In fact, he felt quite warm, in an odd and tingling way, in his head and in one leg.

The sun flashing in his eyes brought back memory of the night before. And then he knew that his head was ringing, his leg hurt terribly, and rocks prodded his back. Grunting, he lifted his head. But he did not lift it far; as the muscles of his neck strained, his head began to swim and his leg to throb. And what he saw made the hot pain in his leg go cold.

He lay on the brink of a cliff that plunged toward a glacier, far below. Glancing about, he realized he was perched on a narrow ledge, some distance below the trail. Actually it was hardly a ledge, more a part of the cliff that was a little less steep than the rest. Already one of his feet wobbled over the precipice, and his hand curled over the brink. A sudden move, a single shift, could send him sliding with a shower of pebbles into the void below.

The pain in his leg grew. It was soon so bad that he lifted his head again, slowly, gripping at rubble around him for support. He saw nothing of his leg, only a scarlet stain on the snow beneath it.

He realized his leg might be broken.

Sizing the rocks looming above him, he could not even guess how far below the trail he was. He was lucky, it seemed, not to have fallen all the way. But that was not much comfort.

He had never felt so helpless. His mind tried furiously to think of a way to reach the trail, but came up with nothing. If he moved too suddenly, he would slide from the cliff. And with a broken leg, he could hardly hope to climb the sheer rocks. Even if he reached the trail, without wood for a splint, he would not be able to walk. His horse was gone; he knew that. And his chances of rescue seemed slim; this high pass was used only rarely even in the summer and not at all during the winter. Though Ianwyn knew he had ridden east, she and the search parties she might send would not know where to search for him. The mountains were vast and wild. The only person who knew where Rhian was was the War Lord, who, for all Rhian knew, might be in Fach-ne-Rhoanith or Bellonbain by this time.

Rhian kicked with his good leg and tried to inch farther back onto the ledge, but his boot pushed more air than stone, and the sounds of pebbles scraping and falling into the depths made his skin crawl.

"Canrhion!" he called out. But Canrhion was only a watery sphere of yellow on the white sky, watching him unblinkingly.

It occurred to him then that he might die. Death had been little more than a word—he could not remember the day his mother had died, and his father's passing had been heralded by such a long illness that his death seemed only a sleep. But now death gnawed at his leg, and doom grinned on the bone-white glacier beneath. He felt tears start, not because he feared the teeth of rocks or the sucking-dry of starvation, but because he regretted the things that might have been. He first thought of grand things: his castle, his study, and rainy days he had spent looking over the moors of Canys, realizing the kingdom belonged to him. But he soon thought of Ianwyn; he saw her smile turn into a frown when he did not return. And there was Pinwy, lost and angry somewhere in these mountains, perhaps suffering or dying, Rhian could almost hear Pinwy's voice calling to him, distressed, cajoling . . .

"Rhian!"

He let his eyes fall closed.

"Rhian! Are you all right? Rhian!"

He felt content to listen to the voice from beyond memory. Soon enough, he knew, it would fall silent.

"Stay right where you are! Don't move!" the voice yelled. Rhian heard a faint scuffling of boots on stone and a whicker of a horse. A pebble, striking his forehead, made him open his eyes.

"Pinwy?" he shouted out. "Pinwy!"

"Rhian, I'm coming," Pinwy called from above. "Now don't move. Don't move, or you might drop off. I'm coming down."

"Pinwy! Be careful. Don't come down, or you might not be able to get back up again. Pinwy! Stay where you are."

A hail of pebbles preceded a pair of boots, which grounded themselves between Rhian and the edge of the cliff. "I can hardly stay where I was," Pinwy said, a little tremulously, "because I am here. And I *will* help you." The rising wind caught Pinwy's tawny hair. His eyes were wide.

"But how did you find me? Pinwy, how?"

"You have outdone yourself this time," Pinwy said. He winced when he saw Rhian's leg. "I can see I won't be able to get you up without a rope. Hold on while I climb up and get one."

With this, Pinwy, boots and all, disappeared upward. As Rhian listened, it seemed a long time before he heard Pinwy shout to him from the trail that he had a rope and was coming back.

A few minutes later Pinwy reappeared. He knelt on the ledge near Rhian's head. He had shed his cloak, and over one shoulder he wore a coil of rope, which he took off and began to let out. "This is to keep you from falling," he said as he threaded it under Rhian's waist and knotted it. "I am not very strong, Rhian." Rhian did his best not to cry out when Pinwy lifted his hips to secure the rope.

"What about a rope to keep *you* from falling?" Rhian called after Pinwy when he had begun to ascend again. He remembered that Pinwy had never been fond of heights.

"Never mind. If one of us has to end up at the bottom of the cliff, it ought to be me. I'm the one who ran away from Fach-ne-Canys and got you into this!"

"Be careful, Pinwy!" Rhian croaked. But Pinwy, with apparent disregard for his own safety, dropped back to the ledge and began to examine Rhian. "This isn't going to be easy," he said.

"Not for either of us," Rhian said.

Pinwy hesitated. Finally he checked the rope with a tug, bent down, and began to lift under Rhian's shoulders.

In spite of himself, Rhian cried out in pain. Pinwy released him and stood up again.

Rhian erased his wince. "It is all right," he told Pinwy. "Do what you have to."

Stooping again, Pinwy locked his feet against the ledge and took Rhian beneath the arms. He hoisted him up, and put Rhian's arms around his neck. Then with the rope tied to Rhian's waist and under his arms, he further secured Rhian to his own body. This left Pinwy's arms free for climbing. Rhian bit his tongue as pain shot through his body from his leg. Beyond Pinwy's shoulders he saw windy nothingness threaded with cloud and the distant peaks of the mountains over the great, groping glacier. He felt Pinwy's body straining and his own inching up the cliff away from the ledge. He kept imagining Pinwy's stance breaking, sending them both from the rock.

The next moments were terrifying. Pinwy found footholds more quickly, but Rhian could tell his strength was flagging. He felt his own weight dragging on Pinwy's shoulders, and though he tried to push up the cliff with his good leg, his kicking seemed only to hinder Pinwy, who grunted for him to stop. Rhian felt as if he were being lifted above the roof of the world, step by step. The ledge below was fast tucking itself under the rounded edge of the rock. Pinwy wheezed.

What seemed an eternity followed. More than once Pinwy's hold faltered, and Rhian was sure his brother had fainted or lost his footing. But by the time Rhian dared open his eyes, he saw he was lying on the edge of the trail, with Pinwy moving him toward level ground.

Fighting his way to a sitting position, Rhian glanced back

at the cliff, shuddered, then sighed. He was silent as Pinwy unfastened the rope from a boulder.

"Pinwy," Rhian said at length. "Why . . . ?"

"What else was I to do, Rhian?" Pinwy knelt and began to peel back the cloth around Rhian's wound. "Your leg looks bad. It might be broken."

"Pinwy, after the quarrel we had, after what I said to you, you could have ridden by. You could have at least avoided risking your own life—you could have gone to Fach-ne-Canys for help, instead. I know you didn't want to climb all the way down the cliff. By the Fates, why did you do it?"

"Because you are my brother," Pinwy said, looking at him.

"I suppose," Rhian said, "that is one of the advantages of having a brother, whether one is a king or not." Warmth and drowsiness swept over him as he looked up.

Pinwy reflected his smile. "And of being one," he said. "Whether you are a king or not."

11

Ianwyn could not sleep. A spattering of stars glittered from her window, and the white shape of Rhin the cat made a blur on her windowsill. Pushing her blankets aside, she wondered if she ought to venture down the tower steps to ask the grooms whether anyone—Rhian or Pinwy or the War Lord—had returned.

Her stomach felt hollow as she sat up. During the nights and days since Rhian had left, the hollowness had increased. And it had spread from Ianwyn into the castle itself—rooms like the King's Hall and Rhian's study were empty and cold, and about the only person who even bothered to come to dinner had been Miriel. In fact, if it had not been for Miriel's companionship, Ianwyn felt she might have gone mad. "As long as Mont Cants must be lost in the mountains," she whispered, "why couldn't I be with them?" If they did not return—she shuddered at the thought—there would be no Mont Cants left to rule Canys. Except her and Talwy.

"I wonder," Ianwyn said, "if Talwy had anything to do with

this." She sat on her bed and drew the bedclothes across her
knees.

To comfort herself, she recalled how that evening at supper
Miriel had said she was sure both Rhian and Pinwy would
return before midnight. Ianwyn wished she could share Miriel's
hope, but she had a sense of impending disaster that Miriel
perhaps did not apprehend, for Miriel was not Rhian's sister.

It must be near midnight. And Rhian had not returned.

And yet, the tower room suddenly did not seem as dark as
before. Moonlight glimmered under the crack of her door, and
a silver glow bathed Rhin. Looking up, Ianwyn saw three
stars framed in her window, each bright and distinct, each
shining with an unmistakable flame.

She marked the position of the stars—a large one to the
right, smaller ones on the left to complete a triangle. Circled
in her window, the stars matched a symbol she had seen more
often in stone and wood.

"Serron," she whispered. "Serron."

But a second realization almost made her forget the first.
"Serron would not give her sign for only me to see. Rhian must
be near!"

She flew to the window. As if the stars themselves were
sprinkled on it, the snow glittered around the walls of Fach-
ne-Canys, darkened only by clumps of hemlocks near the village. But a shape detached itself from the trees and followed
the road upward. Ianwyn saw the horse and its riders and knew
the sign had not been mistaken.

"Rhian," she whispered. Pinwy was with him. That they
would return together had been her hope, but there had seemed
so little chance of it.

This was like a miracle. Serron's miracle, she realized. Her
father had often talked about finding wisdom in the mountains.
If Rhian and Pinwy now shared a horse, they had indeed found
wisdom. But suddenly she wondered why Serron had waited
to give her sign until their return. Perhaps Serron had delayed
giving her sign until the journey was finished. But, Ianwyn
realized, the journey had really only begun.

IV
Fing

When Rhian woke, he felt drowsy and warm. He found himself wrapped in sheets and covered with quilts. A cloth hugged his head and another bound his leg. The room was warm and smelled of pine logs and candlewax. From somewhere near the foot of the bed came the crackle of a fire, and Rhian, gazing over humps in the blankets, saw flames licking in a familiar grate. He realized he was lying in his own bed.

"Sire," a voice said. Looking into the shadows, he saw the servant girl he had met in the King's Hall the night before he had gone after Pinwy. Her name returned to him slowly. *Miriel*.

Her eyes shone in the candlelight, and her hair, now bound in braids around her head, glowed slightly from the firelight behind it. Her eyes paused on him, and she smiled. "So you are awake at last," she said. "How do you feel?"

"Bandaged, mostly," he said.

"That is Ianwyn's doing," Miriel said. "She did not leave your side all night. She didn't, that is, until I persuaded her to get something to eat. I'm afraid she will be angry with me when she finds you awakened just as she left."

"How is Pinwy?"

Miriel turned toward the fire. "Better off than you," she said. She ladled something from a pot over the fire into a wooden flagon, which she brought to Rhian's bed. She knelt, helped him raise his head, then tipped the cup to his lips. A draught tasting of honey warmed his throat, but soon it was gone, and Miriel put the cup aside. "We were afraid you might not wake up, Your Majesty. You have lost blood, and your leg was badly broken."

Rhian winced. "When my brother Talwy and I were children," he said, "Talwy fell from an apple tree and broke his arm. I remember how everyone in the castle worried about him, how old Lord Varan brought him a jeweled chest for a get-well present. Everyone, especially my mother, worried over him and brought him things to eat. I was jealous, but what I didn't know at the time was that breaking a bone hurts too much to be worth any number of golden boxes or well wishes." Miriel laughed gently. "Has there been any sign of the War Lord?" Rhian asked.

"The War Lord?" Miriel said. Her eyes flickered up. "No. He has not returned to Fach-ne-Canys."

They looked at each other for a moment, then Rhian said, with a frown, "When I was a boy, I dreamed of perishing heroically in a battle. But now I am a little wiser, I think. Wise enough to know that there are things about life I would not like to give up." He glanced around the room. "Even little things, like the feel of heat from a fire, or the smell of newly washed sheets, or the sight of snowflakes. I suppose it takes facing death to make a person realize the beauty of life."

Rhian's eyes caught Miriel's. He saw his own face reflected in her storm-blue eyes, and he extended his hand toward her. She continued to watch him, her smile fading as his hand closed around hers. For a moment she seemed hurt, and then she looked away.

"My lord," she said in a whisper.

"I am hardly your lord."

She took her hand from his grasp, and still looking away, she rose slowly from her chair. "With your leave, Your Highness, I think I should go." She took up her skirts and pushed out the door.

Rhian looked at his hand, almost expecting to find it thorned. He laid it at his side and stared at the beams of the ceiling. "Canrhion's rise," he muttered. But before he could say more, the door opened again.

When he saw it was Ianwyn, he was both relieved and disappointed.

"By the Fates, you're awake!" She spent several minutes asking him how he felt, and she winced when she lifted the blankets to look at his leg. Next she adjusted his blankets, put more wood on the fire, and brought him another flagon of Miriel's brew. "I am no healer," she said. "I have been afraid all night that you would not wake up. When Ienan the groom and I set your leg, you didn't even stir."

"That," Rhian said, "is probably just as well."

"Without Miriel to comfort me, I might have gone mad with worry," Ianwyn said. She stopped. "By the way, was Miriel here?"

"She left only a moment ago."

"She left? Why?"

Rhian let his eyes fall half-closed.

Ianwyn, drawing a chair toward the bed, changed the subject. She explained her understanding of what had happened in the mountains according to Pinwy's story. Rhian was happy enough to fill in what Pinwy did not know, how the War Lord had deserted him at the pass, how his horse had thrown him, and how Pinwy had risked his life bringing Rhian up from the ledge.

"Pinwy's version was more modest," she said. "I am proud of him! I will have to think of some kind of a medal to give him."

She seemed less eager to speak about the War Lord, however, and when Rhian pressed her on the subject, she only stared out the window toward where late afternoon had darkened the clouds over the mountains. "The War Lord was too ambitious for a peaceful Mont Cant king," Ianwyn said. "Perhaps it is best he is gone. His anger will keep him away from Canys, but I don't think he is bitter enough to become our enemy."

"He was bitter enough to leave me in danger," Rhian said. "If he dares return to Canys, he will have the dungeon he wanted for the smith and his son."

A pause followed, then Ianwyn said, "We will have a feast when you can walk again. It will be in honor of both you and Pinwy, naturally, but of Pinwy in particular. Do you know, Rhian, that he has been waiting to see you. I sent him away to look after the servants, but he should be back soon. When he comes, see if you think he looks more like Father than he used to. He is sorry about running away—he kept asking me if I thought you would forgive him."

"Why wouldn't I forgive him?"

"I see," Ianwyn said, "that Pinwy isn't the only one who has changed. Indeed you deserve the third sign!"

"The third sign?" Rhian felt a twinge of anticipation.

Ianwyn's eyes went wide. "I forgot to tell you," she said.

She told Rhian how she had seen the stars in her window that formed the sign of the Third Fate.

"Are you sure?" Rhian said, feeling cold.

She nodded solemnly.

"But Serron is only the third," he said. "There are Seven Fates, Ianwyn. And perhaps you are mistaken about the sign—"

"You must not doubt the Fates," Ianwyn said. "Three of them have given you their signs. The rest may soon do so." Ianwyn bent nearer and said in a low voice, "When you were still in the mountains, Miriel had a dream. She told me only reluctantly."

"What did she dream?"

"She dreamed you were king of all Rhewar, and—"

"And?" Rhian frowned. "Is there more?"

"Dreams come for many reasons," Ianwyn said. "They may come from the Fates as warnings or prophecies, but they may also be figments of our own imaginations. What Miriel's dream was I cannot say—"

"What did she dream, Ianwyn?"

"She dreamed she fell in love with you," Ianwyn answered. "She dreamed she became your queen, but that when you kissed her at your wedding, the walls of Fach-ne-Canys melted away, and waiting outside were your enemies, who brought out daggers and killed you."

2

"I don't understand what Rhian sees in that girl," Pinwy said after Ianwyn had closed the door to Rhian's room a week after their return to Fach-ne-Canys. "And for that matter, I don't understand what *you* see in her, either. Both of you seem to have made her an honorary Mont Cant."

"Come on, Pinwy," she said. "What bothers you about Miriel? She is lovely—she seems to shine, and all of us need that. And she is terribly clever."

"Too clever," Pinwy said, narrowing his eyes. "She knows too much to be a servant."

They moved away from Rhian's door. But Pinwy stopped

under the first torch and repeated, as if Ianwyn had not heard, "The girl knows too much to be a servant from Fach-ne-Armad, as she says she is."

"If she isn't from Armad, where *is* she from?"

Pinwy looked away. "I haven't worked that out yet, but I know she doesn't come from Canys. Take one look at her and you can see that. Have you ever seen anyone in Canys with *blue* eyes and *black* hair? Have you? My guess, Ianwyn, is that she comes from the south, probably from Armei. I remember a ballad about the House Arma-ne-Ithy, the rulers of Armei, that said they had 'cloud-blue eyes.'"

"You are probably right," Ianwyn said. She herself had no suspicions about Miriel. Her suspicions, rather, centered on Pinwy. "You are probably right," she said again. "Miriel was probably born in Armei and brought as a slave to Fach-ne-Armad. There is an awful slave trade going on in the Western Sea, and the slavers often rob cradles in fishing villages along the coast. Miriel is not sure of her own background herself. She tells me the only thing she can remember are the slave huts of Fach-ne-Armad."

"What I would like to know, then," Pinwy said, "is how Miriel learned so much in those 'slave huts.' The girl knows more about horses than our grooms do. She told Rhian yesterday that the reason his horse threw him in the pass was because it was ill-bred."

Ianwyn shrugged. "They sell horses as well as slaves in Armad. It doesn't seem odd to me that she might know about them. After all, everyone has his specialty. You, Pinwy, know far more about poetry than most princes do. Miriel knows about horses."

"Not just about horses," Pinwy said. "Two days ago I read her and Rhian my latest poem—a ballad about a boy who tames a wild horse. When I had finished, Miriel said she liked the symbolism in it and thought the assonance was good, but I ought to work on my alliteration. Now where did she hear terms like that—from a slaver? And that isn't all. She told me the poem reminded her of 'Y Maeron, The Windfate,' an ancient poem by one of the first bards of Rhewar. I have never read the poem myself. It is written in an old Armein dialect that is impossible to understand without years of training. I hope you don't think slave traders and wharf folk study ancient languages!"

By this time they had reached the end of the corridor. Ianwyn wadded her apron in her hands and pushed against the doors with her shoulder. "Does it matter that Miriel is educated?" she said. "What difference does that make?"

Pinwy frowned. "Miriel pretends to be docile. But under all of that, she seems very strong. There is a steely look in her eyes, as if she has often been in danger and is almost used to it. I think she is a spy."

"I appreciate your taking food to Lord Toran," Ianwyn said, "but you shouldn't listen to him too much. He thinks everyone is a spy. He even thought Mother's sister was a spy when she came to visit us when Father died. Canys is neither big nor important enough to draw spies from the powerful countries of the south. If there *is* something Miriel is hiding from us, she will tell us in time."

"After she is queen of Canys, you mean," Pinwy said.

"That, Pinwy, was not nice."

"You can't deny that Rhian is fond of her," Pinwy said. "Four times out of five when I visited him today, *she* was there. And the other time all Rhian talked about was what Miriel had said or what Miriel had done." Pinwy sighed. "Have you noticed how Rhian looks at her? Have you heard the way he talks about her? He even asked me today if I would write a poem about her. Hah!"

Ianwyn laughed. "Myself, I think it is about time Rhian fell in love. That business with Princess Sereniel was hard on him. And Rhian is almost eighteen. Most kings—our father was one—marry when they turn eighteen. And the fact that Miriel isn't a princess won't make any difference. One advantage of being king of a small kingdom like Canys is that one does not have to choose from the nobility. Mother wasn't a princess, at least not by blood." Ianwyn took a deep breath. "Anyway, I don't foresee a wedding right away. It isn't as if Miriel is trying to become queen. In fact, she's done her best to keep her distance from Rhian, though I think she likes him as much as he likes her."

Pinwy's face softened. "Maybe I have been seeing too much of Toran," he said. "Have I been imagining things?"

Ianwyn took his arm and guided him toward the courtyard doors. "Your logic, Pinwy, is flawless. The only reason you are concerned about Miriel is because you are concerned about Rhian."

3

In the small hours of the morning, a new storm lashed against Ianwyn's tower. She first noticed Rhian's voice in her dreams, and when she awakened, she realized that shouting, distant and shrill, was coming from the darkness, not her mind. She threw her blankets aside and raced down the stairs. All the torches in the castle had gone out; there was not a glimmer of light anywhere. She ran blindly down the empty corridors, feeling the darkness thunder in her ears and brush against her legs. Darkness blinded her, snagged her feet, closed in around her, and made the screaming only more horrible. And other sounds rose in the darkness: moans from beams, scratching in the rafters, and groans from the castle walls in the push of wind and snow.

She met Miriel carrying a candle to Rhian's door. Both of them hurried into Rhian's room.

"No!" Rhian shouted from the darkness. "No! I won't come with you! I won't! Canrhion! I'm falling! I'm falling! Oh, stop, stop, stop! Miriel! Don't let them. Ianwyn, help me! Pinwy! Help me! Off, you thing of blackness, off!" Miriel fumbled for more candles. Ianwyn dropped to her knees beside the bed.

"Rhian," she said. "Rhian! It's Ianwyn. I'm here." She caught his arms and pinned them to the bed. His wrists were startlingly hot; the muscles of his arms stood out in the candlelight. At Ianwyn's touch he began to relax, though he continued to mutter.

Miriel rekindled the fire then joined Ianwyn. Her hair, disheveled and wound into dark knots, hid her face, but her eyes flickered with worry. Rhian stopped moving when she touched his face, but his sheets and blankets twisted around his legs and tumbled into heaps on the floor. The collar of his nightshirt stretched, torn, between his shoulder and his throat. The bandages on his legs had ripped away, and his leg was bleeding again, though, to Ianwyn's relief, it had not rebroken.

While Miriel gathered up the pillows and covers, Ianwyn straightened the nightshirt and held a hand to his forehead. It was indeed more than a nightmare; she felt fever burning beneath her palm. Beads of sweat collected on his brow. He was breathing hard.

"Fetch some water," Miriel told Ianwyn. Her eyes burned, and her lips were so tightly pressed they were only a pale line. Ianwyn took a candle and fled from the room; she soon returned with a basin of water and a cloth. Miriel had collected Rhian's quilts and had drawn them over him again, for he had begun to shiver. She took the cloth from Ianwyn, bathed his forehead; but his skin remained pale and hot.

"I don't understand," Ianwyn said, fighting tears. "He seemed so well yesterday. He seemed almost completely well."

"It's my fault," Miriel said, her face softening momentarily.

Ianwyn stopped and turned Miriel to face her. "It's my fault," she said again, her voice passionless and dogged.

"Your fault? How?"

"I shouldn't have done it. But I couldn't help it."

Ianwyn took the cloth. "Tell me what you did," she said. "Tell me why it is your fault Rhian is sick."

Miriel's eyes went thick with tears, but her face remained rigid. "I love your brother as much as you do," she said. "But I must be careful. He is the king. And I am...a servant. I cannot let anything happen between us. I cannot let my dream come true." Miriel stared at Ianwyn. "But last night Rhian and I were talking, as we sometimes do, about love‾—how oddly people behave, and such. Rhian began talking about Fing, the Fate of love. Fing, he said, was the kindest of the Fates. She distributes her gifts—both love and fire—ungrudgingly. But I told him he was wrong, that it is good to love someone not when it is easy, but when it is hard, when to love him is to endanger your very life. The love that is hard—not hard to find but hard to keep—is Fing's love, I said. Fing has very little to do with the other kinds. Then he asked me if I had Fing's love, if it was hard for me to love him. I told him it was. Then he said he must not have Fing's truest love, for he had loved me from the very first. He said loving me was as easy for him as breathing. And I couldn't help it, Ianwyn. I said I loved him, too." Miriel paused. "Don't you see, Ianwyn? All of this is my fault!"

Ianwyn guided Miriel to a chair. "It is not your fault. You must be half awake or you wouldn't think such a thing. I think I understand—from your dream you seem to think that by loving Rhian you will harm him. But Miriel, love never harms.

Never. Love always mends. It builds and brightens."

"But the dream!" Miriel said. "You yourself told me that part of the dream—the part about Rhian becoming king of Rhewar—was Fate-sent. If part of it was, the other part was too."

"Nonsense," Ianwyn said.

Miriel looked at her hands; her eyes remained dull. "My dream was real, Ianwyn. And I am not what I seem; Rhian may indeed be harmed if I am foolish enough to let him love me, whether it is easy or not."

Ianwyn stiffened. "You are not what you seem?" She remembered what Pinwy had said, and for the first time she saw in Miriel something deep and sad. It seemed suddenly chill, and Rhian began to moan again. But Ianwyn said, "No matter what you are, Miriel, saying you love Rhian won't bring fever to him. That is nonsense. We both know that."

Miriel looked at Rhian, and the shadow in her eyes sank away. "Maybe I am not awake still, after all," she said.

Ianwyn smiled, but she felt suddenly weary. "When one is awakened in the middle of the night to this," she said, "it is hard to be calm."

4

Daylight brought visitors. Most had heard Rhian's shouts in the night and came half-dressed and groggy to ask about him. Each looked at the still king and fell silent; some nodded knowingly to their companions, for paleness like snow lay on him, and no muscle twitched. Some of the servants offered to bring food to sustain Miriel and Ianwyn, and another servant, one who knew a little healing craft, examined Rhian and nodded gravely. "It is a fierce fever," he said. "If it does not break by nightfall, His Highness may not wake again."

Dignitaries from the village came before noon and looked on Rhian with pity. To Ianwyn's horror, some of them discussed whether Pinwy could be crowned king of Canys if Rhian died, or whether Talwy, the next-oldest prince, should be found. Ianwyn lost her temper when the head of the village council asked her where Rhian kept the Mont Cant crown.

Noon arrived with a brief golden brightness, then paled into afternoon, but neither Ianwyn nor Miriel left the room. Rhian seemed unchanging; he lay motionless. Sometimes when Ianwyn touched his forehead it felt hot, and other times it felt cold and damp.

"I wonder where Pinwy is," she said to Miriel when afternoon had begun to deepen. "I suppose he has to hold the castle together, since no one else is around to do it."

"He will come soon," Miriel said.

But the shadows continued to thicken. Cold set into the room in spite of the fire. Still Pinwy did not come. Ianwyn felt herself ebbing toward desperation.

Then, when Miriel began to light candles, Pinwy came. Ianwyn rushed to him. She meant to reprimand him, but she stopped when she saw him clearly. He was bundled in his riding cloak, and when he threw back his hood, his face was wind-reddened. Bits of ice clung to his hair and eyelashes. He was breathing heavily, so Ianwyn guessed he had been running.

"Pinwy," she said, "if you went to the village for a healer, you wasted your time. The nearest healer is in Armad, and I have already sent for him."

"I didn't go to the village," Pinwy said.

"Did you hear that Rhian was ill?"

"I heard," Pinwy said, "but—"

"Not just ill," Ianwyn said. "He may die, Pinwy!" Ianwyn threw her arms around Pinwy.

"Ianwyn," he said. "Please. Rhian won't die. He won't if you will just listen to me. Of course I know he is sick—but I received a message this morning..."

"A message?" Ianwyn blinked at him.

"A message from one of the pages that there was someone asking for me in the village."

"And for that you went to the village?"

"Who from the village would want to see you?" Miriel asked. "The whole village council came here this morning."

"Not *from* the village, *at* the village. The person who summoned me was not from Canys at all. I met him while I was in Serhaur—yes, I know I never told you about him, Ianwyn. But he is a difficult person to explain and an even harder person to ignore. So when I heard he was in the village, I had to go meet him at the inn."

Ianwyn looked at him, uncomprehending. "But Pinwy, how could you go at a time like this?"

"I went to Rhi—that is the man's name—because I knew he could help Rhian," he said evenly. "The groom told me Rhian was sick, beyond help of healers. That is why my friend was in the village—because Rhian was sick. He came to give me this!" Pinwy produced something that, catching the light from the hearth, blazed like a fire itself.

Ianwyn saw that it was a phial. It was filled with a golden liquid, which in the firelight looked like trapped flame or condensed light. Through facets of the crystal container, it cast odd reflections, like birds or butterflies, on the walls and ceiling. And even though Pinwy held the phial firmly, the patterns of light revolved and spun, flitting like doves around the room.

Miriel stepped back. "Your friend brought that?"

Pinwy nodded. "He gave me a note, too," he said. He brought out a bit of parchment, which he handed to Ianwyn. She unfolded it and held it up to the light. As Miriel edged nearer, Ianwyn read aloud.

"To the princesses of Fach-ne-Canys," she read. Her eyes flickered to Pinwy's. "Whoever your friend is, he doesn't know our family."

Pinwy shrugged.

"I have sent an elixir of healing with Pinwy. Let King Rhian taste it, and all will be well." Ianwyn looked at Pinwy. *"A concerned friend."*

Ianwyn took the phial and held it at arm's length. The neck of the phial felt warm. Certainly she could not consider giving this to Rhian without first knowing more about Pinwy's friend. There were, after all, few men from Serhaur with any love for the House Mont Cant. When she looked at the phial, however, she could not think it was poison. Its warmth eased her tautness, and soon she took it in both hands and knelt at Rhian's bedside.

Ianwyn looked at Rhian and feared it was already too late. The last traces of color were gone from his cheeks, and if he was breathing, his chest gave no sign of rising. His sealed lips were the same color as his cheeks, and even his beard and hair seemed white and stiff. Ianwyn wrenched the stopper from the phial.

Pinwy and Miriel sighed as the fragrance of the liquid spread. The aroma was rich, dark, golden, something like the smell of a ripe pear or baked apple, but not so sweet, and much, much deeper. In the same moment the room seemed lighter, and Rhian's lips parted.

"The liquid is life," Miriel whispered. "Quickly, Ianwyn. Give it to Rhian."

Pinwy lifted Rhian's head, and Ianwyn trickled the liquid on his tongue. She had known since childhood not to give anything to drink to someone who was sleeping, but somehow this seemed different. The contents of the phial did not seem to be a liquid after all, but rather honey-colored light. Rhian absorbed it, but he did not choke or cough, and he did not swallow. The contents, when gone, left no residue in the bottle but an odd glimmer.

Almost before Ianwyn had taken the phial away, Rhian's lips moved. His cheeks darkened with color. His lips turned crimson. His arms shifted under his blankets. He began taking gulps of air. She touched his forehead and found it no longer hot, only warm, and the hair she brushed away was bright and wiry. Before she could speak, he opened his eyes.

Though they were hazy, the fever had left them. For a moment his expression was confused, searching, but then his eyes rested on Miriel, who knelt beside the bed.

"Miriel," he muttered, dragging an arm from beneath his blankets, reaching toward her. "Miriel. I am glad to see you." He smiled slightly. "It is still easy to love you."

She went ashen, and Ianwyn bit her lip and forced her eyes away.

Rhian's arm began to falter. "Miriel," he said again.

Her shoulders relaxed, and she took his hand. Her eyes glittered. "Rhian," she said, "it is easy."

5

"I have decided to go on a campaign when the good weather returns."

Miriel, who had been mending, looked up from her needle. "What do you mean, Rhian Mont Cant? Every day you tell me how you hate fighting and wars and weapons." She tossed her work aside. "Now do you expect me to believe you are going to battle?"

"I didn't say battle, Miriel. I said *campaign*."

"Raiding amounts to the same thing," she said.

"Now why would I want to go raiding?"

"Why would you want to go campaigning?"

Rhian broke into a smile. "You don't see what I mean, do you? You are right about war. I loathe swords and armor and shields. But when I say campaign, I don't mean with a sword. I don't mean to strike across the border into Serhaur or Oerth. I want to shape things up *between* the frontiers, instead. I have been lying in bed too long. It's time I began to be king again. Canys may be prosperous, but it needs a guiding hand. Do you have any idea what state the tax system is in? And from what you have told me about the slave trade in Fach-ne-Armad, I think I owe a visit to the Lord of the City. I won't allow slavers in my realm. And other things need doing—mending roads, herding sheep, and even giving out apples. Ask Ianwyn. And I should find a new War Lord and train a few warriors. I won't attack anyone. But it might be wise to be prepared. Canys has fierce neighbors, Serhaur and Oerth—"

"And Armei," Miriel said.

"And just about every other country on Rhewar."

Rhian's own speech inspired him. He felt the strength of his gradual healing, and though he knew he was not well yet, the past few days had made him restless. That morning Pinwy had brought fresh clothes from the tailors, among them a tunic in Mont Cant gold with an embroidered jerkin of green wool. Pinwy had helped him stand and dress, and Rhian had taken a basin of water and a comb to his matted hair. He had been almost sorry when Pinwy helped him back to bed; he was thoroughly weary of lying down. Pinwy helped him reach a compromise by propping him up with cushions. In this position Rhian received Miriel when she came later that morning. Out of his nightclothes, shaved and combed, he felt much more presentable.

But Miriel laughed when she saw him. She said she wondered if she had found the right room—she was looking for Rhian Mont Cant. Rhian laughed, too, but not hard.

Miriel smiled slightly. "What I don't understand," Rhian said, looking at her needlework, "is why you have had to sew all day. I seem to recall releasing you from servitude. You are a lady now, a lady like Ianwyn—"

"Which is precisely why I am doing mending," Miriel said. "Ianwyn works harder than five servants, and now that I am a lady, I have learned my lessons from her." Miriel pinched the seam of the garment. "Do you think I can keep idle with your sister around?"

Rhian laughed. He could imagine Ianwyn now, hurrying through the corridors with her skirts in her fists, alighting here and there like a bumblebee.

Glancing at Miriel, he saw she was again buried in her work. He watched her, as he had watched her all during his illness, and he could understand her expression. Each twist of her lip, each narrowing of her eyes, each glint of her teeth was familiar; her very face, the mere familiarity of it, made him smile to himself.

Pushing the tip of his tongue between his teeth, he swung his legs from the bed. He winced when his feet met the floor, and his head began to swim, but in a moment he stood, one leg cocked.

"Rhian!" Miriel said when she looked up. "Just what do you think you are doing?"

"I'm standing, of course."

She frowned, raising her needle toward him. "It's dangerous for you to be on your feet without one of us helping you. Here, let me help you sit down again."

"Not yet," Rhian said. "I didn't stand to vex you, Miriel. I stood for a reason. I won't lie down again until I have done what I need to."

Miriel folded her arms.

He limped across the floor toward the fire, to an oak cabinet. He braced himself against it with one arm and opened one of its doors with the other. "Now close your eyes," he said. "Close them tightly, Miriel."

Miriel pressed her eyes closed. "Is it a surprise?" she asked.

"I hope so," Rhian said.

"A surprise," Miriel said, "could be anything from a bag of gold to a poke in the ribs."

"Hold out your arms—no, as if you were carrying something—that's it."

"I hope it's nothing *alive*," Miriel said, giggling a little.

"You'll find out," Rhian said. Gently he lowered his burden into Miriel's arms.

Her eyes sparkled when she opened them. "Rhian! A gown! For me? It's beautiful!" Indeed, as Miriel unfolded it and held it up against her, Rhian thought it *was* beautiful, as beautiful as Ianwyn had promised it would be. The color of the dress matched Miriel's eyes, which turned to him, wide with tears. "Rhian," she said, giving him a brief hug. "Rhian, this is a gown for a princess, or a queen..."

Rhian beamed.

Turning her head sideways, she looked at him. "But when will I wear it? And what would I wear with it?"

Rhian brought his other hand from behind his back. Candlelight caught on a bright object in his fingers, and silver stars reflected from it to freckle the ceiling. It was a hoop of white gold, wrought, thin as wire, into a coronet. "You can wear this," he said.

At Rhian's bidding Miriel knelt, and he put the coronet on her head. Then he took her hand and drew her to her feet. "But this is nothing to hold back my hair," she said. "It is the crown of a queen."

"Precisely," Rhian said. "Fach-ne-Canys has been too long without a queen. But it will have a queen again, this spring."

Miriel said nothing in answer, for Rhian had never really asked her a question.

6

Darkness gathered in the east and spread westward, shrouding the gloomy clouds and swallowing the last glimmer of blue. The ridges of the Monte Serhaur vanished behind the curtain of evening, but the hill of Fach-ne-Canys stood out against the sky, golden squares in its walls and tower. On a distant hill, two men knelt in the snow among dead thickets of current and gorse, watching the tower.

The distant light gleamed in the gray eyes of the first man, who looked at Fach-ne-Canys with a frown. "I will not wait any longer, Enrhi," he said. "Let us go at once."

"Patience, my prince," the black-robed man said beside him. "Do not be foolish. You are tired of waiting? I have waited countless years, cursing the passage of time, but I am careful not to move too soon. Haste is often death, my prince."

Talwy tasted acid in the back of his throat. "I didn't ask for your help, Dark One. I asked only for the wish you promised me." Talwy shuddered in the shadow of memory; the snow suddenly chilled his knees, and the wind brought prickling to his neck. But no matter how dreadful the granting of the wish had been, he was now immortal, and the dark strength of that knowledge brought flecks of purple fire into his eyes. "Now that the wish is granted," he said, turning to the sorcerer, "I want only my freedom, creature of Enrhion. I don't need you to claim my throne for me. I need only this." He drew a dagger from his cloak and lifted it toward the sky. It gleamed dully.

The sorcerer only laughed, a sound like the click of iron. "You overestimate yourself," he sneered. "You seem to think you are more ruthless than you really are. How many would you kill at Fach-ne-Canys before that knife faltered in your hand, before that spark of loathsome goodness would stop you? Would you cast away that dagger after murdering only Rhian? I see in your eyes that you would—and that would not be enough. The people of Canys would rather place Pinwy or Ianwyn on the throne than you. You seem to forget, Talwy, it would not take them long to realize who Rhian's murderer was. Go this night to Fach-ne-Canys if you want, but you will get only blood, and no crown."

Talwy slipped the dagger into his sheath, but his eyes glittered. "Do not mock me, Dark One. I would gladly turn this dagger against you."

"I have passed the purple fire of Enrhion, just as you have," the sorcerer said. "I am, as you are, the master of my life. I have turned away greater daggers, Mont Cant."

Talwy laughed. "You forget that I know the mastery as well as you do. This dagger, twisted in the right place, could bring you pain enough that you would willingly flee your body. Beware, Enrhi the Dark, or I will show you reason to fear me."

The sorcerer paled, but his eyes burned on.

"I am more clever a fool than you thought me," Talwy said.

Enrhi touched his beard, then began to stroke it. "Perhaps." He looked at the castle, where three stars winked in the windows beneath the battlements. "Enrhion finds many clever fools, for he is the Master of All Cunning, the lord of hooded lies and silent darkness, the Lord of Death." The sorcerer smiled. "But Enrhion's servants are never wise. And when wit and wisdom are thrown together in the arena of night, wisdom often is the victor." Then the sorcerer muttered, so that Talwy could scarcely hear, "If only I had been given the other twin..."

"You have this twin," Talwy said. "And if you had the other, you would not like it. You blame me for the spark of kindness you say is in me. But Rhian has no spark—he is an entire blaze!"

"Not easily quenched," the sorcerer said.

"No."

"Not easily quenched by a foolish dagger, at least. Again, we must be patient. If you want the Mont Cant throne, you must take it in the guise of Rhian, not as Talwy. I have told you I will give you the crown, in spite of your ingratitude. I will fulfill my promise."

"How?" Talwy demanded. "A week ago we came here, and we have done nothing but wait among these weeds!"

"Maybe *you* have done nothing," Enrhi said, "but I have not been idle. While you slept that first night, I conjured up spells and threw them at Fach-ne-Canys. While you slept, my spells brought a killing fever to the king of Canys, and if all had gone well, we would have slipped into the castle to replace your dead brother with you, with the bindings of a broken leg like his. At dawn you would have recovered from your supposed sickness as Rhian. That much I did for you already. No, I have not been idle."

Talwy said, icily, "What do you mean, 'if all had gone well'?"

"Your brother, of course, did not die."

"Your spells failed?"

"I have not cast a spell that failed in a thousand years! My feckless fool, my curse was turned aside, remedied by an enchantment as powerful as my own. As I suspected, my brother, who is also camped in the snowdrifts near Fach-ne-Canys, has come to protect Rhian Mont Cant. He arrived in time to cure my first spell. He has turned away every spell I have cast since."

Talwy seized his dagger. "Then I will settle my own score."

The sorcerer froze Talwy with a stare. "Dark magic is the least of my powers. And even though the hands of Enrhion have been bound, there are other powers that can serve us."

"You have a plan?"

"I always have a plan. My second method will take longer than the first would have—but it will bring a defenseless Rhian to us in Enrhimonte before summer. We should return to Mont Enrhi and bide our time there, setting our snare in the paths of the mountains, where not even Fate-blessed Rhian Mont Cant will be able to escape us. Come." The sorcerer rose from his haunches and towered into the starlit sky over the skeletons of the bushes.

"How will Rhian come to us?" Talwy said, still crouching.

"You have so little faith in me, Magic-son."

Talwy stood and glared at Enrhi. "True."

"Do you think you are the only royal child who has run away from his House? No! Nearly a year ago, a princess of the House Arma-ne-Ithy fled the castle at Armei Nanth after an argument with her uncle, the king. Since then she has avoided her uncle's searchers by taking the guise of a servant. Even now, the princess is secure in her secrecy, undiscovered. Her uncle's warriors are far off her trail, searching for her in the mountains of Fingonlain."

"What does that have to do with Rhian?"

"This very night," Enrhi said, nodding at the lights of the castle, "your brother has asked Miriel, a servant girl, to marry him. But he will not marry a servant. He will marry Princess Marin Arma-ne-Ithy of Armei."

Talwy's eyes lit. "What would happen," he said slowly, "if the king of Armei received an anonymous letter telling him where his niece is and what she has done. The possibilities are endless, Enrhi the Dark. You are truly cunning."

"Now you will have patience. You will let me bring the crown of Canys into your hands."

Talwy smiled. "I will wait," he said.

The last touches of light blurred the western sky as the two broke away from the bracken. The stars above seemed to pale and withdraw as they passed. Soon the lights of Fach-ne-Canys vanished into the gloom of the midnight moors.

Talwy grinned to himself, but he touched the hilt of his dagger.

7

The weather that winter, whenever Pinwy had time to notice it, was bright and cold, broken by a few dark snowstorms, but generally frozen, blue and clear. Except for the hill of the castle,

Canys was blanketed with flat snow that made the land seem to be an enormous frozen pond.

All of it would have made excellent poetry. And though Pinwy was slow to admit it, some of his activities would have made good poetry, too. One task he both liked and dreaded was bringing meals to Lord Toran. Pinwy had been afraid of the man since he had been small. And Toran's illness, if anything, had soured his disposition. His voice grated and crackled. His eyes flashed with black fury, and his tongue seemed to lash sparks into the darkness of the room. But Toran's other moods made up for his madness. And one afternoon Pinwy forgave Toran everything.

In unsteady candlelight, Toran lay sunken, a shadow among the other shadows of the room. If his hair had been silver before, it was now white. "Mont Cant," he said, turning half-lidded eyes to Pinwy, "my time is growing short. There is something I must tell you before I pass into the Dimmer Lands."

Pinwy leaned a little closer. He was not really concerned. Toran often said such things, that his end was creeping on him, and often he confided in Pinwy secrets about spies and demons, phantasms of mighty foreign powers. Toran's condition now seemed neither better nor worse than it had for most of the winter. Pinwy prepared himself for more news of spies.

"I have a warning for you, Mont Cant."

"A warning," Pinwy presumed, "that I should give Rhian?"

Toran's face constricted. "I am through with spies, Mont Cant," he said. "I am through finding evil in men's eyes—my own sight is fast blurring. You must discover your own spies, Mont Cant. But do not discover too many—" His voice faltered; when his next words came, they were hushed. "That is what I must warn you about. I see that you are much like me. We have the same look in our eyes. You, unlike your brother, see deeply into men, wonder about what they think, watch their secret frowns. It is a blessing, Mont Cant . . . and a curse!"

Pinwy said nothing. The stale darkness of the room and the thickness of Toran's voice disquieted him. For the first time Pinwy thought Toran might indeed be near death. His forehead grayed, and his eyes became only ragged slits on his face.

"You are not well," Pinwy said. "I will bring Rhian."

Pinwy stood up to leave, but a hand caught his elbow. "Stay," Toran said. "Stay."

Kneeling at the side of the bed, Pinwy saw the grooves

around Toran's mouth relax. "You are young, my prince," he said. "I am old, cold, empty, filled with only the hollowness of suspicion. I wanted to see clearly, but I only blinded myself." Toran paused, and Pinwy for a moment feared he had died. But when he spoke again, his voice was a little louder and smoother. "I told your brother once to read eyes, not lips." His eyelids fluttered. "But Pinwy, read hearts."

Pinwy fought back tears when he brought Rhian to Toran's room. He felt like crying not because Toran had died but because throughout the days of his illness, Toran had called him by the name of his House, and only at the last did his frost yield enough to say Pinwy.

As Rhian lifted the blankets over Toran's face, he grimaced. He stepped back and laid a heavy arm on Pinwy's shoulder. "Toran was bitter, but he was strong," he said. "He was as cold as snow or frozen earth, but he was as strong as an icy boulder."

Pinwy listened for the sounds of the storm through the walls. "Strength fails in the end," he said. "But so must cold, Rhian."

Rhian nodded. "But it is unfortunate that Toran's spring came so late. Still, some never warm at all, and Toran served my father well for many years." Rhian sighed and pushed the hair back from his forehead. He glanced at Toran.

"He won't be buried, then?" Pinwy said. He knew that the earth of the moors claimed the poor, the evil, the sad, and the hard-hearted.

"No," Rhian said thoughtfully, "no. Toran will have a pyre."

8

The night before Spring First, snow still crusted the ground. The hill of Fach-ne-Canys, it seemed, was cast in snow for good; the drifts were inches thick, shallower around stones and ruts but somehow tenacious. Ianwyn feared there would be snow for the first day of spring, for Rhian's wedding day.

But an abrupt change came at sunset. As soon as the sun brushed the horizon, stripes of silver shot through the clouds, and before long, the whole western sky flamed yellow. The snow itself took on a gold tint, and the bleak, ashen colors of winter burned away. At twilight a warm, moist west wind lifted, bringing with it sun-drenched clouds out of the sea, so that even when the sun was gone, there were glitterings of yellow in the clouds, as if bits of the sun had been trapped there. Dusk brought purple drapes across the mountains and quenched the fire in the east. But lightning flickered out across the moors, and its flashes were warm and ruddy, distant promises of spring.

Ianwyn saw sunset from her tower and was pleased. Rain would do little to help those traveling to the wedding; it would muddy the roads, dampen spirits, and perhaps soak wedding gifts. But Ianwyn knew a good rain would wash away the shell of snow and make the next day seem to be spring.

She smiled when she heard the first drops of rain. By dawn a steady rain fell, and when she peered from her window, the rain had already done its work. The earth was brown and damp. Ashen clouds floated over the moors, and streams of mud crossed the stones on the road. Rain made iron-colored puddles around the hill and washed the peak of Mont Cant clean of ice. The air smelled of spring, of mud and newly unearthed leaves, of willow buds and rain and mist and wind.

"I wonder," Ianwyn said as she hurried down the tower steps, "if all princesses in charge of their brothers' weddings leave everything to do on the last day."

The silence of the corridors convinced her she was the first person up. But tenseness had risen before her, a hope and a dread, a gloom that made her press her hands uneasily against her ribs.

But she smiled when she saw the King's Hall. Shafts of light broke through the windows to fall on tables and chairs on either side of a gold carpet leading to the empty dais. Flax-colored tablecloths embroidered in blue matched new tapestries hung along the walls. A blue cloth emblazoned with the sun-burst of Canrhion dominated the dais.

It will all be glorious, she thought, when there are hearth fires and lanterns and harps and guests and platters of food. But she allowed herself no more idleness. Hurrying to the kitchen, she found that she was not the first person awake after all. Twin fires crackled on the cooking hearths, and someone stood in front of the farther one, palms down toward it.

Ianwyn took a step nearer. Though she meant to call Miriel's name, she closed her mouth. Miriel, gazing into the flames, sighed. Her lips twisted. A tear glistened on her cheeks. "How could this have happened?" she muttered.

Ianwyn hurried to Miriel and touched her shoulder. "Good morning," she said.

Miriel started. "Oh," she said in a wobbly voice. "Oh, Ianwyn. You startled me."

"I didn't mean to, Miriel. I didn't mean to disturb you. Miriel, is there . . . something wrong?"

Miriel hesitated, and her face went hard. "Does there have to be?"

"No, of course not." Ianwyn smiled. "I suppose," she went on, "that anyone about to be married has a perfect right to be up early looking into a fire. I know I would be frightened if I were being married. And I might not even be sure—in the rush of the moment—that I loved who I was going to marry—"

"It isn't that," Miriel said. "I am sure I love Rhian. I am more certain of that than ever. But . . ."

"But what?"

For a moment a kind of longing pierced the dullness of Miriel's eyes, but then she turned away and pressed her lips. "I can't tell you," she said. "I can't."

"You don't have to tell me," Ianwyn said, "though I will be happy to listen should you decide differently. Whatever it is," she went on, "I am sure it is hardly as bad as it seems. It will be lovely tonight, and I think your worries will go away."

"I wish they would," Miriel said. "I wish I could forget them."

"My problem seems to be," Ianwyn said, "that I forget too much. For instance, have you seen the guest list anywhere? I don't know where I put it, and I cannot remember for all the Fates how many people are coming!"

9

Rhian stared at the stack of clothes in Pinwy's arms. "If I had known I had so much clothing to put on, I would have begun dressing last night. Why so many clothes? Pinwy, Ianwyn hasn't planned an *outdoor* wedding, has she?" Rhian glanced at the raindrops lashing against his window.

Pinwy laughed as he laid the clothes on a table. "Look on the bright side. It could be worse. Such things aren't as complicated nowadays as they were in the days of the great kings of Rhewar. I read a poem once in which a prince took five days to get dressed for his coronation at Enfach Fawr."

Rhian chuckled and went to the fire. He poured steaming water into a tub while Pinwy brought towels. While Rhian began washing, Pinwy wandered across the room and found himself in Rhian's looking glass.

Seeing himself was disappointing. He thought himself much less handsome than his brother. Though Pinwy and Rhian were both slender, Rhian was wiry and angular. Pinwy was simply skinny. Pinwy was so engrossed with looking at himself in the mirror that he did not notice Rhian had finished washing until he felt a tap on his shoulder.

"If we can't get me in all these trappings on time," Rhian said, looking at Pinwy mirrorwise, "we can just have Miriel marry *you.*"

Pinwy frowned, but crossed to the table, where he took the top garment and handed it to Rhian.

"You look like a duck," he said when Rhian had put on a pair of gold tights. "And a wet one, at that. Did you ever dry off?"

"I will be happy when all of this is finished," Rhian said. "Now that the rain has cleared the snow, I have so much to do."

Pinwy interrupted Rhian by pulling a tunic over his head. "Kingly duties are all very well, but you don't have to finish all your winter schemes all in one day, or for that matter, all in one summer. And, in case you have forgotten, you are getting married this evening."

Rhian pulled the tunic over his shoulders, threaded his arms through the sleeves, then straightened it around his waist. "I haven't forgotten," he said. "It's a little frightening, Pinwy."

"Of course, it is," Pinwy said. As if he, Pinwy Mont Cant, had any idea of what it was like.

"It is a great decision," Rhian went on. "To fall in love is easy, Pinwy. I loved Miriel from the first day I saw her. To love her seemed only natural—"

"Now you regret your choice?"

"By the Fates, no! That isn't what I mean at all. I love Miriel a hundred times more today than I loved her the day I asked her to marry me. I am completely given to her, Pinwy.

I only doubt my own wisdom. I fear I love much too easily, as Talwy told me once."

"That doesn't seem to be a fault to me," Pinwy said. "And you shouldn't think of Talwy at a time like this, either. He looked at things in an odd light."

They were silent while Rhian put on his slippers and donned his doublet. Pinwy meanwhile battled a horrible notion that made his arms go cold. What if Talwy himself should return for Rhian's wedding?

"I have heard," Rhian said cheerfully, "that you have written a poem for the feast after the ceremony." He looked at Pinwy with mock suspicion. "I hope there are no hidden meanings in your poem. I am not good at subtle and hidden messages—"

"Neither am I," Pinwy said. "My verse will be simple and direct."

"What is the name of the poem?"

"Your belt," Pinwy said, "needs to be done up a notch."

"That is an odd title," Rhian said. "And I can guess its meaning already." He grinned and cinched his belt. He patted his stomach. "Is that better?" Pinwy nodded. "Now, what is your poem about?"

"It is about thirty lines, not counting refrains," Pinwy said. "I won't tell you the title, because that would spoil the whole poem. But I will tell you what it is about. It has to do with fire."

"Fire?" Rhian said. "What does fire have to do with a wedding?"

"Not all the winter blazes are on hearths," Pinwy said, smiling with satisfaction, "and often fires are not formed of flame."

Rhian broke into a grin.

"You must admit," Pinwy said, "that both you and Miriel have been glowing lately. If we snuffed out the lights, we could find both of you from the sparks! Anyway, I first got the notion for the poem when we had Toran's pyre. I saw the parallel at once. Fing is after all the Fate of both love and fire." Pinwy's eyes left Rhian's. "Love and death," he went on, "both cause change. Fire warms us or burns us, depending on how close we stand to it."

Rhian patted him on the shoulder. "I think," he said, "that the only one who is too warm will be Ianwyn, now that we have taken so much time. Now, where did I put my circlet?"

10

"You can't be serious, Ianwyn," Rhian said. "At our own feast Miriel and I have to wait in the kitchens until it is almost half over?"

"That is precisely what I mean," Ianwyn said. "The ceremony at weddings is never held until the guests have had enough to eat; it improves their dispositions. At any rate it's traditional that the bride and the bridegroom are not seen until later."

Rhian sighed. "It will be a wonder if there is food left for us." He sniffed at the air. "Especially with those Mont Encants. Did you see that fellow, Aradyn? He has twice the bulk of any man I have ever seen—"

"There is plenty to eat," Ianwyn said. "If you begin to starve, take something from a platter as it goes by." Noting the rising hubbub from the King's Hall, she paled and brushed back her hair. "I will fetch you when the time comes. Meanwhile, stay here."

Rhian was sorry when Ianwyn was gone. For one thing, he felt odd standing alone with Miriel, in such dazzling clothing, in the kitchen among servants, who hid smiles and kept staring at him. Miriel wore the gown he had given her, but she seemed unfamiliar. Unfamiliar, surprisingly, because of a twist in her face and an odd dullness in her eyes.

Part of Ianwyn's preparations had been to hang a gold curtain over the door at each end of the passageway that linked the kitchens with the King's Hall, so Rhian could see nothing of the feast. But he heard, above the faint drum of rain, the sounds of voices in low conversation. Occasionally he heard a chair scrape back or an outburst from a loud voice followed by laughter. Listening more carefully, he heard footfalls, the crackle of fires, and scattered notes on a harp, as if it was being tuned. He imagined what the room looked like; he could almost see Aradyn Mont Encant rolling in his chair, guffawing. He imagined Pinwy and Ianwyn grinning at one another.

"How many people are out there?" Miriel asked, staring at him.

He shrugged. "A hundred or so. Hardly a throng, but all the King's Hall will hold. You can thank your lack of relatives that we did not have to hold the wedding outdoors."

Miriel's cheeks drained of color. The flame in her eyes flickered, then died. The last traces of familiarity paled away, and Rhian found himself facing a fearful-eyed and tight-lipped stranger. He took her arm and drew her toward the King's Hall.

"I didn't mean that remark about relatives the way it sounded," he said. "It doesn't make any difference to me that you have no relatives to ask."

"But that's just it!" Miriel burst out. Her lip began to tremble. "Rhian! I won't let myself do this to you!"

He looked over his shoulder and saw several servants watching them. He pulled Miriel to his side and hurried her through the first curtain into the passageway.

There was scarcely room for the two of them to stand between the drapes. It was dim; the only light came through the weave of the fabric. Rhian could barely see Miriel's face. From one direction came the sound of the feast, now more pronounced, and from the other came noise from the kitchens, more distant.

"Miriel," he whispered. "What's wrong?"

Her arms were stiff but trembling. The glow had gone out of her eyes, and a glittering path wound down her cheek. "Rhian," she said, "listen to me. Try to understand. Please. I . . . I cannot marry you."

"You can't marry me?" he said. "Miriel? Are you saying you don't love me?"

Miriel stared away. "Love you?" she said. "Love you? I love you more than I have ever loved anything or anyone. I love you so much I forget the pain. I forget the horrors of my past when I am with you. I love you more than anything. But I cannot let myself marry you. I have known that all along."

"If you love me you can," he said, striving to understand. "You can!"

But before Miriel could reply, the drapes parted on the kitchen side of the passage, and servant girls, blinded by overloaded platters, swept through. The last girl muttered an apology, then pushed through the far curtain. Rhian caught a glimpse of the firelit hall beyond, the draperies and tablecloths, the ranks of guests. Ianwyn was standing up, apparently welcoming them.

Rhian caught the last servant by the arm and whispered to her, "Don't come back this way into the kitchen. Tell the others." The girl's face flickered when he added fiercely, "On pain of punishment," before he let her go.

He looked at Miriel again. The shock of disruption, however, did not dissipate quickly, and they listened to the rain, each avoiding the other's eyes, for a few minutes. "Miriel," Rhian said, forcing the words, "do you have doubts? Are you afraid of something? You are, aren't you? But if something is wrong, I will make it right. If you are afraid of something, I will drive it away. I love you, Miriel."

"Lies destroy love, Rhian," she said, her voice stiff. "And one of my lies—an evil, selfish lie—has destroyed all chance of our being married. You have to understand—"

"Lies can be healed," Rhian said. "What is wrong, Miriel?"

Her frown did not soften. Her eyes seemed more desolate than before. "I . . . I don't think you know who I am," she said.

"But I do," Rhian said. "I do. You are the woman who will soon be my queen," he said. "That's enough." But he paused, sensing her pain, suddenly uncertain, then sure again. "And it doesn't make any difference if your real name is Miriel or not."

"It is not Miriel," she said. "Miriel is a liar. Miriel was a runaway, so fierce with fear and so hardened by desperation that lies didn't matter to her. Lies masked her past. Lies let her love you, even when love, as she knew all along, would come to this." She kept her eyes low and her chin upraised. "You knew me as Miriel the servant girl," she said. Her eyes flamed with fierce pride. "But I am not Miriel; I am Marin."

"Marin?"

"Marin," she said. Then she added, almost angrily. "Marin Arma-ne-Ithy."

Arma-ne-Ithy. The ruling House of the kingdom of Armei. Rhian's mind spilled out memories, scattered fragments of his knowledge of the House Arma-ne-Ithy. He remembered having seen the hosts of the House Arma-ne-Ithy in march on Bran, for King Elevorne his father had granted them leave to take the mountain trails, northward toward Branfach. He had given them permission because they had given him no choice. Emerald-and-sapphire-colored banners had risen against the rain-peppered wind of summer, and warhorns had screamed at night from among the hills. When the princes of the House Arma-ne-Ithy had visited Fach-ne-Canys, Rhian had been in the King's Hall, sitting beside his father. He still remembered tall helms and blue capes, blue eyes and raven-colored hair.

Shaken, Rhian stepped back. Marin. The name touched his mind. Marin Arma-ne-Ithy. Again the doors of his memory swung open, and he found himself in the King's Hall once more, but this time the day was not so distant, and the Prince Rhian who sat beside his father looked much more like the King Rhian who now stood in the passageway. It had been a rainy autumn evening, not more than two years before—Rhian saw again the mud-marked traveler from Armei who had brought news that had seemed trivial at the time. "The heir-princess Marin has quarreled with her uncle, the King of Armei, and she has fled, and her uncle cannot find her."

"Miriel!" Rhian gasped.

"I am not Miriel," she said. "Miriel is dead. I am Marin."

Rhian fought dizziness, then indignation. "Why didn't you tell me? Why did you lie to me? I . . . I love you still. I can't change that. But—"

"Love doesn't change," Marin interrupted, her eyes sparkling. "But everything else does! You could have married Miriel with no fear. But you should beware of loving Marin Arma-ne-Ithy! She is a perilous princess! She is the daughter and only child of Atlantan the Tall, once king of Armei. Her father is dead and his throne is occupied by his younger brother, Cerican, her uncle: by the laws of Armadon the Fifth Fate, she should receive the crown after her uncle." Marin's eyes burned with fury. "I do not want the crown of Armei," she said, "but Cerican wants the kingship for his son, my cousin Merican. He tried to kill me. He did! The nobles of Armei think I ran from Armei Nanth after a quarrel. Hah! I ran from the city because my uncle sent assassins to kill me!"

"But you are safe now," Rhian said. "You are in Canys!"

"You don't understand! I am not safe. I will never be safe! As long as I live, I am a threat to my uncle. He is hunting for me, even now."

The truth of the situation struck Rhian only slowly, and in spite of an urge to take her in his arms, he turned away. "If your uncle is searching for you," Rhian said, "he will find you if you take on the robes of the queen of Canys." He lowered his head and tried to sort out the threads of pain weaving through his mind. "Perhaps," he said, his voice straining, the lines of pain broadening, "perhaps you are right. Perhaps we should not get married."

Marin said nothing. But by her silence, Rhian knew she must be weeping.

"We . . . we have to consider what the consequences would be," Rhian went on, pressing his eyes closed. "For me, and for you. If you are Marin Arma-ne-Ithy, you must stay hidden. Your uncle's power is great. The garrison of Armei-Nanth alone could overrun my kingdom in a single day. The fleets of Armei could bring Canys to her knees. Your secret will be hard to keep. And I could not protect you, Marin." He hesitated, wishing he could face her. "How could I justify endangering my kingdom and my people, just because I love you? How could I?"

"As I said," she answered evenly, "you must not marry me."

He faced her, but when her eyes touched his, he looked away. "Then again," he said brokenly, "what is my kingdom, or its king, without you? If I don't have you—Miriel or Marin— what am I? What is left of me? Oh, Marin, it would be better for me to love you and die by your uncle's sword than to turn you away now."

"Don't be a fool, Rhian Mont Cant," she snarled. "To marry me would bring ruin—for you and your kingdom."

"I know," he said, blinking back tears. "I know."

11

Ianwyn decided after a first sip of ale that she must settle her growing uneasiness at once. Something like a whisper told her all was not well. It was not something Ianwyn had forgotten to do, but she could tell it was not something that would burn itself out, dissipate, or vanish.

"Something is wrong," she told Pinwy.

"I know," Pinwy said. "The Minstrel is giving his poem before I am."

"Pinwy, I am serious. Can't you feel it?"

He shrugged. "So far, Ianwyn, everything has gone well. I haven't noticed anything unusual—" Pinwy stopped short. "Except one little thing." He nodded at the doors to the courtyard. "Two of our serving maids have emptied their platters, but both have gone out the back way."

"Into the rain?" Ianwyn said incredulously. But at that moment, as if to confirm Pinwy's words, a girl with a platter tucked under her arm slipped through the courtyard doors.

Ianwyn stared at Pinwy. Pinwy called a servant with a snap of his fingers. "Tell me," he asked in a low voice when a girl came, "is there something wrong with the passage into the kitchens? Three other girls have gone into the court."

"Orders," the girl whispered.

"Orders?" Ianwyn said, leaning across Pinwy. "Arawyn, who gave you these orders?"

"The king," Arawyn said. She pointed toward the curtain. "He and Lady Miriel are in the passageway, and he said for none of us to pass that way." Pinwy burst into a fit of coughing.

Ianwyn stood up. Feigning a smile for her guests, she strode toward the dais, and the door behind. Before she climbed the first step, she heard Rhian's voice, tense and strained.

Expecting the worst, she slipped through the drape.

She found Rhian with Miriel in his arms. Miriel was crying, and from the distant look in Rhian's eyes, she guessed that he, too, was near tears. She froze and then turned to leave. But something made her stay. "Rhian," she said, "Rhian. We will soon be ready."

Miriel's face lifted from Rhian's shoulder. Her eyes were big with tears and round with longing. Rhian simply looked determined. And Ianwyn could understand neither look.

"Is . . . is anything wrong?" As soon as she had spoken, it struck her what a silly question this was. Miriel looked at Rhian, then back to Ianwyn.

"Nothing is wrong," Rhian said, a little huskily. "We will be ready in a few moments."

Ianwyn narrowed her eyes. Something, she was sure, was very wrong indeed, no matter what Rhian said. She drew a kerchief from her sleeve and gave it to Miriel. Whatever the trouble, Ianwyn thought, it was best left alone for the time being. Rhian looked at her, expressionless, then turned away and raised his chin in a way that reminded her of Talwy.

Ianwyn cleared her throat. "Very well, then," she said. "Come out when you are ready."

When she emerged, she felt stares on her. But she smiled, then moved to Pinwy and laid a hand on his shoulder.

"What is it, Ianwyn?" he muttered. "Nothing serious, I hope."

"I don't know," Ianwyn said. "But we had better start the ceremony. Is the Minstrel ready?"

"He should be," Pinwy said.

"Find your place," she said. "The Minstrel will catch on."

Ianwyn and Pinwy moved to the dais and stood together on the right of the door. A hush swept over the throng. Knives found plates, tankards thumped to the tables. The last bit of noise, a snicker from the fat Mont Encant, cut itself short. The Minstrel stalked to his place on the left of the dais, collected the harp in his arms, and poised trembling fingers on the strings.

Nothing happened.

Ianwyn felt her hands tighten into fists. The hush became silence. Ianwyn felt she might have heard the thoughts of her guests had it not been for the music of the rain.

But then Rhian and Miriel appeared, heads held high, arms joined. Miriel's face was red with weeping. Rhian looked decidedly grim.

Edging nearer Ianwyn, Pinwy whispered, "They both look splendid. A little sober, maybe; but I might, too, if I suddenly realized I was about to be married for life."

After a fanfare of thunder and a flourish of increased rain, the Minstrel began, striking a chord that coursed through the hall and made Ianwyn's arms prickle. Surprised by his own mastery, the Minstrel stumbled out several more strains of music, then began to chant:

> *"O Fing, the Fate of flame and love,*
> *We wait below, and thou above*
> *Dost send thy falling fire down;*
> *Ever stand the West,*
> *Bless the West,*
> *Sing the Seven Fates."*

The Minstrel's runs chilled Ianwyn, and she found herself apprehensive. This time, however, she could pinpoint the source of her concern; as a bolt of lightning unfolded the sky beyond the windows, she nodded in understanding. "Love is hard," she whispered. She looked at Rhian, read the lines on his face. "Love is now hard for Rhian."

> *"A crown, a pledge, a hope from thee;*
> *A union for eternity*
> *With the Fates of Westerrealm;*
> *Ever stand the West,*
> *Bless the West,*
> *Sing the Seven Fates."*

Others began to sense uneasiness now, and though the notes of the Minstrel's harp sang pleasantly on, though the hearth blazes glowed, many, including Pinwy, began to tremble with what they perhaps supposed to be a draft. Only Ianwyn knew better. It was now Miriel's turn to carry the wedding melody, and she stepped forward to the table. Her eyes had cleared, though the stars in them were gone, and when she lifted the golden coronet and turned toward Rhian, her voice was high, clear, and soft:

> *"In my night sky thou art the moon,*
> *On my yew tree the guarding bark.*
> *And to my ocean, thou, the sun,*
> *Shalt send warm rays where waters run."*

Miriel's eyes locked on Rhian's, and she raised the crown, then let it descend on Rhian's head.

The restlessness in the hall rose toward fever-pitch. Rhian hesitated, and every moment that went by extended into an eternity. Ianwyn heard the rain building on the roof, the fires filling the hall with a roar of flames. And still Rhian waited. In a moment, Ianwyn realized, the chance would be gone. She wanted to scream to him to hurry, or everything—she was not exactly sure what everything was—would be lost.

Rhian strode ponderously toward the table. The silence screamed. Gently, with curved fingers, he reached out for the circlet, biting his lip. He seemed to be fighting something—each movement was stiff and hesitant. And his words sounded thick with reluctance:

> *"In my night sky thou art the stars,*
> *On my yew tree the waxen leaves.*
> *In my dark desert, thou, the sea,*
> *Shalt bring the rains and fogs to*
> *me."*

Rhian took the silver hoop in his fingers. It seemed at first that he would drop it, but slowly and deliberately, face taut, he lifted it high. Ianwyn stared in wide-eyed awe, almost in disbelief, as she made out the perfect silvery circle of the crown against the distant black of the rain-starred window behind.

With a clap of ear-bursting thunder, a spear of lightning threaded the silver circle, and Rhian brought the crown down to rest on Miriel's head. The tearing suspense ceased.

For a long moment, puzzled silence filled the hall. All who were there had felt the tautness that had raged there, but none but Ianwyn understood it. Rhian himself stood, pale and blank, as if he had forgotten what he was doing. But the icy expression on his face melted away. His lips rounded into a grin. Miriel took a deep breath; the sparkle came into her eyes again. The two of them looked at one another in silence.

Someone tittered in the back of the hall.

As if Rhian had forgotten, Ianwyn thought with an indignant glare back across the tables. But her smile returned when Rhian kissed Miriel.

The noise that followed was deafening. A dozen courtly ladies sighed. The servant girls giggled. The sword-bearing young men opposite the Minstrel's table cheered. Scattered clapping came from some of the older gentlemen and hooting from one or two of the Mont Encants.

Then, as Rhian caught Miriel's hand and turned toward the crowd, there was a roar of applause. Ianwyn clapped louder than the rest, for she knew that the kiss, somehow, had been hard-won.

V
Armadon

Though the sun had not risen, a pale thread of light burned at the bottom of the window that looked eastward toward the mountains. The dimness made the panes of glass gray, and beyond Marin saw the cloaked forms of sleeping trees, the drab fabric of the moors, and the wooly outlines of the Monte Serhaur. All was still.

She first mistook the silence for peace. But bit by bit she realized it was enchantment; bewitchment rather, the same bewitchment that had caused her sudden awakening. It was neither the drowsy quiet of a summer afternoon nor the frozen silence of a winter morning; it was a dusty quiet, an in between quiet, a final, dismal quiet something akin to death.

She shifted, but her movement was constrained by heavy blankets. Her arm brushed Rhian, who lay beside her in a patch of dust and half-light, his hair tousled by sleep and silvered by the dimness. His eyelids were almost closed. But no breath moved his lips or made the blankets lift and fall.

Maybe, she thought abruptly, he was dead. The notion came from the nightmare she had just had. She put out her hand and slowly brought her fingers to rest on Rhian's cheek.

The spell lifted. Rhian's eyebrows twitched, and the blankets swelled with a sudden breath. At the same moment light on the windowsill flamed to orange, and through a gap in the mountains sunlight poured, a flood that washed away the gray and sent shadows scurrying behind rocks and trees. The brightness swept over Rhian, lighting his yellow hair and making his eyes flutter open. He smiled drowsily.

"Is it morning?" he asked. "Marin—"

She frowned. "You should call me Miriel, as we agreed,"

119

she said, pulling blankets over her arms.

Rhian squinted at her. "But no one else is here."

"Keep from making Marin a habit," she said. "A slip of the tongue, just one, could bring the might of Armei into Canys. I learned to be cautious when I fled from Armei. I had to be. You must be, too. You must learn to be careful, Rhian."

"I'm sorry," he said. "I sometimes forget. I know what you and I and Pinwy and Ianwyn agreed after the wedding. But I thought my calling you Marin when we were alone made you feel more honest. Isn't that what you said?"

"If I did," Marin snapped, turning away, "I have changed my mind. I must be shrewd and unbending, as I had to when I was in hiding."

He closed his eyes and pretended to sleep again.

She frowned, for she had indeed told him to call her by her true name. But when he had said it, with the tatters of the nightmare still inside her . . .

"Rhian," she said softly, at length. "I am sorry. I'm a little out of sorts, I think. But understand my fear, Rhian. I dreamed . . ."

After a moment, Rhian prompted, "What did you dream?"

"You know," she said with a sudden, self-reassuring smile, "I'm not sure *what* I dreamed. I can't remember now. But it was horrible. I remember that. Don't look at me like that, Rhian. It isn't funny. You know how I feel about dreams. I told you that a dream warned me to leave my room the night my uncle's men tried to kill me. I have the same feeling now— that something dreadful is going to happen today."

Gold from the sunrise glittered in his eyes. "I *know* something dreadful is going to happen today," he said, "and I dreamed about it all night, too." Sitting up, he threw his blankets aside and glared at Marin. "Before the sun sets," he said ominously, "Pinwy and I will have to weed the garden!"

2

When Pinwy left the courtyard of Fach-ne-Canys, he saw that new leaves on the sycamores had begun to unfurl. Already new branches extended shade over most of the yard.

Once out the castle gate, he saw that the progress of spring was as swift on the castle hill. Rains during the previous weeks had teased a carpet of bright green from the earth and turned the moors yellow with new heather. Even clumps of hemlocks, trees that hardly ever changed, seemed brighter, more green, than gray. Pinwy decided he liked spring even when he smelled upturned earth and saw the furrows of Rhian's garden.

The garden was one of Rhian's new ideas. "Change," he had said, loudly and often. "Spring means change, and if we make no changes ourselves, the world will make our changes for us. We may not like what it does, so we had best stay ahead of it. Stay ahead, yes. We have to make changes to stay what we are!" Pinwy had never been fond of change. He was not sure it was a virtue, even if Armadon, the Fifth Fate, said it was. And now he wondered where Rhian's changes would end. Since the weather had improved, Rhian had scarcely been inside the castle except at night. There had been no feasts and hardly even meals. Rhian had gone to Fach-ne-Armad several times to stop the slave trade. He had been off at least that many times to villages and remote parts of Canys to speak with the people, to recruit warriors, and to look for a new War Lord. He had been back at Fach-ne-Canys for a week now, but that had not curbed his new ventures. Instead, he had taken it into his head to plant a garden.

"It doesn't seem fair," he had told Pinwy and Ianwyn, "that we should feast on food we have had no hand in raising. The peasants have hard enough a time feeding themselves without our taking a share of their harvest." Choosing a semicircular plot of land at the foot of the hill, Rhian had borrowed an ox and plowed the very next day. Pinwy was even now sore from bending to sow the garden after Rhian had furrowed it.

Pinwy found Rhian already at work. He was kneeling among his bean sprouts, plucking shoots of grass. "It is about time you got here," Rhian said.

"I came," Pinwy said. "I came when I would rather have done just about anything besides weed this garden."

"Poetry, you mean?"

"At the top of the list, naturally," Pinwy said.

"You can't eats poems," Rhian said.

Pinwy scrutinized him. In burlap trousers, with dirt on his hands and in his hair, Rhian looked like a crofter from the village. Pinwy said so.

"I am more dressed for the occasion than you are," Rhian said, looking at Pinwy. "What did *you* expect, that a princess would be waiting here for you?" Rhian grinned and moved on, picking his way along the hillward side of the field until he had passed the vegetables and had come to the new wheat. "It isn't as if *I* am fond of pulling weeds, either," he called back to Pinwy. "But I am sure the peasants like it little better than we do."

But Pinwy only smiled. He stepped onto a boulder and sang out a verse he had thought of only a moment before:

> *"The peasant king in burlap robe*
> *Loved slopping pigs and brewing swill.*
> *'Tis not,' said he, 'indignity.*
> *If I don't do it, someone will—'"*

A well-aimed clod stopped Pinwy short. Rhian, apparently, was not amused. "Sorry," Pinwy said. "I was only trying to be funny. Though I don't know why I try to be clever at all, considering what hard luck my humor has had this morning. Just after I got up, I met Ianwyn. I don't know if she ever told you, but I knew Miriel wasn't who she said she was all along." Pinwy lowered his voice. "After the wedding, I couldn't help but tell Ianwyn, 'I told you so.' I'll always remember the look on her face. At any rate, Ianwyn usually has a good sense of humor. So this morning I thought I'd have some fun with her. I told her I needed to ask her something. You know Ianwyn. She stopped and asked me what was wrong. I told her, in a very serious voice, that I suspected Ienan the groom was really the High King of Fingonlain in disguise."

Rhian chuckled.

"That was what *I* thought," Pinwy said. "I thought it was at least *mildly* funny. But Ianwyn got upset. She told me not to make light of something so serious. She said something about being uneasy, and *not* in the mood for jokes."

"Mischief in the air?" Rhian asked. "That almost sounds like Miriel. This morning, when I called her by—her real name, she got angry."

"Women," Pinwy grunted. "They're all alike. So few of them have a sense of humor."

Rhian shrugged and glanced across the moors. "Ianwyn has the best sense of humor in the castle," Rhian said. "And Miriel can laugh, too. Pinwy, the difference between men and women is that women like Ianwyn and Miriel sometimes know better when to *stop* laughing. Perhaps they are more sensitive to the unseen forces of the world. Now that I think about it"—Rhian's voice went low—"there *is* uneasiness in the air this morning. Something like smoke in the wind."

"Bosh," Pinwy said. "All three of you have good imaginations."

"Or good perception. Look at the mist."

Pinwy did not bother to do so. "If every time we had a mist at Fach-ne-Canys it meant disaster," he said, "we would all be dead by now."

Rhian hesitated. "Maybe you're right."

"What could be wrong?" Pinwy said. "We have a runaway Armei princess in our castle, but by the Fates, her uncle thinks she is somewhere in Fingonlain. He will never think to look for her here. There is absolutely nothing to worry about."

"There is always something to worry about," Rhian said. "Now that I think about it, odd things have been happening in the past few days. The man the grooms found dead of an arrow wound on the moors—"

"But you said that was an outlaw killing. Canys is a highway for rogues in the spring. You know that. And it isn't unusual for those brutes to quarrel and end up shooting one another. We've found dead men on the moors before."

"Yes," Rhian said, "but the arrow was of foreign make."

"Outlaws come from other kingdoms," Pinwy replied. "That isn't strange."

"But the man himself looked like one of the sea folk from Armad."

"Some of the sea folk join outlaw bands," Pinwy said. "That isn't strange, either."

"But it is odd that I have not heard from the Lord of Armad," Rhian said. "When I was in Fach-ne-Armad last week, he said some of the fisherfolk had seen ships far out on the sea, signaling to one another at night."

"Fisherfolk have good imaginations. So do you, Rhian."

"But I should have heard from the Lord of Armad," Rhian said. "Why haven't I?"

"Because he is probably too busy trying to enforce your new laws to worry about writing messages," Pinwy said. He paused and sniffed at the breeze, which smelled of new grass and leaves—and perhaps, far off, woodsmoke. "You're making something out of nothing—you and Ianwyn and Miriel. Remember, you are Rhian Mont Cant, chosen by four Fates."

"There are seven Fates," Rhian said. "And the next Fate is Armadon. The sea Fate. The Fate of change. Armadon may admire those who can suffer some changes but refuse to make others, but she herself is as changeable as the sea. I lived by the sea one summer, Pinwy. Some days it is flat and blue and shining. But the next it may rise in storm and destroy even that which before it granted life. Armadon is the same way. She respects only those things that can weather her storms."

Pinwy kicked at a furrow. "But four Fates already side with you."

"The greater the forces that side with me," Rhian said, "the greater the forces that side against me. Lately the forces against me have been growing more powerful, I think. These past few days I have been haunted by the memory of . . ." Rhian's voice faltered. He squinted at the sun. "I have been thinking about Talwy."

"Didn't we come here," Pinwy said, "to weed the garden?"

Rhian took Pinwy by the elbow. "Indeed we did," he said. "And I suppose none of the grass will come out by itself. Shall we begin?"

3

Though Ianwyn raced the darkness toward home, she did not fear it. Even though light was draining from the western sky, she was not afraid. She had never feared darkness, not even as a child. Her discomfort, rather, came from the mist. Fog curled on her heels, hounded her steps, and made her heart thump faster. Darkness was predictable, but fog seemed to bode of peril.

When she had left the castle that morning, the mist had been distant, blue and narrow, tinged with gray and pale scarlet as if it were smoke, as if it were seeping through cracks in the earth from an immense subterranean forge. Later that morning, about the time she had reached the family she had gone to visit

with her basket of fruit and bread, the fog had advanced over
the moors, rolling in enormous wheels across the heather. Ianwyn had first smelled it then and perceived in it the taste of
something resinous, like smoke from a great oily burning.

That she would become lost in the fog was not her worry.
The trail would take her nowhere but to Fach-ne-Canys. The
castle was distant, but nothing dangerous lay between. The
way wound over the moors past nothing more frightening than
outcroppings of stone or stunted hemlocks. And the fog was
heavy but not opaque; she could see some distance ahead.
In fact, she could see someone standing on the trail, not ten
steps away.

A tall man, blurred by the fog that whirled between them,
stood beside a thorn hedge. Ianwyn knew about the moors in
spring. Men of all kinds traveled through Canys once the snow
melted in the Serhaur passes, once the ice broke on the beaches
of the Western Sea. Wanderers came from the coastal villages,
adventurers from over the mountains, travelers from the southern kingdoms, ruffians from the north. She guessed from the
stranger's stature he was foreign and from his mantle that he
was a traveler. She took a step toward him.

"Hullo," she called out, squinting into the mist.

"Good evening, there," the man returned.

This and the man's clothing told Ianwyn he was no ruffian.
He wore green, a very dark green that was almost blue in the
dimness. A great traveling cloak, hoodless, fell from his shoulders almost to his ankles. And from beneath the cloak came a
gleam of polished steel. She halted. "You have no need to be
afraid," the man said. "I will not harm you." He lifted his cloak
to reveal a long sword. "Don't grudge me the right to wear a
weapon. There are dangers on the moors at twilight. Wolves,
for instance."

"And you," Ianwyn said. "Are you as fierce?"

The man chuckled and threw back his dark hair. "I am not.
I am a traveler, not from these parts, and I wear a sword to
keep away wolves and outlaws, not maidens." He threw his
hands vaguely into the fog. "And I have no outlawish companions." This, at least, seemed to be true. But only a moment
before Ianwyn had noticed tall shadows deep in the mist on
her right, tall forms like men on horseback. Now, though, she
saw nothing but mist.

"A man doesn't need friends to do harm," she said, as the man turned dark blue eyes on her. "The worst deeds, my lord, are done by those who are alone. What is your business in Canys?"

"I might ask the same of you."

"I am on my way home," Ianwyn said, "to Fach-ne-Canys."

The man's eyes momentarily lit then went dull again. "Fach-ne-Canys! Call this coincidence, but I myself am going there."

Ianwyn would not have called it a coincidence.

"Since both of us are going to Fach-ne-Canys," the man went on, "we could go there together. There are evil things on the moors at night."

"Indeed," Ianwyn said. Looking at the man's face, she felt she had seen it before, or a face very much like it. The man might have been called handsome, but under the circumstances she found him only haunting.

"Shall we go?" he said. "Or must we stand here until the fog kills us with the cold?"

Biting her lip, Ianwyn nodded. They started along the trail, the stranger walking ahead. Eddies of fog trailed over his shoulders, and once Ianwyn had passed, fog fell closed behind her. It was almost as if they were both enclosed in a moving cage.

Ianwyn was not sure why she dreaded the man so. She was not always so cool with strangers. But she did not intend to make a friend of this one until she saw him in better light. She could not wholly believe his destination was Fach-ne-Canys, for if it was, what business would he have that she would not know about?

"Why are you going to Fach-ne-Canys?" she asked, catching up to him.

"I want to speak with the king."

"Rhian Mont Cant?"

"Rhian Mont Cant *is* the king of Canys, my lady."

"I know," Ianwyn said, vexed. What his business might be with Rhian, though, she could not guess. But when the village lights began to appear from the gloom, she remembered many tall, sword-bearing men had come to Fach-ne-Canys in the past few weeks. This man, of course, was another candidate to be War Lord.

"Might your errand to Fach-ne-Canys have to do with war?" she said.

The man stopped. His face turned the color of the mist. He said carefully, "It might."

The stranger, suddenly, seemed no older than Pinwy. "What I mean," Ianwyn said, "is that I have just realized you probably want to talk to Rhian about becoming our new War Lord. Rhian has been looking for one all spring."

The stranger smiled. "Oh, yes. I do hope to become your War Lord. But tell me," he said, "are you related to the king? If you call him Rhian—"

"Rhian Mont Cant is my brother," Ianwyn said.

"Then," the man said, "you must be Ianwyn Mont Cant."

"And you," Ianwyn hazarded, "must be a Mont Cant relative—with a little southern blood. Let me guess. You are coming from the north, so you must be a Mont Encant."

"Precisely," he said. "That makes us distant relatives. My name is Averan—Averan Mont Encant, and I am pleased to meet you, Princess Ianwyn. I hope you will forgive my rough manners."

"Heaths were not made for smooth manners," Ianwyn said, relieved.

"By the Fifth Fate, who would guess I would meet Ianwyn Mont Cant on the moors?" He took her arm. They started southward again, this time side by side. "Princess Ianwyn's fame is not small," Averan said. "But most tales mention your wisdom, not your beauty. I see that travelers have ignored your greatest virtue."

Ianwyn felt disarmed, for she was sure this man meant what he said.

She might have been heartened before to see the lights of the village, but now she found the glow of the lamps unwelcome. The moors fell behind, and the two of them moved onto a track that led among the hedge-hidden cottages. The roofs and chimneys of the village, however, did little to hinder the fog. But if Ianwyn was still afraid, she was no longer afraid of the mist. Or of the stranger.

Soon shafts of gold from the hill of Fach-ne-Canys penetrated the gloom. But Ianwyn scarcely noticed the bright windows set like beacons high above the moors. Her eyes wandered instead to Averan, for the light of the lamps at last allowed her to see him clearly.

Averan, she guessed, *was* young, but closer to Rhian's age

than Pinwy's. His face, smooth and ruddy, gave the impression of pride. His hair was black; his clothing was sea-green; and his brooch no longer seemed of bronze but of silver. He seemed a different man from the one she had met on the heath.

"We are almost there," she said. They reached the hillward side of the village. "When we reach the King's Hall, I will take you to my brother."

"Your graciousness has not been exaggerated," Averan said.

"You will find," Ianwyn said quickly, "that my brother is equally kind."

"I hope you are right. I have an inkling your brother won't like me as much as you seem to think."

"Rhian needs a War Lord," Ianwyn assured him. "Badly."

"Indeed," Averan said.

The moon appeared as they passed through the hemlocks. Its crescent seemed so brittle that a puff of wind would shatter it, or that the clouds passing over it would soon break or block it.

"Fach-ne-Canys is fair even at night," Averan said when they left the trees. "Rumor has it your brother loves beauty. He has not only a lovely sister but also a lovely wife."

"Queen Miriel, who was before a servant, is indeed beautiful."

To this Averan did not reply. By the time they reached the gate, the lights of the village formed a blur beneath, and off to the west the hills were ringed with a crimson glow, here and there twinkling scarlet. It might be campfires of wanderers, Ianwyn thought, but enough fires and enough travelers to make the moors glow? It must be twilight.

Ianwyn brought Averan to the doors of the King's Hall and stopped for a moment to imagine Rhian's impression of Averan. He would certainly make a good War Lord. She could see Rhian cocking an eyebrow, as if he had encountered no more ideal prospect. Then she saw Rhian and Averan shaking hands, smiling to seal their agreement.

But when she followed Averan through the door, a scream jolted her from her daydream. Pinwy, Rhian, and Miriel stood together just beyond the dais table. Pinwy, gaping with surprise, looked at Ianwyn. Rhian looked at Miriel. And Miriel stared at Averan.

Turning toward him, Ianwyn understood. The two shared

a color of hair and eyes, and their eyes mirrored one another's familiarity.

Miriel murmured, "Merican."

"Marin," the man said. "It *has* been a long time since I last saw you. I thought you might have changed, now you are a queen and a Mont Cant. But you still go pale when you see me."

Ianwyn backed away. How could she have been so blind? And how could she explain to Rhian—and Marin—that she herself had brought him?

Merican's eyes found her. Starting now for the dais, she froze, bewitched by Merican's eyes, which, once they lifted from Marin, lost their malice. They shone, deep blue, just as she remembered them from the heath. "I am sorry, Princess Ianwyn," he said. "But could I have told you the truth?"

Overwhelmed by fear and shame, she looked away.

"Merican of Armei," Rhian said, standing in front of Marin, "You should not have come here."

Merican's smile persisted.

"You are either brave or foolish," Rhian went on. "Perhaps you have not heard how ruthless the Mont Cants can be. Why have you come?"

Marin broke away from Rhian. "You won't have me, Merican," she stormed. "I will never go back to Armei—never!"

"You won't have Marin," Rhian said. "She is my queen, and even if she were not, I would not let you take her. Leave this castle now. Leave my kingdom at once!"

"Not until Marin leaves with me," Merican said. He put his hand on his sword. "You have no choice, King Rhian. I see what you are thinking. You plan to throw me in your dungeon or perhaps even kill me. But you can do neither. I am the crown prince of Armei, and I am not as alone as you seem to think." He smiled. "My father, Cerican of Armei, would not put me in danger, even though I insisted on coming here by myself. Horsemen followed me from the moor. They will be at your gate by now. Don't be rash, King Rhian."

Ianwyn did not remember hearing hoofbeats on the heath, but she could not be sure. She wanted to say something, but dread made her mute. "I don't want to hurt you or quarrel with your father," Rhian said. "I only want you to leave here now, and your horsemen with you. Neither Marin nor I want the wealth or power of Armei. By the Fates, we want only peace."

"How little you understand of Armei," Merican said. "It doesn't matter whether Marin wants the throne of Armei or not. She is the daughter of Atlantan the Tall, so she holds the allegiance of certain rebellious barons in Armei, barons who will not be silent until—she returns to Armei. Marin's place is in Armei Nanth, with her true kin."

"True kin?" Rhian burst out. "You worm!"

Merican's hand flew to his sword. His cheeks sank beneath their high bones, and his knuckles whitened. "You are building your own gallows, Rhian Mont Cant," he said. "Beware and hold your tongue, or the wrath of Armei will crush you and your petty castle. Do you think a dozen horsemen is all I have to call on? Do you think I intended to take your wife from you with words?" Merican spat. "You call yourself king of Canys. But you don't even know what has happened in your kingdom."

Rhian swallowed, but he returned, "I am the king but not the country. And my people," he added, eyeing Merican, "are good fighters and stout folk."

"Not so stout as you think," Merican said. He grinned. "Your people are strong, but they bend their strength to furrows and apple trees, not to armor and ships. They have made garden fences with their spears and pear buckets of their shields. They have lost their swords in root cellars. We had rumor that you had been among them, trying to prepare for war. But you have been here for a week, and a week was all we needed. Your stout folk troubled us when our galleons first anchored at Fachne-Armad, but the lord of the city surrendered to us when he saw our might. He tried to warn you, but his messengers died. Those stout folk who defied us in Armad died for their bravery. We took other coastal villages without even a stone being thrown against us. The inland villages were little more trouble, and there are not many of them. My father has more resistance from the northern provinces of Armei than we got from your people. Some tried to escape, some fought, and some tried to bring word to you. But the day we took Armad we sent horsemen to keep news from reaching you. We wanted to surprise you, King Rhian, and it seems we have. You gape to hear that your kingdom is no longer yours."

"I don't believe you," Rhian said.

Merican smiled. "Look for yourself."

"Pinwy," Rhian said. "Go to the window."

Pinwy moved to the nearest window and peered out. He hesitated, cupping his hands around his eyes. "There are watch fires," he said dully, turning to Rhian. "There are dozens of them in the north and in the west. Fifteen miles away, perhaps less."

"There are hundreds of fires," Merican said, fastening his eyes on Rhian. "There are two thousand warriors of Armei, all circling Fach-ne-Canys now. Release Marin, or my father will tighten the circle like a noose. You cannot win, Rhian Mont Cant. The might of Armei is launched against you. You have no more than a handful of men in this castle and a few more in the village. Few against many."

"You will not have Marin," Rhian said. "Bring your warriors if you want, but you won't take Marin until you have killed me first."

"As you wish."

Talwy is behind this, Ianwyn thought with sudden despair. The fire in Merican's eyes told her that much. Only Talwy could have made this nightmare. "You won't have Marin," Rhian said. "By the law of Armadon, your own Fate, many things can change—but some must not. I would sooner give you my kingdom than my queen."

"But you have no kingdom."

"I still have a life. I will give it, if I must."

"Martyrs are fools," Merican said. "And I do not think you are a fool. There is a saying in the rite of Armadon that the true test of a king is how he behaves without a kingdom. You no longer have a kingdom. Armadon has changed that much. So who are you to defy Armadon by keeping your queen? If you say there are some things you must not give up, some things that do not change, you may inspire Armadon's favor with your doggedness. But what good will that do you if you are wearing my sword in your heart? Come, Rhian. Listen to me. You must give up Marin. There is no other way." Merican paused. He looked at Ianwyn. "Unless . . ."

"Unless what?" Marin said, her voice high and thin.

"Unless we might arrange an alternative exchange." Merican stared at Ianwyn. "You, Rhian Mont Cant, married Marin without her uncle's consent. My father is of course hurt; he craves restitution of his loss. There will be an exchange between our kingdoms. Our two lands will be allies, after a fashion. Since a daughter of the House Arma-ne-Ithy has been given to Canys, it is only fair a daughter of the House Mont Cant should come to Armei."

"You want to take Ianwyn," Rhian said slowly.

"Instead of Marin. To be a guest in Armei Nanth."

"Rhian," Ianwyn whispered, "I will go—"

"Merican doesn't want a guest," Marin said. "He wants a hostage."

"Call it what you want, cousin," Merican said. "It is my offer."

"But how would I know whether you treated Ianwyn well?" Rhian said.

"Still you do not understand. I can take *both* Ianwyn and Marin and treat them how I please. Look at the chance I am giving you. I am not known for my mercy—I intended to give you no such alternative. But mercy constrains me, and it gives me patience. I will give you time to see the folly of your thinking. I will come back at dawn to hear your decision, whether you will yield to me Queen Marin or Princess Ianwyn—"

"Or neither," Rhian said.

"Or whether I will be forced to kill you," Merican said, lips tight, "and destroy this castle and make Canys a province of Armei and take both Ianwyn and Marin to Armei Nanth. This third alternative, which you seem to prefer, is hardly pleasant. Especially for you, Rhian Mont Cant. Think carefully, or it may be your last choice." Ianwyn lifted her eyes to see Merican turn and disappear from the hall.

The King's Hall was dark now, more shadow than light. The hearth fires had all burned down and cast only a rumor of light on the tables. "Look on the bright side," Pinwy said at length. "Even at worst, we are bound—all of us—to get an incredible elegy."

4

Rhian stepped into the armory. His torch did little to light the room or warm it; a chill left over from winter lingered there. It hid in the racks of weapons, smelling of iron and cold ash.

It was as if he had discovered some ancient trove: the unsteady light cast cruel shadows on the pikes and maces and glimmered off sword points.

Coughing from the torch smoke, he drew the nearest sword and lofted it, testing it before replacing it. He tried more swords before he came on one that satisfied him. The sword he chose was beaten of rough iron—it seemed almost a clumsy thing, but its weight in his hand was almost familiar, as if he had practiced with it often. As he sheathed the weapon, he recalled other mornings, the autumn before, when he had lit the armory torch to choose a blade for practice with the War Lord.

"Blast Ander." He heard his voice echo, and wondered where the War Lord was now. But he no longer grudged any hour he had spent in practice.

He climbed the stairs, not realizing how near dawn was until he reached the second flight. A few more stairs, and dapples of light appeared, sporting around his boots, flashing across the sword. And when he reached the landing, light slanted through narrow windows at the end of the passage. A glimpse of the heaths revealed no mist, no vapor to delay the coming of dawn.

He turned from the windows and started down the corridor. The brush of his fingertips against his tunic, the click of his boots, the rattle of the sword—all seemed suddenly deafening. While many mornings at Fach-ne-Canys were quiet, mute like the moors, this dawn was different. The silence was complete and heavy.

A sense of finality haunted his walk. It was as if familiar doors, windows, and patterns of flagstones were passing him for the last time. When he reached the courtyard, he lingered beneath the dawn-whitened sycamores and noticed how pleasant their dusty fragrance was.

But he did not delay long. Even now Marin, Ianwyn, and Pinwy would be worrying about his return. He should spend his last moments—if these were to be his last—with those who meant most to him. "Armadon," he muttered. He was not sure why he appealed to the Fate whose kingdom held his own by the throat. "Let me lose my kingdom. Let me lose my life if I must. Let the whole world turn upside down and perish in dawn. But let Marin and Ianwyn and Pinwy be unharmed." His words were only words. They lost themselves in the dawn silence.

He opened the doors to the King's Hall. Though the first
dawn light streamed through the hall, Rhian saw no further
than a few feet. "Marin?" he called, squinting. "Ianwyn?"

No answer came; the dawn silence seemed only to deepen
with the brightening walls. Touched with fear, he found the
hilt of the sword and strode forward eyes pinched narrow. He
nearly stumbled over a bench. The grating of wood against
stone resounded hollowly.

"Marin? Ianwyn? Are you there? Pinwy!" His words boomed
as if he were in a canyon. The hall, with its dusty tapestries
and long rows of tables, rarely echoed so.

He groped along tables to find his way and glimpsed the
rim of the sun, rippling over the far mountains, casting a flood
of light over the moors. Dawn, his mind muttered, sensing
emptiness. Dawn.

"Marin!" he cried out. "Ianwyn! Pinwy!"

He clawed his way onto the dais steps. The end of the table,
where a few minutes before he had left the others, was bare
and crusted with sunlight. It was as if they had never been
there at all. There was no imprint in the dust, no feeling of
warmth in the air; it seemed even the chair where Marin had
sat had not been moved.

"Marin!" Rhian said. "Ianwyn!"

His mind reeled with images. He imagined Prince Merican
again, climbing the hill under the colors of Armei, a hundred
grim warriors at his back, spears raised, teeth set. He saw the
company pause at the gate; Merican, sword ready, came through
the doors into the King's Hall. The rest of the vision was swift
and sharp; Rhian saw Pinwy shoved into sword-scarred hands
and Ianwyn dragged away. And Marin, head erect, eyes blazing, as the warriors of Armei bore her away.

He ripped the sword from its sheath. "Fates of Westerrealm"
he cried. "Why?" For a moment the sword gleamed. As it
turned downward in Rhian's hand, he pointed it toward his
throat.

But the moment passed. The sword point dropped to the
stones with a crack. A moment later cool air made him look
up. The draft, he found, came from the kitchens. He took up
the sword again and went to the threshold. He gulped cold air.
The sharpness of the air made him realize it might not be too
late.

Raising his blade, he charged through the kitchens toward a rectangle of silver light. But not many steps from the door, he noticed a faint jingling sound, like small bells sifted by the wind. Slowing, he heard more puzzling noises, the whisper of voices, a creak like a leather strap stretching, a muted clank of metal. As the doorway broadened, he saw shadows, silhouettes of horses, forms of men in saddles, lines of spears against the sky. A dozen horsemen waited beyond the doors.

He bellowed a battle cry and leaped into the blinding dawn, his sword rising toward the sun. The horses nearest him wheeled to meet him. One reared and screamed. Voices rose to meet his shout; but rather than war cries they were shouts of surprise, and the voices were not all unfamiliar. "Rhian! What in Rhewar are you doing?"

"Rhian, it's all right!"

"King Rhian! You have nothing to fear."

Rhian's sword came down. He stood among horsemen, some two dozen of them, all on the sunward side of the castle. As he had guessed, all of them wore mail, and all of them sat on war horses, and all carried spears. But the color of their capes was blue, not green, and on their round shields shone the crescent moon, not the fish of Armadon. An unmistakable blue and gray banner crackled in the breeze, and from the high helms floated plumes of winter-gray and white. These men were not from Armei.

"Bran?" he gasped. He looked from one horseman to the next as he sheathed his sword.

"Bran," said a familiar voice, from the horse nearest him. "But more than Bran." Rhian saw Marin seated behind a warrior. "These are the Crescent Knights of the House Branmawr."

"Why you yelled and waved your sword I don't know," Pinwy said from behind a horseman on Rhian's left. "By Canrhion's rise, fight the men of Armei, not these men. They are going to save us."

"They are going to try," Ianwyn said from a mare near Pinwy. "We have no time to waste. Rhian, we must go."

A warrior faced him. "Your sister is right," he said. "We have no time. The prince of Armei will be at your gate in a few minutes. Our men in the hills cannot hold the noose of Armei open for long."

"I don't understand," Rhian said.

"We will explain," the warrior said. "I am Ianbrin Bran-mawr, brother of the King of Bran, Lord of the Crescent Knights. I am at your service. Mount behind, quickly."

Rhian did so, balancing himself on the back of the saddle. The horse turned sunward. Ianbrin lifted his arm and cried out, "Ride!"

Rhian pitched back as the horse lurched forward. Before he had properly regained his balance, the stallion was in gallop. The earth blurred to pale green. The roar of the wind deafened him. The speed of the horse threatened to knock him from his seat.

"Take hold of the saddle, Your Majesty," Ianbrin shouted at him. "We are in for rough riding. We left none too soon."

Rhian gripped the saddle and looked back. Already the hill of Fach-ne-Canys climbed above them; the castle on its crown seemed remote. Rhian ached to see Fach-ne-Canys left behind so swiftly. But clumped on the hill, where the Bran horsemen had been only moments before, were more horsemen.

A jolt made him look forward again. Ianbrin urged his horse beyond a gallop, to a speed so reckless Rhian thought the horse's hooves must not be striking the ground at all. The other horses were equally as swift; they all galloped nearly abreast, legs and manes made invisible by their speed. Rhian saw plumes and cloaks trailing like smoke, spears bent against the wind, and somewhere, fancied perhaps, a billow of copper-colored hair. Such swiftness Rhian had never imagined. It was only when he saw a silver moon on the shield of a nearby rider that he remembered the full significance of the Crescent Knights.

He had seen some of them the past autumn, at Princess Sereniel's feast. There had been only a handful of them, as the princess's personal guards. He remembered asking Sereniel who they were. Her answer was still clear in his mind.

"Those are the Crescent Knights, the most dependable war-riors in my kingdom. They are chosen for the king's service the moment they turn eight and are brought up in a fortress on the north headland of the Bay of Branfach. In older days they were called the Long Spears and were used by the kings of Bran in the Winter Wars. Nowadays, though, we use them only for show and for special tasks—"

"Special tasks?" Rhian remembered asking. "Such as?"

"Such as rescuing spies or tracking down marauders," she had said.

Soon the hill of Fach-ne-Canys was only a hump behind them. Their pursuers were almost invisible. Sun and wind swept out of the gaps of the Monte Serhaur, pouring over the moors. Gripping the saddle horn, Rhian saw that the warriors of Bran had spread out only a little; two horses only, one which Pinwy rode, lagged behind the rest. A number of other horses matched Ianbrin's. Several pairs of hooves beat the same cadence.

Mont Cant, free of its usual festoon of mist, rose against the sky in the northeast, its great western face in shadow. Weaving in and out of shadow and forest was the Mont Cant trail; Rhian realized that the Crescent Knights had already taken them almost as far as they could walk in a day. "Lord Ianbrin," he said. "You have saved us!"

"Perhaps," Lord Ianbrin said. "Armein arrows, at least, will not find us. But we cannot stop yet. We must take advantage of our lead—and quickly. We are a score against a thousand, no matter how swift our horses are."

"The Fates were kind to bring you to us at such a time of need."

"Begging the Fates' pardons, they had little to do with it," Ianbrin said. "This escape is planning, not providence. We were dispatched from Branfach several weeks ago, the moment the first rumor of King Cerican's ambitions reached us. We camped in the winter valleys of the Monte Serhaur as we made our plans and sent sentries and spies into the moors to mark the approach of the ships and hosts of Armei and to watch Fach-ne-Canys. We tried to get a messenger to you to warn you, but you were not at the castle at first, and then it was too late. But fortune let one of our spies discover Prince Merican's plan to take Marin at dawn. I received the news and ordered the jaws of the Armein trap to be pried open. But our plans, so far well-laid, may have been made hastily—"

"Sometimes haste is prudent," Rhian said.

"Sometimes haste is vital."

"I owe you my life," Rhian said, suddenly overwhelmed. "And I owe you the lives of my wife and family."

"You owe me nothing," Ianbrin shot back. "For one thing, Your Highness, I have not saved your life yet. For another, I am only following a command. If I weren't escaping with you, I would be riding in front of some Bran spy in Serhaur or Oerth."

"But I am no Bran spy; why are you saving me?"

"It is my duty."

"By whose orders?"

"Those of my niece, heir princess of Bran."

"Sereniel?" Rhian said, his eyes widening.

"Yes. It was she who first heard tidings that you had wed the lost heir of Armei and that King Cerican was sailing from Armei Nanth to retake his niece. The news came from an old man in white who simply appeared one day in her garden. She came to me and commissioned me, with her father's approval, to come to Canys and preserve you and your family from harm."

"Princess Sereniel is farsighted," Rhian said. "She guessed the future well. But she remembered the past better. Tell me, Lord Ianbrin, did Sereniel give you a message for me?"

Ianbrin's head turned suddenly. "She did indeed. I had forgotten. I hope you won't ask me to explain her logic because her message defies understanding: 'All favors must be answered, but no true debt can ever be repaid.' That, Your Highness, is all."

"It is enough," Rhian said.

The company soon moved into a long, narrow valley between Mont Cant and its southern foothills. Beyond the hills the land, he knew, was broken and stony. There were notched gorges and flat ridges. Over the south a yellow haze hung.

Rhian soon realized they could not forever follow the valley east; and when a southward twist brought the sun from his eyes, he saw a cliff wall ahead of them. They must veer north or south. But seemingly heedless of this, the Crescent Knights urged their horses onward.

Just as Rhian was about to warn Ianbrin, the knight shouted for the warriors to halt. Ianbrin pivoted his horse suddenly, hurling Rhian forward. Horses screamed, and some of the riders shouted. All the riders dismounted. Rhian did so clumsily—his legs ached from gripping—then helped Marin from her horse. Ianbrin ran to where other warriors were standing, but quickly returned and gripped Rhian's shoulder. "If you and your queen will mount my steed . . ."

A little puzzled, Rhian nodded. He helped Marin into the saddle and climbed after her. The horse side-stepped. Its strappings squeaked as Rhian settled himself and took the reins. Rhian steadied the horse and hardly noticed a pair of warriors helping Ianwyn and Pinwy onto a milk-colored stallion on his left. The other riders, Ianbrin among them, mounted up again, two of them behind other men.

A mare trotted aflank of Rhian's horse. Rhian looked at Lord Ianbrin.

Ianbrin pointed southward, toward a notch between two hills. "Take that valley," he said. "The ground there should be stony enough to lose anyone who follows you. There will be cover of woodland farther in—"

"You mean us to ride there ourselves?"

Lord Ianbrin frowned. "I do," he said.

"But I thought we were going to Branfach with you," Marin said.

"Yes," Ianwyn said from somewhere behind Rhian. "Aren't we going to Branfach?"

"*We* are going to Branfach," Ianbrin answered. "But you are not. There are two reasons. First, we cannot avoid all of King Cerican's war parties if we stay in one group; they will surely track us for a long way. Because they have a fresh supply of men and horses, they may overtake us. Therefore we must draw them away from you, so if they catch us, they will not find you among us. By that time you will be far enough away that all Armei will not be able to follow you."

"By Canrhion!" Pinwy said. "I am all for having these southerners drawn off our trail, but where are we to go? We can hardly go back to Fach-ne-Canys. Not yet, anyway."

Rhian eyed the notch between the hills. "Where *are* we to go?" he asked. "Couldn't we circle through the foothills and rejoin you farther north, and from there go to Branfach?"

"No. Our parting must be final. We can do no more for you than we have already done. King Caldwy Branmawr agreed to let us help you. His Majesty holds no ill will against you because of your broken betrothal to Sereniel. His Majesty has never liked Armei and has never forgiven them for their raid into his country ten years ago. But he gave us one caution— we were *not* to bring you to Branfach—"

"Why not?" Marin burst out.

Ianbrin shifted in his saddle. "Bran is not a large land. The House Branmawr has little power besides the Crescent Knights. Bran has only a few ships, a few warriors, and a few, distant allies—too few to afford making a real enemy out of a kingdom like Armei. Though we risk our honor to rescue you, we cannot

harbor you at Branfach. Cerican would take the city from the
sea. He would make our own folk captive. Can you understand?"

Rhian was silent for a moment. "I understand," he said.

"You must ride now," Ianbrin said.

"The warriors of Armei must not see us separate," another
knight said.

"Your help to us," Rhian said to Ianbrin, "will not be forgotten. If I live to see the end of this thing, you and your
knights will be rewarded."

"Farewell, then," Ianbrin said. "Ride, quickly!" His horse
jolted away, and the Crescent Knights rode off, gathering into
a gallop.

Rhian wheeled the horse. He dug his boots into his flanks.
Keeping his attention fixed on the passage between the hills,
he turned only to see that Ianwyn and Pinwy rode close behind.
Only once did he glimpse the Crescent Knights; already distant,
they galloped in the trough of the valley northeastward. Their
mail shone like stars and their white plumes arched like waning
moons over their heads.

It seemed a miracle that no horseman appeared behind them
before they reached the hills. The passage, he discovered, was
not so much a dip in the ridge as it was a canyon, a wide ravine
between two bald knobs. It was stony enough a place to mask
tracks; there was no grass and only a few trees. A muddy
stream disappeared into rubble at the canyon mouth.

The place, though not hospitable, was welcome. It took
them from the open valley and kept hoof marks from betraying
their path. The last trace of the valley and of Mont Cant beyond
it soon disappeared. As Ianwyn and Pinwy moved up beside
him, he saw that their white stallion's neck was lathered. It
would do no harm, he decided, to continue at a trot to give
the horses some rest.

But the slower pace frustrated him. It seemed slow after the
gallop. A trot, too, was rougher than a run; Rhian shifted from
one side to the other. The saddle groaned, and Marin clutched
his waist.

The clatter of hooves became a voice. Its rhythm echoed
on the canyon walls above the chatter of the stream. Soon
Rhian increased the pace back toward a gallop. But before his
horse had changed its gait, a lurch snapped back Rhian's head.
His circlet, which he had forgotten, tore from the tangles of

his hair. He heard it fall with a sharp splash a few hoofbeats later.

"Bother!" he snapped. He whirled the horse and walked it back to the stream, then dismounted to search the riverbank for a sign of the coronet among the stones.

Ianwyn, though, had followed its fall. The milk-colored stallion drank at the stream while Ianwyn and Pinwy, also afoot, stooped on a sand bank. They were looking at something at their feet.

Rhian first mistook their expressions for fear. Ianwyn had gone pale. She pointed shakily at something on the sand. "Rhian! Your circlet."

"Bothersome thing," Rhian said. "I put it on this morning with the thought of dying as a king—I had forgotten about it until—" He stopped himself. "Ianwyn, what's wrong? You look as if you have seen a Fate."

Ianwyn lifted her face toward Rhian's. "I have seen a Fate," she replied.

He followed Pinwy's eyes to where his crown had fallen. It lay in the sand. But something else lay there as well, contained within the circle of gold. A recent flood had washed a fish there. The creature was dusted over with sand and half-buried in it. The tips of its tail touched the perimeter of the crown, and on the far side of the circlet its mouth approached the metal again.

Rhian stared at it. Marin's eyes went to Ianwyn's, then to Pinwy's. "By all the Fates," she said. "The fish in a circle—this looks almost like..." She faltered. "...like the symbol of the House Arma-ne-Ithy, the badge of Armei—"

"The sign of Armadon," Ianwyn said.

"Unmistakably," Pinwy said. He looked at Rhian.

"Do you suppose it is a bad omen?" Marin said.

"It is the fifth sign," Rhian said. "But how have I earned it?" His voice echoed among the rocks. "I have lost my kingdom, my castle, and my people. I have given up my garden and my study and my King's Hall. I have nearly lost my queen, my brother, and my sister." Rhian brought his hand to his forehead. "The only thing I have not lost is what I was not willing to give up." His hand fell to the hilt of the sword. "And in exchange for all of it, for changing and not changing, I have gained the favor of the Fifth Fate."

"Then you have lost little," Ianwyn said.

"But much all the same," he said. He bowed his head when he thought of Fach-ne-Canys and his kingdom, both gone. As king, he deserved to be ruined with his kingdom, and his escape was somehow as much a curse as a blessing.

Ianwyn seemed to understand his torment. "And much," she agreed.

VI
Erd

Pinwy thought it would have been frightening to be alone in the night wilderness if it had not been for the campfire. Their fire, though small, cast orange light onto trees and boulders, and the rising sparks smelled of ash and reminded him of other fires and more pleasant times.

Pinwy was glad Rhian had insisted on building a fire. Márin and Ianwyn had been against the idea, for, they said, the light was sure to draw King Cerican's war bands to them. Rhian had pointed out, a little wearily, that fires, especially small ones, might be seen at great distances only if they were in the open. Building a fire in the trees would alert only those who were already close enough to find them anyway. Besides, they needed light and warmth. Pinwy could not agree more.

He stretched his fingertips toward the flames. "This is really a lovely fire," he said. "I don't suppose any of you thought to bring along ink and quill?" Pinwy said this to be cheerful, but none of the others seemed amused. Only Rhian even tried to smile. Since they had climbed out of the canyon that morning, Ianwyn and Marin had spoken little, and each time Rhian had tried to cheer them, they had only snapped something at him. Gazing across the fire, he saw that Rhian's eyes were half-closed. They opened only when Marin laid a hand on his knee.

Pinwy looked at Ianwyn. She did not seem well. Hunched toward the fire, she gathered her mud-spattered skirts about her knees. She cradled her arms beneath her shoulders as if she were cold, though she did not shiver.

Pinwy stood up and walked around the fire until he could

sit down beside her. She did not look up even when he laid a hand on her shoulder, and he noted that she no longer smelled of rosewater. Instead her hair smelled of wind, the same smell Pinwy sometimes found in his cloak after he had been out in the cold.

When she looked at him, he grinned and patted her shoulder. "You aren't looking yourself. Are you feeling well?"

She forced a smile. "I am doing well enough that you don't need to worry about me," she said. "I will be all right," she said, "in time."

"I see," Pinwy said. But he was not sure he did.

"I don't mean to be dismal," Ianwyn said quickly. "But there are memories, haunting memories..."

"Bad memories?"

She touched the hand he had placed on her shoulder. Her fingers were warm. "If so, it would be easier. I could understand bad memories and defeat them. But they are pleasant, Pinwy. All pleasant."

"Then I don't know if I understand."

She gazed through the rising smoke at the glistening traceries of stars. "I once thought that Fach-ne-Canys was simply a stone castle, and not a spectacular one at that. Fach-ne-Canys may really be no more than a name for a pile of stones. But maybe it is more. Maybe it was a body, and I was its heart. Or maybe, it was the other way around. But I can hear its voice even now, the creak of the tower stairs, the groan of the rafters, the whisper of rainwater against the window. I can still see the rusty iron locks and the dusty tapestries in the King's Hall." Ianwyn looked past the fire to the shadowy pines. "We were born in that castle, you and I and Rhian. Our parents died there. I see people I brought apples to: Father and Mother, Talwy, Oenan, Ander, and Toran—"

"But Ianwyn," Pinwy said, "Toran is dead and the others are gone. They would be gone even if we were at Fach-ne-Canys now. We are here—Rhian and Marin and I."

Ianwyn glanced across the fire toward Rhian, who was talking to Marin in a whisper. "But there are some who are not here," she said. "I shudder to think what will become of them when the Armei warriors move into the castle. What about Rhan and Eriel and Merta and the other servants? And Ienan, the groom? He will mutter that it is all a bad dream. He will talk to the horses in puzzlement, but he will not understand!" Pinwy looked away; he had not given the servants even a thought. "And I keep thinking about Rhin," Ianwyn went on. "After what happened last night, I forgot to feed him. He is so old he can't take care of himself. What will he eat?"

"The servants will feed him," Pinwy said, although he knew they might not. Ianwyn's mention of Rhin made him remember her tower room, which reminded him of his own room, his writing table and ink, his quill and the neat stacks of parchment by the window overlooking the road.

Pinwy fought sadness. "We have fine servants at Fach-ne-Canys," he said. "They will take care of everything, and when we go back, it will seem as if we had never left at all." Pinwy peered at Rhian. "When do you think we will be able to go back, Rhian?"

Rhian did not answer; he kept his eyes on the flames. Finally Marin spoke. "My uncle Cerican is thorough. He will not only scour the country with searchers, but he will seize Fach-ne-Canys as well. He will put the servants in the dungeon, and turn the castle into a garrison fort. As long as Cerican or Merican lives, Fach-ne-Canys is theirs."

"We can never go back," Rhian said.

Pinwy coughed. "Never go back?" he said. "Never?"

"We can never go back," Marin said.

"But how can you say that?"

"I have had experience with these people," Marin said. "Cerican, my uncle, is ruthless. He will stop at nothing to be rid of me. And now to be rid of you. And as long as he has Canys (who will take it from him now?) we cannot go back."

"Rhewar is a wide island," Rhian said. "There are many places that could be our home."

"Yes," Pinwy said suddenly. "We might live in the wilderness, in some valley or forest. We could build a log house with a warm hearth, where we could make a pleasant task of hiding."

"You misunderstand me," Rhian said with a faint smile. "When I say lands, I mean kingdoms. We must seek the protection and hospitality of some king in Rhewar—"

"But what king will take us in?" Pinwy said. "What kingdom would dare give us shelter? It would mean emnity with Armei for whoever did."

"We can't go to Bran," Ianwyn said. "We know that already."

"I don't think we can go to Serhaur, either," Pinwy added. "The House Esteran would like nothing better than to see us captive in Armei. The wilderness is a much better idea."

"There is always Oerth," Rhian suggested.

But Ianwyn shook her head. "Canys is not Oerth's enemy, but Canys has never been Oerth's friend, either. No one has. The House Bellyr is ill-tempered and treacherous."

"They fear Armei too much to help us," Marin added.

They fell silent. Shadows seemed to press close around them. But Rhian's drooping shoulders squared suddenly. "Wait," he said, "we have left one kingdom out."

"Fingonlain!" Marin said. "Of course." She began laughing along with Rhian. "To think that name used to bring such fear. What a pleasant sound it has now!"

"Fingonlain?" Pinwy said. "Do you think we could find friends in Fingonlain?"

"Of course," Marin said. "Since the Winter Wars, Fingonlain has been Armei's greatest enemy. Even in years of peace there have been battles in the Monte Fingon along our border. The House Arma-ne-Ithy has sworn oaths against the House Tanrhiar. The High Kings of Fingonlain have vowed eternal emnity against the kings of Armei. When there are rebels in the mountain provinces of Armei, Fingonlain aids them. When a royal relative seizes the throne in Heithernheda, Armei supports the usurper. There are few years of peace. Armei, being narrow and mountainous, bordering the sea, has many ships. But Fingonlain raises horses, and there are no warriors in Rhewar to match Fingonlain horsemen. We will have a mighty friend if we can win Fingonlain's help."

"They will help us," Rhian said. "Since Marin is dangerous to King Cerican, she would be a sharp weapon in their hands. The House Tanrhiar will not turn us away."

"But Fingonlain is far away," Pinwy protested. "Heithernheda is far to the south. And suppose we reach the city and are refused?"

"We would be little worse off than now," Ianwyn said. "Your plan is sound, Rhian. I think it is our only choice."

"We have enough food in the saddlebags for two weeks," Rhian said. "Marin, you have traveled beyond Canys. How long will it take to reach Heithernheda?"

"When I fled from Armei Nanth, I was hardly in the mood
for measuring distances. But it seems as if it took me, alone
and on foot, two weeks to reach Bellonbain. Another week on
board an Oerth slaver brought me to Fach-ne-Armad. But I did
more hiding than walking in Armei. And there were squalls
on the sea. It was winter—"

"Three weeks," Rhian said, considering. "It may take us
that long to reach Fingonlain, for we will have to avoid Armein
patrols all the way to the Oerth border. Perhaps beyond." He
took up a stick and with it knelt in the smooth earth by the
fire, sketching a map. "We will have to keep to these mountains—here, until we go south out of Canys—thus. We should
cross the frontier into Oerth near the mouths of the River Bellain—here—at the Rock of Stars, on the sea. From there we
can follow the River Bellain southeastward to its springs, cross
mountains into Gonoth, and follow the sea to Heithernheda.
That way we can avoid both Armei and Enrhimonte altogether."

"The hardest part of our journey will be from here to the
Rock of Stars," Ianwyn said. "After that, the searchers of Armei
will be less thick and the land less rough."

"Less rough?" Pinwy said. "How do you mean?"

"Safer, for one thing," Marin said.

"Warmer as well," Rhian said. "Here in Canys spring has
only begun, but in Fingonlain it is summer-warm already."

They all nodded. It was settled, insofar as anything could
be.

2

Ianwyn had never dreamed Canys was so vast. The foothills
of the Monte Serhaur were wide and woody. The country al-
ternated between high ridges and open moors, tight forests and
sparse river groves. There were pine woods along the knees
of the mountains, forests where a beam of moonlight, if it
passed the tangle of the branches, would fall on a forest floor
knee-deep in needles. There were windy valleys where only

current bushes grew. There were gorges carved in among the mountains, long networks of granite canyons with sheer walls four hundred feet high, where hidden brooks ran. At dawn, when mist lay in the deeps, these gorges seemed to be deep rivers brimmed with vaporous water. It was treacherous indeed to venture out before the sun cleared the morning smoke away. Every vapor could hide a craggy drop.

There were still remnants of winter everywhere. The peaks of the Monte Serhaur were capped with snow. And when the orange sun climbed above the morning shadows, it lit crystal frost on the rocks of the higher hills. New grass pricked up in the valley bottoms and along the creeks, but in the hills only white skeletons of grass and gray heather remained.

If they had remained in one place, the morning cold might have been unbearable. But Rhian insisted on leaving just after dawn. This to Ianwyn was just as well; climbing into a horse-warmed saddle was welcome. By noon the world became warm and pleasant again.

They followed trails among the hills. The paths were beaten ruts among the weeds or in forest clearings, but they formed a great network, branching, winding, converging, coupling and parting almost like streams. Ianwyn could not help wondering, as Rhian led them southward, who had made these trails. She wondered what wanderers had passed the silent ways among the weeds. At night she wondered what lanterns had swung along the dark curves, trailed by footsteps and laughter and voices.

They saw no one, though. As Ianwyn thought about it, she wondered if the trails had been made by men after all, or if beasts or ghosts or nature had carved them instead.

The third day out of Fach-ne-Canys, she spotted a war band. She and Pinwy had dismounted to lead their horse down a defile into a burn between spurs of the mountains when a distant trumpet brought her attention eastward. Through the trees she spotted green-cloaked horsemen, a dozen or so. Before she could count them, they disappeared into a canyon.

Rhian had seen them, too. Long after their disappearance he remained crouched on the trail, reins in his hand, his eyes toward the canyon mouth. When Marin stopped beside him, his hand went back to her. The intensity of his grimace warned Ianwyn to silence. It was only after the horn sounded again, echoing far in the east, that Rhian once more stood up.

"An Armein war party?" Marin asked.

Rhian nodded. "But not the first."

Ianwyn chilled. "There have been others?"

"This morning I spotted banners and rising smoke on the mountain shoulders. I heard horns from the west last night. I have seen signs of camps in the hills. Maybe there are wanderers as well as warriors in this wilderness, but I have done my best to avoid them."

Looking at Rhian's eyes, she noticed how deep and bright they seemed. They moved restlessly, mirroring the branches of the trees, the sky, and the mountains. But beneath their brightness, his cheeks were hollow and dull. He had slept little, she knew suddenly. He had kept them safe but had burned up his own strength to do so. His sharp eyes must be Erd's gift, for the earth-Fate gave all such powers. But Erd had given no gift, she realized. Erd was by far the most practical of the Fates, the most shrewd: he gave no gifts. He demanded physical sacrifice for the physical prowess he gave.

She decided they must all help Rhian watch. That afternoon she rode erect in her saddle, starting in the stirrups whenever a long stalk of grass brushed against her ankle. She watched the sunlit trees for signs of rising smoke and the heaths for the glint of armor. Her ears opened to the slightest movement in the leaves. She sniffed for the smell of smoke among the budding rowan and new sage. But she spotted no more than a knot of smoke lifting from the mountains that might have been no more than a shred of cloud.

3

They camped in a valley running between tall hills on the north and sheer cliffs on the south. There were no trees, and only a few bushes, grayish mulberries, growing against the cliffs.

Ianwyn wanted to object when Rhian decided to camp in the valley. But she could not put into words her reasons for disliking the place. It seemed an ideal place to camp; a brook trickled in the lower shadows, and the high mulberry thickets provided cover. But she somehow felt dreadfully exposed.

While Rhian secured the horses, Ianwyn and Marin looked for a place to sleep. They could not build a fire in such an open valley, so they had only to find a dry place where nettles from the bushes had not fallen, where the earth was soft and bare.

"Have you seen Pinwy?" Marin asked as they arranged sleeping spots.

Ianwyn saw nothing but twitching dark branches. "He must have wandered off," she said. She added, squinting into the darkness, "I hope he hasn't gone too far. He may not be able to find his way back again in the dark . . ."

But Pinwy appeared only a moment later, followed by Rhian, who had just come from the horses. "I have found something," Pinwy said. "I was trying to find the stream, but I found a *thing*, instead."

"What is it?" Marin asked.

"I don't know," Pinwy said. "It was high and long enough to be a cliff."

"Maybe it was a cliff," Rhian said.

"No." Pinwy frowned. "It was *like* a cliff. But it was *in the middle of the valley.*"

Rhian started with Pinwy toward the valley bottom. Ianwyn was not curious about Pinwy's *thing*, and she hated to imagine what it might be, but she went along as well.

She saw it the moment they emerged from the brush. It was perhaps a stone's throw away, in the center of the valley, but it was neither as high nor as bulky as she had expected.

"Canrhion!" Rhian exclaimed. "This is a road."

"A road?" Marin said, drawing closer to Rhian. "Here? In this wilderness?"

"A very old road," Rhian said, "built long before the First Mont Cant, before the Winter Wars, when an Adracan Great King ruled all of Rhewar. A great network of roads once connected all the provinces in the old realm of Rhewar. Most of them were battered down in the wars or have since fallen into ruin. This may be a remnant of the Old Realm Road that led from the old city of Fach Wenath on the sea through Bellain Pass toward Bellonbain."

"Then we may have found the quickest way out of Canys,"

Pinwy said. "If this road will take us into Oerth..."

Ianwyn eyed the mountains. "This valley is too barren to travel in. Any watcher on the cliffs would see us coming miles off."

"Ianwyn is right," Rhian said. "And Bellain Pass, of all the ways over the mountains, will be the best guarded. Cerican and his warriors will have guessed that we went southwest from Fach-ne-Canys and that we are trying to reach Oerth and the countries beyond. We should not follow this road. We should continue in the hills until we reach the sea. We should cross into Oerth at the Rock of Stars."

4

They crossed the road at dawn. Time had made the Old Realm Road only a ridge of earth. Flagstones along its edge had broken away and now lay in the weeds below. The stones that remained were matted by creepers and tussocks. The road had crumbled over the years, and now, at least to Ianwyn, it was no longer a work of men but a creation of ghosts. She was happy enough to leave it behind.

It was so good to climb back into wooded country that she scarcely noticed the weather. She hardly marked the advance of clouds from the west, the stubborn shadows lying under the trees, the shifting wind. She did not realize a storm was brewing until she heard thunder.

First it began to sprinkle, in drops that might have been mistaken for dew. But moments later rain began. The horses whickered when thunder rolled overhead. They shook water from their flanks and drove their noses angrily into the rain. Pinwy buried himself in his cloak and huddled behind her. When she glimpsed a profile of Rhian's face, she saw that his features had hardened with concern. Then she heard sharp coughing and saw that he held a hand to his mouth.

The real drawback of the rain was the mud. Before noon the paths were deep in it. The horses labored to keep up their pace. On the hillsides gathering rivulets notched the edge of the trail or broke it away entirely. Even when the storm dropped eastward onto the plain, the mud seemed to worsen with the water dripping from the trees.

The sky cleared before nightfall, but the brief appearance of the sun was not enough to dry the forest. At twilight the trees dripped still. And Ianwyn realized that night would be unpleasant at best.

They stopped at a soggy grove of fir trees. The bed of needles under the boughs, Ianwyn pointed out, would be drier than grass in the open or leaf-strewn mud. Rhian suggested that they build a fire—it was safe, surely, for the rain must have washed most of the war bands from the hills. They halted, and Pinwy and Rhian set off to find dry wood.

Sharp coughs alerted Ianwyn to their return. She saw them coming far off through the trees. "There isn't a dry stick of wood in this whole forest," Pinwy said. "Not so much as a twig!" Both of them were doused from their excursion into the trees. Ianwyn helped Pinwy shake his cloak dry, but when she offered the same service to Rhian, he refused with a dark nod. He pushed between Marin and Ianwyn on his way to see the horses. Ianwyn watched him go.

Pinwy sneezed. "If I ever write another poem praising rain," he grunted, "may my parchment curl. This is miserable!"

They soon bedded down among the trees. It seemed impossible to sleep. As if the dampness of her clothing were not enough, Ianwyn thought, there was a dreadful wetness in the air. Occasionally a load of water fell from the branches overhead. But most disconcerting of all was a cough—deep and damp—that came from the direction Rhian lay. At each cough Ianwyn's jaw tightened; she had heard just such a sound at night when she was a little girl. It echoed still in the hollows of her ears, faint but persistent. The coughs rumbled, hovered, built toward a climax as they had the night her mother died. Then, as they had years before, they sank into a chill silence.

When Ianwyn heard the shriek, she thought it was her own. But it was more a shout than a scream, and it came from Pinwy.

"Pinwy!" Her voice was thick. "What is it?"

He cried out again.

She sat up. Pinwy was kneeling, pointing into the trees. "Ianwyn," he said. "Ianwyn! Look *Look!*"

She saw nothing. She could scarcely make out Pinwy's hand.

He stood up, shedding damp pine needles. "Can't you see

it? It's gone now! Gone! But it was there. It was a light," he said. "I saw a light!"

"What kind of light?" Ianwyn asked, still staring into the blackness.

"It was a lantern," Pinwy said, trembling with excitement. "It couldn't have been far away. It was there among the trees, there at the top of the hill."

"I think someone's poetic imagination is getting the better of him," Rhian said gruffly. "All of us were awake. But you are the only one who saw the light."

"I didn't see anything," Marin said.

"But *I* saw something," Pinwy said. "I saw it. I know I did."

"Lanterns don't simply appear," Marin said. "Not out of the wilderness. You must be dreaming."

"I was not dreaming," Pinwy said. "I saw that lantern as plainly as I have ever seen anything. I even saw who was carrying it."

Ianwyn imagined lamp-bearing monsters, each looming beyond the nearest tree. "What did you see?"

"I saw Rhi the Bright," Pinwy said. "The wizard."

"There aren't such things as wizards," Rhian said.

"Except in poems," Marin agreed. "I seem to remember hearing a rhyme about Rhi."

"Rhi the Bright," Pinwy said.

"Yes, this Rhi the Bright. He comes into many of the old tales. But one should not really take him seriously. It would be splendid if there *were* such magical people, but you must realize great enchanters are only made-up."

"Great Ynysandra! Did you believe Rhi the Bright was my imagination when he saved Rhian's life with that elixir?"

"All the same," Rhian said, "your wizard isn't here now."

"Rhian is right," Ianwyn said quickly. "We ought to depend on our wits, not wizards." She stared into the blackness. "Besides, if your magician was really here, he will probably come back."

5

In spite of increasing signs of spring, Ianwyn soon wearied of watching the scenery. The further south they traveled, the more the hill country narrowed and the more the heath encroached, until they traveled along the margins of the trees, between the mountain slopes and the moor itself. Only a stream from the mountains or an outthrust mountain arm broke the emptiness of the plain.

Ianwyn paid more attention to Rhian. She was worried about his cough; by this time it was constant. By itself a cough might not be dangerous; Rhian insisted it was bound to go away. But Ianwyn, and Marin as well, suspected the problem might run deeper. Perhaps the cough was only the symptom of a worse sickness. She saw dullness in his eyes. Marin constantly asked him whether he felt well.

"I am just tired," he would say. "Just tired."

This did not satisfy either Ianwyn or Marin. Marin told Ianwyn she feared Rhian's winter sickness might be coming back. But Rhian refused to cooperate with either of them. Instead of taking care of himself, he ate little, much less than even Ianwyn, who was doing her best to curb her hunger. Each evening when they struck camp, he tethered the horses, brought the wood, and made the fire, refusing help from any of them. Whenever they came to a stream broad enough to ford, he dismounted and led the horses through with everyone else high and dry on horseback.

Once Ianwyn woke at night and found him awake, staring into the shadows. She urged him to sleep. "If I sleep," he said, "who will watch?" She offered to watch for him, but he refused. When she said that if he did not sleep, he would burn himself out, he only said, "Erd will give me strength. We are in the wilderness, Erd's country, and she will guide us through it only if one of us is watchful enough to pay her price."

"Even Erd cannot demand this of you, Rhian," she said. "We are away from most of the Armei warbands. Sleep. For your own sake. For Marin's sake. For my sake." He lay back against a stump, but when she woke just before dawn, his eyes glinted in the dimness.

But in the midst of all this, she began to notice a change in him. It appeared first in his beard, which after days without trimming curled along the edge of his jaw and on his upper lip. It was no longer like sparse gold thread; rather it was the color of rain-wetted earth and thick like fine copper wire. It reminded Ianwyn of her father's beard, though Rhian's was much darker.

The beard, however, was only the beginning of the changes. Somehow Rhian no longer appeared boyish. He seemed both broader and taller. He stood straighter. Traces of lines appeared above his eyebrows and shadows beneath his cheekbones.

Then Ianwyn began to have nightmares. Mild at first, they were simply glimpses of black mountains. But each night they became more vivid. She dreamed the same story again and again, adding more to the dream each time. A beast with lightning eyes began the dream. It chased them—the four of them—down a canyon walled by soot-colored cliffs. They ran to a black river that emerged from the rocks on one side of the canyon and disappeared on the other. The only way to cross was a slender log balanced between the banks. The beast, always at their heels, forced them to try the bridge, one at a time, beginning with Pinwy because he was the smallest. In each dream, Pinwy, Marin, and even Ianwyn herself crossed safely. But under Rhian's weight the log broke, and Rhian fell into the river. Only his shadow remained. It scampered from the river to join Ianwyn, who now found herself alone. The shadow looked exactly like Rhian except that it wore on one dark finger a curious golden ring. Ianwyn somehow knew the only way to bring Rhian out of the river was to look at the ring, to understand its insignia. But she also knew that to recognize it would mean death. The nightmare ended with her decision still unmade.

On the seventh night out of Fach-ne-Canys, she awoke with the dream still in her mind. She stood up, gathered her cloak around her, and moved to join Rhian, who stood among the trees. He was watching shafts of moonlight steal across the heath. It was bright enough that she could see his face. "You ought to sleep," she said.

He nodded, but his features, stony in the moonlight, did

not change. "I will sleep," he promised, "in a moment."

She started back into the trees. She had meant to wish him a good night, but the unexpected glitter of starlight on his eyes had made her speechless. Only when she was half asleep again did she realize why. For the first time in her life, the depth of his eyes was too great for her to fathom.

6

Pinwy could see how the Rock of Stars had inspired so much poetry. It rose almost directly from the sea. Carved out of a thick fin of sandstone, it was a last spur of the Monte Serhaur at their southernmost extremity, on the Firth of Armei. Some strength in the rock had kept it standing above the slopes to the sea, and some combination of wind, waves, and rain had hollowed out a great opening in it, perhaps a stone's throw across, which was almost circular. From their camp at the base of the cliff, Pinwy saw nothing but blue through the window, but he guessed that at night the famed spectacle of stars through the rock would be marvelous. There was a path twisting away through the alders that led to a ledge above the sea and below the opening. Marin and Ianwyn had already climbed there and back, but Pinwy himself had not been able to go. He was gathering wood for the fire.

Breaking off branches, Pinwy wondered if he would have time to scale the rock before dark. It hardly seemed he would, so he suggested to Rhian that they stay here another day. Rhian returned that the Rock of Stars was far too dangerous a place at which to "loiter."

Loiter indeed, Pinwy thought. He simply wanted to stay in one place long enough to collect his wits. This place seemed perfect. He liked it most because of its silence. It was the kind of silence in which important things seemed to happen. It was a reverent stillness that touched something inside him.

Pinwy let his sticks tumble from his arms. Brushing the wood chips from his sleeves, he noted the size of the heap of wood he and Rhian had gathered. "We have enough wood to

burn for a week," he said to Rhian. "At least a week. As long
as we have all this wood, we might as well stay until we can
use it all."

"We will not stay past dawn," Rhian said. He glanced at
the rock then at the sea. "This place is watchful. It is full of
hidden things, and it is dangerous for us, Pinwy. It is the least
known pass into Oerth, but there is little chance Cerican has
left it unguarded. It is watched, from one side of the rock or
the other."

Pinwy kicked at the pile of wood. "If we are in such great
danger, why are we building a fire? If there are enemy sentinels
in the rocks, the fire will draw them to us. And a fire would
be a beacon to any Armein warship that happens to be out on
the firth."

"Indeed," Rhian said, "we will not make a fire tonight. The
wood is for the fire we will make at dawn, just before we leave.
As you say, the light and smoke will draw the men from the
rocks and the ships from the sea. I hope it will draw them from
their hiding places long enough for us to slip by. They will
gather to our fire. But they will not find us warming our hands
by it."

Pinwy blinked. "Oh, I see." Because it had begun to get
dark, he decided to walk to the sea instead of climb the rock.
As he started to the beach, the wind came up. It rattled the
reeds and ruffled the sand above the waves' reach. When he
came to the sand, he sat down in it and looked over the ocean.

How could Rhian be uneasy? It was a still and peaceful
place. Before the sun set, he thought, he ought to write a poem.
The words began to flow almost before he was ready. First he
tried to memorize the verse, but it came too quickly. So he
plucked a reed and tried to write his poem in the lower sand,
where the breakers had made a damp, smooth slate. He hoped
notes on the sand would help him remember the verses long
enough to keep them in his mind. But the tongues of the waves,
occasionally lapping higher than usual, hindered his work. Before he had finished the first line (after rewriting it a dozen
times) it was too dark for him to see what he had written.

Looking up, he saw shadows gathering in the trees. The
sky behind the rock had turned black. A single bright star
peeped through it. The wind was coming up; it hissed in the
reeds.

He started back. Because it was dark among the trees, he had to walk slowly. Even so, he might have lost his way in the trees if it had not been for a pinprick of orange light, which appeared now and again among the distant tree trunks before being swallowed by dark branches.

The light seemed to be coming from the exact place where he and Rhian had piled their wood. But would Rhian have started a fire? Pinwy approached warily, almost expecting to find Armein warriors holding the others captive. But as he rounded a bend in the trail, he saw that what he had thought was a fire was instead a lamp, something he faintly remembered seeing in one of the saddlebags. Set on the ground, it cast shifting light on tree trunks and on Ianwyn, Rhian and Marin, hunched over it.

Pinwy hurried to them, but arrived to find himself completely ignored. Ianwyn and Rhian did not look up. Even Marin did not notice him until he touched her elbow. "What's happening?" he asked her.

She nodded toward the lamp. Ianwyn's hair fell over much of the parchment she and Rhian held.

"What is it?" Pinwy persisted. "A message?"

"It could be," Marin said.

"Where did it come from?"

"We have no idea," Marin said. "The letter is signed by somebody named Oenan-ne-Fach, but Rhian says it cannot be from him. It must be an Armei trick. No one leaves a letter lying in the rocks—"

"It was not simply lying in the rocks," Ianwyn said, lifting her head. "You saw it as well as I did—it was propped neatly on the rock face above the trail, directly at eye level. Where the two of us would be sure to see it as we climbed up—"

"Still," Marin said, "there was no one on the trail. There were no footprints. Either someone climbed from above, through the window in the rock, or this was delivered by that raven we saw."

"It could have been the raven," Ianwyn said. "In the days of the great kings ravens were trained to carry letters."

"But how would he know we were here? How would he even know that we have been 'disinherited'?"

"It doesn't say 'disinherited,'" Ianwyn said. "It says 'distressed.' That could mean almost anything. And Oenan could have heard about what has happened in Canys."

"By raven?" Marin hazarded.

"I don't pretend to understand what is happening," Pinwy broke in, "but at least in poetry, ravens are evil birds. They are omens of disaster. If a raven brought this message, I would not trust it."

"I think no raven delivered it," Rhian said. "I think a warrior planted it as part of some plan of Cerican's to trap us."

"But it is Oenan's writing," Ianwyn protested. "You said so yourself."

Rhian stood up. "That is the part that worries me," he said. "The note *is* written in Oenan's hand. Or a good counterfeit of it. What is more, the words are his; I recognize their patterns, as if Oenan were saying them himself. Then . . ."

"Then?" Ianwyn prompted.

Rhian hesitated. But he soon shook his head. "No. No matter how well made this ruse is, it is impossible. The message cannot be from Oenan. And even if it were—"

"Maybe," Ianwyn said, "we should read it again."

"Read it, Ianwyn," Pinwy said.

She opened the scrap into the light. *"To all the distressed Mont Cants,"* she read. *"Things are not as bad as they seem. I need your help, but in return I can give you help against your enemies. Come quickly to Enrhimonte, to Mont Enrhi, where I await you. With all hope of your swift arrival here, Oenan-ne-Fach."*

"It *does* sound like Oenan," Pinwy said. "It sounds almost like a summons he wrote once to the Lord of Armad."

"But part of it does not sound like Oenan," Rhian said. "His full name is Oenan-ne-Fach, but I have never heard him use it. He never signed it to any of the royal papers. He told me once he used his full name only when he was very, very angry. Maybe that is a warning."

"It should be warning enough that the message comes from Enrhimonte," Marin said as Rhian knelt beside the lamp. "Nothing good has ever come out of that land. Not, at least, since the last great king died. Even Armei, with all its might, cannot match Enrhimonte's ancient power. Rhian, I have lived nearer Enrhimonte than you have. If Oenan is at Mont Enrhi, he must be a sorcerer or a phantom. Nothing else has lived in Enrhimonte since the city of Enfach Fawr vanished into darkness . . ."

As Marin said "darkness," Rhian snuffed out the wick of

the lamp. Blackness, thick and cold, closed in. Marin went on, a little tremulously, "If we went to Enrhimonte, we, like the royal city of the Adracans, would be lost in darkness. There are forces among the Monte Enrhir with power that can swallow a whole city, its palaces, its people, and its twenty-one legions. How are we to prevail against power like that? Enrhimonte will destroy us!"

"Or help us," Rhian said. "There is a force more powerful than the Seventh Fate, a force that can be both more cruel and more devastating than Enrhion, but also gentle and constructive. Destiny swept the city Enfach Fawr away. Destiny might also decree that we go to Enrhimonte."

"None of you have been fugitives before," Marin said. "I have. We must be careful. This is obviously a trap."

"Destiny is a trap."

"Rhian, use your head," Marin snapped. "Even if this message had (miraculously) come from this Oenan, would you risk going to the Dreaded Realm for a counselor you say betrayed you? Be sensible!"

"Oenan betrayed me very little," Rhian said, watching the rock. "During my first year as king of Canys, he was my father, my brother, and my friend. If he had stayed longer, I would have given him a Badge of Erd for his service and sacrifice. I should have given him one, anyway. Few counselors have served the Mont Cants as well. I have forgiven him his mistake. All of us make mistakes."

"Fugitives can't afford many mistakes," Marin said, tight-lipped. "Will you make the mistake of going to Enrhimonte?"

"I owe Oenan much. He said he needs help."

"But how can we help him if this is a trap?" Pinwy said. "Can we afford to walk into something like this?"

"I am convinced we can," Rhian said. "To begin with, I am willing to make a sacrifice for the chance to help Oenan."

"Such nobility may win you Erd's favor," Pinwy said, "but it may win you an early grave, too."

Rhian gripped a tree branch. "Without Oenan's help, my kingdom would have fallen into dust during that first year. Perhaps to refuse Oenan's offer now would be equally as dangerous. Yes, I too think it may be a trap. But we have escaped from traps before. We can probably escape from this one, too, and help Oenan in the bargain."

"Enrhimonte lies between here and Heithernheda," Ianwyn
added. "It is the shortest path into Fingonlain. If we came to
Mont Enrhi and found Oenan was not there, we could continue
to Heithernheda. And if Armein warriors shun Enrhimonte, as
you say, Marin, it might be a better path than along the Gonoth
seacoast, in view of Armein ships."

Marin sank to a seat on a log. For a time silence prevailed.
"I think," Rhian said, "we must go to Enrhion."

Marin turned her head away.

I think we should not be hasty about this," Pinwy said.
"We ought to remember Talwy more clearly—he went to Enrhimonte, remember? Any trap *he* might set would not be easy
to escape."

"The trackers lost Talwy in Enrhimonte," Ianwyn said. "But
he may have gone farther south."

"But you and I know he didn't," Pinwy said. "What do you
have to say about *him*, Rhian?"

But Pinwy found Rhian was no longer beside him.

7

By the time Rhian left the trees, the sea wind had risen to a
gale. When he faced the sea, the wind hindered him, tightening
his tunic across his chest and pushing back his hair. When he
moved landward, it snapped at his heels, pushed his cloak
between his legs, threatening to hobble him and fling him to
the ground. Yet for all its force the wind was not unpleasant.
It seemed to hurl away the clot of mugginess around his mind.

For some reason he had an overwhelming urge to climb the
rock. Something was waiting for him there; some power was
drawing him toward it—he had an invitation to meet someone
or something up there, far above the sea. He knew this more
clearly at every step.

Once he left the weeds and began climbing the rock itself,
he could see almost all of the sky except for that blocked out
by the rock itself. He wanted to look up, but he hardly dared
to, for the path grew narrow and precarious. On one side a
wall of stone rose; on the other rock fell away, sheer toward

foam on the rocks beneath. Moonlight through the stone window fell at an odd slant from above; it painted a gray oval far out on the bay. Above he heard the wind howling. Below the waves slapped. It seemed that both the wind and the water wanted to claim him.

When he reached the ledge at the end of the trail, he leaned against the cliff, wheezing and coughing. He looked at the dark waves beneath. He was so high now that no spray reached him, but he heard the waves pounding beneath, pushing against the foundation of the rock.

He backed into the window. But a metallic click made him whirl around and rip his sword from its sheath. A black shadow on a higher crest of rock leaped at him. A sword flashed out of the darkness. It knocked his own sword away. The blade rattled over the stones, caught on a tussock of grass, and balanced on the edge of the cliff. He backed away, edging toward the sword, yet ready to leap or lunge. But the cloaked shadow moved around him, keeping him at bay with the sword. The circle fish of Armei flashed on the man's belt buckle. Rhian moved back against the rock.

"King of Canys," a voice said, "you are a fool. From what I hear, you could have saved your life and perhaps even your kingdom if you had given up Princess Marin at Fach-ne-Canys. But you tried to escape. You had to cross the mountains, though, and there are few ways of crossing the mountains. This is one of them, one that King Cerican himself did not think of. But I, Engoth of the Guard, knew of it. I knew you would come here. I deserted my troop on the coast yesterday—they would not listen to me. I risked losing my honor. I risked my life to come here. But Fate has brought us together. And Fate will let only one of us come away."

"If you kill me," Rhian said, "you will die, too. I have warriors below—"

The man laughed. "I have watched from this rock. I have seen your *warriors*. A boy and two girls, one of them Marin Arma-ne-Ithy, the king's niece. When I take her back to him, I will earn the reward I deserve. Perhaps, King Rhian, I will take your brother and sister to him, too, so he can toy with them—if they will come without resistance."

Rhian was breathing hard. "Kill me if you must," he said, eyeing the sword. "But at least spare my family. Is my blood not enough?"

"Perhaps I will like shedding royal blood, once I begin," the warrior said. "Perhaps King Cerican will let me do his work with Princess Marin, too."

Rhian tensed, readying to spring. But a spasm of pain gripped him. He clutched his chest and doubled forward. Violent coughing ripped his throat. He collapsed on his side.

The warrior jerked his sword back in surprise. In the same instant, Rhian recovered his breath, gathered on his haunches. He lunged up and rammed his head into the warrior's midriff. The warrior staggered back, and Rhian snatched up his sword. Stumbling to his feet, he prepared for the warrior's next blow.

But the warrior, Rhian saw, had lost his footing. He lay on his stomach, legs dangling over the long drop to the sea. Starlight revealed a grimace of pain on his face—perhaps he had fallen on his own sword. One of his hands groped toward Rhian, and in spite of everything, Rhian found himself slowly extending his arm, ready to pull the warrior to safety.

But thunder sounded in the depths of the sea. The Rock of Stars trembled, then shook. Shards of stone rained from above. Rhian ducked back into the arch, and only a moment later a chunk of stone crashed down in front of him. Shards of rock flew. The sea roared below. The ledge groaned. Rhian heard it tearing away. Coughing again, he sank back, throwing his arms in front of his face, so he only heard, not saw, rocks thundering into the breakers at the base of the cliff. Then all grew silent.

Groping his way to his feet, he blinked the dust from his eyes. There was a wide triangular gash in the ledge where the Armei warrior had lain. Only a few broken boulders remained, split away from the rest of the rock. He winced and looked away.

As his eyes turned toward the stars, suddenly he felt as if he were standing among them, for they shone all around him, more beautiful, clearer and brighter than he had ever seen them. The window was only a few steps away. It appeared in the night like a great ring of gold. Beyond it, pale stars glittered over black lands. The moon had lifted and stood behind the slopes of a great mountain, one of the nearest peaks of the Monte Bellain and the mountain gleamed through the rock window.

Then Rhian understood what had happened. The nightmare of falling rock was forgotten. He gripped stone to keep himself from falling backwards. The mountain, ringed with moonlit stone, was the device on the banner of the House Bellyr. He did not need Ianwyn to tell him what it all meant.

"Erd!" At last he spoke in a gruff whisper. He coughed and steadied his footing. "Erd." The Sixth Fate. The Fate of Earth. She had given her sign. He thought about his sleepless nights, then about the cough that had somehow saved his life. He realized what sacrifice he had made and what sacrifice was still ahead, past the dark mountains, in Enrhimonte.

Already the moon was lifting away from the mountain, letting it melt back into the dark sky.

In awe, he again watched the stars. Brilliant overhead, they faded beyond the window, and there were great patches of black over the eastern mountains. Suddenly his heart slowed its beating. The answer he had originally sought came to him. "I do not fear Enrhimonte," he said suddenly. "I do not fear for myself—only for the things that must be lost. And the things that must be gained . . ."

He turned from the window, lay back against the rock, and bowed his head. "I fear that the seventh sign will be like the Seventh Fate," he whispered. "It of all in the earning will be most bitter."

VII
Enrhion

Ianwyn had just touched the bread crusts when she heard voices. They came from beyond the horses, which were tethered in the rocks along the road. She stilled her hands in the saddlebags and listened. She thought at first the voices might belong to enemies out of the hills of Enrhimonte—Rhian had told them all to be careful. But the voices, she found, belonged to Rhian and Marin.

"He isn't here," Marin said. "Or if he is, he must be buried under the rocks: I haven't seen him. I haven't seen *anyone*, not since we left Bellain Vale last week. We are as close to Mont Enrhi as we can come, unless you fancy climbing. There is nothing but rocks!"

"But we have done no harm in coming here," he said. "We have made good time along this road. We have seen no Armein warriors since we left Oerth."

"There are times when an Armein warrior might be welcome," Marin said.

"You shouldn't be angry."

"Angry? Frightened is what I am. I don't like this place at all."

"Do you think I do?"

"Yes, from the way you dragged us here even when you knew it would be like this and would probably be a trap," Marin said. "Will you wait now until the trap closes down on us?"

"If it will make you feel any better," Rhian said tautly, "we will not wait here much longer. If we see nothing of Oenan by tomorrow morning, we will ride on to Fingonlain. You yourself said you have seen nothing. Perhaps there is nothing to fear. The trap may not be ready to close at all—"

"Yet," Marin said.

Ianwyn took the bread crusts from the saddlebags and started away. She was in no mood to hear bickering; she fought unaccountable uneasiness.

They had chosen to spend the night in the very shadow of Mont Enrhi, in a black glen between the mountain's arms. The glen was quite inhospitable, but they had slept in worse places since coming into Enrhimonte. They had camped on barren uplands, on the lips of gorges, on the road itself. It was indeed fortunate that Rhian had recovered from his cough while they traveled in spring-warm Bellain Vale, occasionally resting at inns; for since coming to Enrhimonte, they had had no pleasant nights. This place, at least, was sheltered from the wind on two sides; ridges of stone and the pale strip of the crumbling road marked off the glen from the vastness of the mountains.

The mountainward end of the glen held ranks of thornbushes, long dead and bare, like barbed iron pikes. Occasionally ravens lifted from the center of the thicket, winged languidly into the sky, wheeled about the valley with scarcely a wingbeat, then descended into the thorns again. Ianwyn had never liked ravens, but since they were the only birds she had seen in Enrhimonte, she pitied them. She wondered what they might eat—the only possibility seemed to be the gray leaves of the thornbushes. She could not remember whether ravens were the kind of birds that ate insects or seeds. But she decided it was worth a handful of bread crusts to find out.

Pinwy watched her from a perch on a boulder. He was scratching at a flat stone with a shard of rock. As she approached, he stood up. "Ianwyn," he said, "I have done it!"

"Done what?" she asked.

"I have found a way of writing down a poem at last," he said, eyes bright. "By Canrhion's rise, these black stones are softer than they look. I have managed to scratch out two verses on this one. Would you like to read them?"

"Of course," Ianwyn said. Pinwy led her to the stone.

"I should tell you something about these poems first," he said. "They are not my usual. At least I hope not. They are a bit bleak—no, very bleak. Keep in mind the kind of inspiration this place gives. When we were traveling in Bellain Vale, among the farms and inns, in pleasant glades and across shady rivers, I made up a dozen poems, but I never got to write them down, so I have forgotten most of them. How could I memorize them when we were sneaking through the woods every time Rhian thought he saw an Armein warband? This dark place inspires a different kind of poetry. But, as one of the ancient bards said, you have to see death before you can see life. Isn't that part of the rite of Enrhion, the Seventh Fate? Anyway, this first poem has to do with the old legend about the disappearance of the great city of the Adracans, Enfach Fawr, and the prophecy of its return. Part of that city might have been right here in this glen; have you noticed the old well by the thorn thicket and the squarish stones along the hilltops? I imagined that the city could very well be hidden in that cloud atop Mont Enrhi, that we could very well wake up and find Enfach Fawr set right on top of us."

"I think there is little danger of that," Ianwyn said with a smile. "If I remember correctly, legend says the city will return only when a new great king is ready to take the throne of Rhewar. And I doubt if such a city could fit in this valley. I think this is instead the site of one of the ancient way stations along the Old Realm Road. But I am sure your poem is very good, all the same."

She squinted at the thread-thin scratchings on the stone and read, with prompting from Pinwy:

> "Beware the darkness, for it brings
> Silent cities in its wings
> And sets them at our feet to rest,
> Made of clouds out of the West."

"That is good," she said.

He beamed. "The next poem is called 'Thornraven Heath.' That is the name I would give this place. Do you think it fits?"

"Oh, indeed. You read the poem this time."

> "Between the nightmare mountain's arms,
> A notch, a nook, a haven,
> Where death lies low among the thorns
> And dark flies with the raven."

Perhaps the intonation of his voice made Ianwyn shiver— perhaps only the cadence of his words, coupled with the breath of the wind in the thorns. A chill rose inside her.

"Do you like it?" Pinwy said, noting her expression.

"Yes," she said. "I suppose I do. But it does bring on odd imaginings."

"That is the work of good poetry," Pinwy said.

"Would you like to come with me to feed the ravens?" Ianwyn asked, showing the crusts in her palm.

"I don't care for ravens," Pinwy said. "Thanks all the same."

She nodded. But by the time she reached the thorns, she, too, had lost interest in the ravens, so she simply threw the crusts as far into the tangle as she could and turned to go.

A few paces away was the well Pinwy had mentioned. It was little more than a dark hole. Rimmed with black stones loosely fitted together, it had an opening the height of a man across and roughly circular. She knelt on its edge and peered into its depths. Because the sun was already low in the west, she could see no more than a few feet down. But she guessed it was very deep.

Then, like a cold hand reaching out of the pit, dread seized her.

It was not new dread. She had sensed it twice before: once when she had first seen the Monte Enrhir rising from the steppes of Oerth, and again when the Old Realm Road had crossed a narrow-spanned bridge over a black canyon. She stood up and stumbled away from the well.

Her eyes went to the steep walls of the valley, and she suddenly remembered where she had seen such faces in the rocks before. They—the rocks, the cloud-swept sky, the wind, and the thorns—all were to the last detail what she had seen in her nightmare.

She lived her dream again: crossing the black river, watching Rhian disappear, seeing the shadow hand wearing the golden ring, hesitating to make the choice that meant her own death. A shadow from Mont Enrhi seemed to reach out across the ridge, across the thorns, across the well, across the cracked ground to net her in blackness. The ground seemed ready to open and swallow her. The wind hissed in her ear, "You will die, Ianwyn Mont Cant," it seemed to say. "You will die."

She ran back toward the horses, her hands pressed against her ears. The voices, the wind, and the shadows chattered at her heels. She would escape. She would go to Rhian. He could save her. She knew he could. She cried his name. The rushing shadows faltered. The voices grew quieter. Running still, she called his name again. The darkness halted, hesitated, cowered at bay. The voices sank into silence. She murmured his name again. At last the shadows receded. The wind fell back to its fortress of thorns.

She was halfway to the horses. Rhian had bolted to his feet. Slowing, she saw his alarm. But she stopped, turned around, and winced when the wind met her again. "I am Ianwyn Mont Cant," she muttered. "I will not run any more. If this place is my dream," she said in a whisper, "I will meet it here. I will not run or hide. I am Ianwyn Mont Cant. If I cannot face up to what she must face, then I am Ianwyn no longer."

The dread and menace vanished. They became what perhaps they had always been—wind and shadows. Ianwyn stopped thinking about her nightmare; she made herself think of Rhin the cat and how he always liked to be scratched on the side of his neck. She remembered a sunset she had seen from her mother's arms, how the golds and yellows had spread across the whole sky, obscuring the clouds. She wished she had an apple to put in Marin's cloak as a surprise.

"Ianwyn!" She looked up at Rhian's anxious face. "Ianwyn! Are you all right?" He shook her shoulders. "Ianwyn!"

She pretended to be puzzled. "All right? I am fine, Rhian. Fine."

He released her shoulders. "You cried out to me!" he persisted. "Marin and I heard you scream, then you called my name three times, as if you were hurt or as if you had seen something. I thought . . . I thought . . . Are you sure you are all right?"

She blinked back tears. "Of course I am all right," she said. "I am sorry I frightened you. I didn't mean to. I simply wanted to show you something."

"Show me something?"

"The sunset."

"The sunset?" Rhian frowned.

"Yes," she said. She pointed at the alternating bands of purple and yellow in the clouds above the sun. The last tremor of horror left her. "Have you ever seen the ending of a day more beautiful?"

"Yes," he said. He folded his arms. "Ianwyn," he said, "be

honest with me. So much excitement over a simple sunset?"

She shrugged to hide the strength of her resolution. "Sometimes," she said, thinking of the death of the sun, "I am excited by small things."

2

Touches of purplish light flickered like lightning on the tops of the rocks and on the undersides of the clouds. Dusk made the shadows black. Twilight came with a hush, and the world became a violet cage of stillness and hovering silence.

Talwy's eyes caught the color of the sky as he glanced over the rocks. He snarled emphatically. Hunched between shadowed boulders, he frowned at the hooded sorcerer beside him. "Have you cast some spell to make the sunset linger?"

"Patience, my prince. That is a lesson you need most to learn. Patience is the greatest virtue of the Death Fate. I would love to seal your mouth with death, impatient one. You forget that all may not go well for us, even now. The Death Fate is far more powerful than either of us, Magic-son, and far less committed to our cause than you perhaps think. Enrhion himself may turn his raven of death on us if we are not careful— Enrhion pities death as well as imposes it, and he may well grant favor to your brother if we do not go about this thing carefully. We must wait for Enrhion's darkness."

Talwy frowned. He placed his hand on the dagger in the breast of his tunic. The iron seemed to burn against his skin. "Do not tempt my anger to come against *you*, Dark One. I may end your miserable deeds here in these rocks. You want me to be patient, but you tease my desire and keep my kingdom from me. I would have gotten farther with a dagger than with you, sorcerer."

Enrhi hissed. "Speak so to me, fool, and you will curse the Fates for putting a tongue in your head. How ungrateful you are, how foolish. You grudge an hour's wait when you have seen months pass. Faugh! You still harp on your dagger, even when *I* brought your brother into our hands. *I* made him ripe for the switch we will make tonight." The sorcerer spread a pale hand on his chest. He smiled. "Look over the rocks. Look at what I have done. Without me, your precious siblings would be dining with the House Tanrhiar at Heithernheda. Perhaps they would still be secure in Fach-ne-Canys. But my craft has brought them here."

Talwy squinted at the campfire in the glen below. "They are here," he said. "But chance more than sorcery has brought them. It was luck that Oenan-ne-Fach stumbled into Enrhi-monte—"

Enrhi smirked. "So you think. But was it luck that I tortured him into writing and signing the message my raven took to the Rock of Stars? Luck would not have helped us without my magic and cunning."

Talwy remembered how Oenan had spat on him and cursed him the day they had chained him in the high dungeon. He narrowed his eyes. "If you had not been such a coward," he said, "I could have twisted my dagger twice in that counselor, and he would not trouble us again."

"Again you have no patience. We must keep the counselor alive for now. We may need him again, if our plans tonight miss—"

"Should your plans miss," Talwy said, "you will not live to make more. I am tired of your plotting and muttering. When your wits fail me, I will use my knife—first on you, then on them."

"You would not kill them," Enrhi said. "You would not kill them all. You are weak. Your evil is swelling, darkening, deepening, but it is still polluted by virtue. Your flaw persists, Magic-son."

"I have no flaws!" Talwy snapped. He snatched the dagger from his tunic and put it to the wizard's throat, just beneath the clipped hairs of his beard. "My dagger will show you how flawed I am!"

The sorcerer plucked the dagger from Talwy's hand and stabbed it into the earth. "Fool!" he said. "I have no doubt you hate *me*. I know that. But there are other throats you would less like to cut. For, evil as you are, there is one whom you love. Your sister, Ianwyn."

"No," Talwy croaked, his throat dry. "No."

"If we fail," the sorcerer said, "it will not be my fault, or the fault of my spells. It will be your weakness!"

Talwy stared into the rocks. Instead of heeding the sorcerer, he nursed his scorn and swore by his very blood that he would kill the sorcerer once he had established himself as Rhian. The sorcerer did not fear him, but Talwy knew that place, at the juncture of the ribs, where a dagger, if twisted correctly, could cause such pain that even immortal Enrhi would give up his life to escape it. This Talwy had learned from Enrhion himself. For this knowledge, as for his own deathlessness, he had suffered dearly. But the knowledge was now his. It was his weapon against Enrhi. And he would use it.

Talwy for now found patience in his fury. He crouched behind the rock as the darkness deepened, and at each deeper nuance of darkness, Talwy twisted his golden ring of immortality in anticipation.

3

When Rhian awoke, his cloak, laid over him, felt hot and constraining, as it never had since they had left Fach-ne-Canys. Even when he had covered the cloak with leaves, he had often awakened shivering. But now he felt as if he were closed in a small room on a summer's day.

He kicked and pushed nightmarishly before he got himself out of the cloak. Then he felt cooler but no less restless. The lavender coals of the old fire shed an odd light. It highlighted each sleeper, and when a log snapped in the ashes, sudden purple light revealed the horses on the edge of the road, Pinwy's poem stones, and other shapes further off. Though the age of the fire told Rhian it must be past midnight, no stars were out. No moon broke the blackness overhead. Even when Rhian strained his eyes, he saw no horizon between earth and sky. Without the fire, he was sure, he would not be able to see even his own hands.

More than black, though, the darkness was thick and oppressive. He felt it slide across his arms, hot and damp. He felt it hiss in his throat as he breathed it. Though the fire burned at his feet, he could not smell smoke. He smelled something like spoiled milk. "By Canrhion," he said in a whisper he could not hear, "I will be glad to leave this place."

To make sure he had not disturbed the others, he squinted at each of them in turn, then set off in the direction of the thorns. He knew he would not be able to sleep. And he was sure if he stayed by the fire, he would awaken the others with his restlessness.

Although he had not been able to make out the horizon before, he now saw that faint reddish light silhouetted the mountain. The glow seemed to come from a point just behind the summit of Mont Enrhi—there the light was brightest. If it was a star, it was the only one that had broken the darkness. Rhian, looking at the sky, felt as if he were in some great, unlighted hall at midnight. He imagined that if he cried out, his voice would echo back. But he had no intention of violating the silence. Instead he listened. Once he heard a cry from a raven in the thorn. Twice he heard a howl—unlike that of wolves or wind—from the upper rocks.

He slowed down, knowing the well was somewhere near and not wanting to blunder into it. Finally he decided to go back to the camp and try to sleep. But when he turned around, he could not see the fire.

He stared into the gloom. He knew he had not come far enough to lose the fire unless the darkness was thicker than he had guessed. The only other explanation was that something had come between him and the fire. But he had passed no rock high enough to do that.

"Blast this darkness!" he said aloud. He craned his neck forward. "I ought to be able to see a little light, at least."

There was light, after all, he determined at last. It was like rising purple mist lit from beneath by some feeble glitter. The coals of the campfire had indeed been blocked by something. Something tall but not particularly broad. Something like the trunk of a tree. Something like a man.

Footfalls sounded faintly, soft and even. The shadow in the purple light began to swell and shift. He heard breathing. The shadow advanced until all the light from the fire was swallowed behind it. Then the sound of footsteps, very near, ceased.

"Hullo!" he called out, stepping back. "Who is there?"

A hiss of breath replied.

Rhian thought he glimpsed two specks of lavender light. "Who is there?" he repeated. He put his hand to his hip, but his sword was missing. He had placed it aside when he slept. "Who is it, I say? Pinwy? Is that you?"

The shadow was too tall to be Pinwy.

Rhian wanted to make a dash for his sword. But the shadow stood between him and the camp. Surely it was armed, in one fashion or another, and even if he were lucky enough to get past, he would be vulnerable from behind.

Rhian sprang. Each of his outflung hands struck clothed flesh. Because he had taken the man by surprise, they both went crashing to the ground. But it took him a few moments to anchor the body below him with his legs. He searched for the arms to pin them down, but before he could find them, something slashed across his cheek.

He reeled back, clutching his jaw. A second blow freed the man from Rhian's knee-hold. Rhian staggered to his feet. His cheek was damp with blood. The man was at once upon him, growling like a wolf. Rhian saw the glint of steel in the darkness; he kicked and sent the weapon flying. But the man only shrieked with rage and redoubled his attack. Hands flew to Rhian's throat. Rhian pulled the man down and rolled on top of him, trying to push the man's hands away. But the man unseated him again, threw him to the ground. Rhian's cut cheek met bare earth. His eyes filled with blackness. His mind went dull from loss of blood.

When he regained his senses, he could not move. He lay on his back, bound to the earth by a furious weight on his chest. His arms were pinned against his body. His legs and head were free, but in lashing them he did nothing but make himself giddy again. He stopped struggling.

"Fetch my knife," a thick voice said. Rhian heard his enemy breathing hard. He shuddered. The voice was familiar—it sounded almost like his own.

"And why do you want your knife, my prince?" a cool voice, frighteningly deep, answered from the blackness. "What will you do with it?"

"Blast you, sorcerer! You know what I want to do with it!"

Rhian heard scuffling, then the click of iron against stone. He soon saw a second set of eyes glint above the first, and a smell he had only half-noticed before, a smell like motheaten cloth, made a taste like tarnished silver in his throat.

"Give it to me, Enrhi!" the familiar voice said. Rhian began to squirm again, but his strength was almost gone.

"Talwy!" Rhian sputtered in recognition. "Talwy, you vicious, wicked wretch!"

"Beware!" Talwy hissed. The disks of purple fire widened. Talwy pinched Rhian more tightly with his knees. "Beware, Rhian, or I will take out your tongue before I kill you. My knife can do bitter things."

Rhian let his head fall back.

"The knife," Talwy persisted. "Wizard, give me the knife."

"You shall not have it," Enrhi said.

Talwy spat in the sorcerer's direction. "Troublesome fool! Give me the dagger now. You rob me of my revenge!"

Time crawled on before Enrhi answered, in a voice so placid that it brought goosebumps to Rhian's throat. "I will not deprive you of vengeance, Magic-son. I merely think it a pity that you slice up your twin so soon, so mercifully—"

"His death," Talwy said, "will not be merciful."

"If you mean to discomfort Rhian with your dagger, you are more a fool than I thought you," the sorcerer said, his voice edged with scorn. "Because you would fear, that does not mean he will. No, Magic-son, Rhian Mont Cant is made of stouter stuff. If you really want to pay him back for all the years he treated you badly, you must do as I say. Sharper than a knife blade will be his sorrow, if you leave him living long enough to see our plan fulfilled, long enough to see you set up as Rhian, King of Canys." The sorcerer chuckled dryly. "Besides, if you cut him up, you will bloody his clothing, and we will not be able to make the switch."

Rhian kicked fiercely at Talwy's back with his knees. But Talwy only cuffed him on the cheek. "You will not become me!" Rhian cried out. "You will not! I will shout! I will warn Marin and Pinwy and Ianwyn!"

"Even if you shout, you will not be heard," Enrhi said. "You will only waste your breath. My spell will keep the others from awakening."

The sorcerer lit a purplish lamp. The lantern, a twisted bit of iron, cast only enough light for Rhian to make out the features of Talwy and the wizard. Enrhi the Dark stood a few paces off, clothed in shadow, clutching Talwy's dagger, which was tipped with crimson. He grinned icily. His eyes, even in the light, burned with violet fire.

But Talwy was even more alarming. He too was dressed in black, but except for the grimace of hatred on his lips, he was the very image of Rhian. His eyes, except for a hint of lavender, were the color of polished iron. His hair, except for the russet beginnings of a beard, was the color of clean straw.

He stared at Rhian. But when the light of the wizard's lamp touched his eyes, he turned them away.

"Talwy!" Rhian said. "I was not sure we would see each other again."

"I was," Talwy said.

Rhian closed his eyes. "I had hoped the darkness had deceived me. I would rather have anyone else in Canys cut my throat. Anyone. There has never been real love between us, Talwy, but—"

"Never been love?" Talwy said. "Why, there has never been anything but hatred from the moment we lay together in the cradle. I have always despised you, and you have always loathed me. From the moment we were born, you were fair and I was foul. From the moment we were born, you were given all the favors and pleasures of life. I was given only the sorrows. Simply because you were born first, you inherited the kingdom, the treasury, and the admiration of Mother and Father and Ianwyn." Talwy bared his teeth. "But I do not need to say anything more about that. You know the injustices well. You know how you have robbed me of happiness. You know how I have always hated you. And I know how you have always hated me!"

"You are wrong, Talwy," Rhian said. "How you have blinded yourself! You have robbed *yourself* of happiness! And you are wrong about another thing, Talwy. I do not hate you. I hate the evil things you have done, but I do not hate you. I thought—almost to this very moment—that I did. But I see now that Ianwyn was right, as Ianwyn is always right. You are my brother, Talwy. I do not hate you. I only pity you."

"Silence, fool!" Talwy bellowed. "Be silent, or by Enrhion, I will kill you now."

But Rhian's words had done their work. Enrhi withdrew from the circle of light. Talwy paled to the color of ice. The glint left his eyes, and his hands went limp and dropped to his side.

But after only a moment it passed, and Talwy assumed a mocking smile. "I think Enrhi the Dark is right," he said. "You, Rhian, will be spared long enough to see me take your place as Rhian Mont Cant, until, with the help of the powerful High King of Fingonlain, I am set back on the throne of Canys. As you might have been. If you had lived."

"And what about the others?" Rhian asked. "What about Ianwyn and Pinwy and Marin?" Talwy did not answer. Rhian went on, clenching his teeth. "No matter what you do to me, you must not harm them."

"You do not deserve it, but I will give you that promise. I will care well for Ianwyn and Pinwy. And as for your pretty Armein wife—"

"Touch Marin," Rhian said, "and the Fourth Fate Fing will smite you down where you stand."

Talwy only smirked. "Such anger," he said. "Such ingratitude. Such arrogance. I am after all granting your last wish. I will take care of the others and do as I will with you."

"I warn you, Talwy, to stop while you still have the chance. Give up your scheme. Call out to the Fates to pardon you for what you have done already! For by the Fates of the West, you will not accomplish what you plan to do!"

"You think I will not?"

"No. You and I may have been mirror-images when we were young, but evil has changed you, Talwy. You and I are no more alike than any other two men in Rhewar. Your scheme will fail!"

Talwy's eyes flickered. "It will not fail."

"It cannot fail," the sorcerer said. "No two closer twins have been born in the history of Rhewar than you and Talwy. With the aid of my spells, no one will be able to tell the difference between you. Not even Marin Arma-ne-Ithy. And if, by the Six Weaker Fates, one of the others guesses Talwy is not Rhian, I have already set a curse on them, on Princess Ianwyn, on Prince Pinwy, on Queen Marin. If any one of them recognizes Talwy, the spell will strike. To recognize Talwy will be death."

4

Rhian awoke to pounding in his ears. Blood throbbed in his wrists and ankles. He felt it pumping in his shoulders and welling up in his cheek, gathering around the bruises in his back. He felt it tickling the skin of his throat. He saw it race across his eyelids to the beat of his heart.

Memory struggled within him as he opened his eyes. But his memory, like his wounds, smarted.

Rhian moaned.

"Sire?" A voice came from beyond the crimson light on his eyelids.

Raising his head slightly, he opened his eyes. "Sire," the voice said again. "Sire, don't try to move, not in your condition. Fighting those cords will only make it worse."

Rhian knew the voice. "Oenan! Oenan, is that you?"

He heard the clatter of chains and the creak of a turning bolt. "Yes, sire. It is Oenan. I am glad to hear your voice—I thought you were dead when they brought you in. You must be sorely hurt, sire, and I am helpless to do anything for you. The reach of my chains is too short."

Rhian nodded slightly, eyes pressed closed again. "Oenan. It is good to hear you again. I thought—" A sharp breath cut Rhian off. "When I met Talwy, I was afraid they had done away with you."

"I am sure Talwy wanted to," Oenan replied, "but that other brute, the sorcerer, insisted on keeping me alive." Oenan laughed dryly. "The pair of them combined have yet to do me in. I am determined not to let them. My one regret is that they tricked me into writing that note. Their cunning be blasted, and their cruelty, too. Please, sire, was it my message that brought you here to Enrhimonte?"

Rhian did not answer for a time. He tried to squeeze his wrists through the ropes lashed around them. His hands grew numb from lack of blood, so he relaxed them. "More than your letter brought us here," he said. "What is this place?"

"The sorcerer's tower," Oenan said. "We are at the top of Mont Enrhi, in the very highest cell of the tower. A pretty place, indeed. Even without bonds, shackles, and locks, we could not escape unless we were birds, and very daring birds at that."

Rhian managed to open his eyes again. He knew he was lying on his side, wrists and ankles securely bound, on cold flagstones, wearing nothing but a rough pair of trousers. He had faint recollections of Talwy stripping his clothes from him once the necromancer had cast the spell that had left Rhian powerless. He had many bruises, and a few wounds. The knife gash in his cheek, now turned against the stone, seemed to be his most serious injury. The stripes on his shoulders ached only slightly, as did his hands and feet where the thongs had cut off the flow of blood.

The room, he saw, was no more than a cubicle, built of dark stone welded thickly with soot-colored mortar. On one side of the cell there was a small iron door, bolted. On the other was a tiny window barred with a thick grate, through which fragments of light glittered. Inside the cell crimson sparks of light from the grate revealed not so much as a stick of wood or a lump of straw.

When Rhian saw Oenan, he gasped. Oenan's voice had carried no hint of his condition. Where once he had been barrel-chested and thick-necked, he was now gaunt and lanky. Though his hair had been golden-brown, it now hung in dirty clumps around his ears. His black eyes had lost their glitter, his lips their fullness.

"Come, now, sire," Oenan said, "it isn't as bad as all that. I am not my usual self, but I was not so well off when I first came here, either. My last feast was in your hall at Fach-ne-Canys. I spent most of the winter in an inn just this side of Bellonbain, where I carried wood for bread crusts. When spring came, I thought I would go to Fingonlain. A cousin of mine raises horses there. But not having much food for the journey, I decided to take a shortcut over the Old Realm Road, through Enrhimonte. I had scarcely crossed the border when Talwy and his warlock set on me and brought me back here. They have done me little good, so I look as you see me this morning."

"Morning?" Rhian said.

"Dawn came almost an hour ago, sire. And may Canrhion's rise be blessed, for nights in this dungeon are cursed. There are phantoms here, murdered spirits moaning for revenge."

But to Rhian, who began to struggle again, the light from the grate seemed hateful. Heedless of the pain, he kicked and squirmed.

"Sire," Oenan said, "stop fighting. You will do nothing but make your cut deeper."

"The cuts are already as deep in the flesh as they can go," Rhian panted. Grunting with effort, he rolled onto his back and kicked his legs into the air. "Oenan!" he said. "I have to free myself—agh—because if it is morning, Talwy is already pretending to be me. I think he means to leave Enrhimonte with the others soon. Once they are in Fingonlain, Talwy will be beyond reach and suspicion. He will have won. And you and I will die upon receiving news of his triumph."

"He must be stopped then," Oenan said. "But we are hardly in any position to do it. I have tried to escape—"

"But you are in chains. I am in rope." Rhian set his teeth, coiled his muscles, then rolled forward and upward until he balanced on his haunches. Dizziness nearly knocked him down again, but he squeezed his eyes closed until the darkness swirled away.

"Blast!" he growled. He lifted himself to his feet. "Blast these cursed ropes!" He glared at Oenan. "Blast Talwy and his knots. Blast this dungeon! Blast everything!" Rhian hesitated, then added, "Blast the Fates, as well! Blast them for all the good it has done to have their signs!"

"The Fates aid those who aid themselves," Oenan said.

Rhian's grimace faded away. He asked Oenan, suddenly, "How cruel are your bonds? Do they cut you?"

"The iron bracelets have not been filed. They are rough and sharp. But I am used to the pain of the cuts."

"Come to me!" Rhian said. Straining against his chains, Oenan pushed away from the wall, but the iron, anchored behind him, stopped him. "I can come no farther."

Rhian steadied himself, fought dizziness, then sprang sideways toward Oenan. He fell to the floor, but he lost no time in struggling to his feet again. "Bring your shackles here," he said. "If their rough edges can fray away these ropes—"

Oenan held out his manacles. Rhian worked his wrists against the edge of iron. It was exhausting work, and the cell seemed to spin as fits of faintness came; his fall had reopened the cut on his cheek. For Oenan the work was no less arduous; he gripped the iron ring in his fist and brought it back and forth along the top of Rhian's ropes. It seemed to take ages to work through a single thread. And before half the top cord had been gnawed through, Oenan fell back against the wall. "It is no use," he said. "Don't give yourself false hope, sire. Neither of us will escape."

Rhian gritted his teeth. "The Fates help those who help themselves, remember?" He threw all his strength into his arms and pulled his wrists apart. At first it felt as if the muscles along his back would snap, but then, in a glorious moment of pain, the rope broke. In another moment Rhian's hands were free.

Oenan gaped as Rhian rubbed the blood back into his hands

and flexed stiff fingers. Next Rhian began to work on the ropes around his ankles. Oenan watched him loosen the knots and shed the coils of rope. "Indeed," he said. "Indeed."

Still stiff, Rhian hobbled to the door. A glance at it told him he could not budge or unhinge it. It had no weld, no seam, no window; Rhian's poundings on it only gave him bruises. The strength of the cell seemed to mock him. But he went to the window grate.

Red glints of morning were on the grill. Rhian threw himself against the grate, bracing his shoulders against the iron and his feet against the floor. The musty iron groaned a little, but it did not give way. Rubbing his shoulder thoughtfully, he moved away.

"Sire?" Oenan said from behind. "May I suggest something?"

"By all means."

"Maybe this is not the same kind of grate we had at Fach-ne-Canys. But the grills in our dungeon there were always fitted from the *inside* and set in only light mortar. I remember a prisoner who escaped when your father was king. The man simply *pulled* instead of pushing."

Rhian nodded and set to work again. This time he meshed his fingers in the grate and began to pull inward. Unyielding at first, the bars soon began to creak, and when he braced his feet against the wall and lunged back, the grate, with a groan, swung open.

As soon as the mortar dust had cleared, he moved to the sill and looked over. It was indeed morning. The crimson sun, lifting from scarlet mountains in the east, hung far above wasted peaks.

From the sill the outer wall plunged down. Reaching outside, Rhian felt no joint between the stones, no stem of ivy, not even roughness in the rock that might provide a hand or toehold. Peering down toward the mountain itself, he guessed this window was at least as far from the ground as the window of the tower at Fach-ne-Canys had been. It was too far to jump and certainly too far to fall. More, almost at the edge of the tower's foundation, the slopes of the mountain fell away in jagged cliffs. It would be easy for a man, if he fell from this window, to drop a thousand feet further, off the cliffs.

"The warlock has beaten me," Rhian said. But when he turned back into the cell, he saw the loops of rope in the center of the floor. He lost no time in binding the two lengths together. He hooked one end of the cord around the still secured bar of the grate. "Will that rope reach the ground?" Oenan asked.

"No," Rhian said, "but it may bring me near enough to jump." He threw the loose end of the rope out the window. "Talwy's cruelty made him wrap more rope on my wrists and legs than he needed," he said. "But each length of rope will bring me nearer the mountain, and if the Fates are willing, nearer to Talwy."

"You are going to try to climb down, then?"

"What choice do I have?" Rhian said. "The Fates have given me a chance. I have no choice but to take it."

"But you have no sword. You don't even have a cloak!"

Rhian shivered. "I may be almost naked," he said. "But I am not unarmed. I have myself. If I survive the work I have to do," he said, "I will return and free you."

A tear came to Oenan's eye. "I am not afraid for Oenan," he said. "I am afraid for Rhian."

Rhian looked away. He swung his legs through the window and squirmed his way out. His grip on the rope, suddenly, seemed loose, and the creaking bar made him afraid the grate might give way.

He soon hung precariously beneath the window. A stiff wind made the rope swing slightly. He did not look down, not even to see how far the rope would take him. His imagination was keen enough: he fancied the whole world spread below him in its misty grandeur. And he could see himself falling, dropping, endlessly dropping toward sword-sharp rocks a mile below.

As he began to descend, hand under hand, his feet found little hold on the rope; soon his arms began to tremble with weariness. He let himself glance down; he glimpsed the interminable fall of the rope, the brush of clouds against the tower cliffs, and the gray of the mountain's shoulders. Quickly he looked up again. The window was only a few feet above his head. His descent had only begun.

He pressed his eyes closed and started down again.

He inched down the rope, fending himself away from the tower with his feet. Soon the tower window was far above him, but the ground was still far below. And only a few more feet of the rope remained; it ended just below him. The ledge below, though nearer, looked narrower than ever.

He held his breath, lowered himself to the last knot in the

rope, then relaxed his arms until he was hanging with them outstretched. He waited until his full flank touched the tower wall, then he let go of the rope.

His side scraped against the stones as he fell. His fingers leaped from the rope to grasp at the wall, but they found no hold. Panic made his mind go dull. He hardly felt his feet, then his knees, meet the ground.

He scrambled up, whirled around, and pushed back away from the wall. His side and knees were raw with scrapes, but beyond that, he seemed unhurt. He had avoided by only a few feet the drop off the mountain.

He cried out to Oenan that he had reached safety. If Oenan heard and replied, the answer was lost in the wind.

It would take him hours, he knew, to reach the bottom of the mountain, for he would be hampered by his own exhaustion, pain, and nakedness. And he could remember nothing of being brought here, so he would be lucky to find the camp at all.

When he rounded the tower, he stopped short. A man stood at the edge of the cliff. Rhian took a step backwards. In the sun's brilliance he could see little more than a great hooded cloak. Enrhi the Dark? Had the sorcerer watched his escape? Or worse, had Enrhi engineered it, so that he could take Rhian prisoner again and crush his will?

But Rhian decided he would not be recaptured. He would rather die. He would not give himself up; he would throw both himself and the sorcerer from the cliffs. But just as he gathered himself to spring, the man's voice stopped him.

"Wait!"

The man stepped into the tower's shadow, and Rhian saw that he was not Enrhi the Dark at all. The man's eyebrows arched when he saw Rhian's surprise. "Well," he said, "are you going to throw me off or not?"

Rhian took another step back. "That depends."

The man examined Rhian briefly, then produced from one of his sleeves a folded gold cloth, which he held out toward Rhian. "Before you push me off, Rhian Mont Cant, put this on. You will freeze going down the mountain otherwise."

Rhian hung back, but when the stranger tossed the garment at him, he caught it. Narrowing his eyes at the man, he slowly shook the folds from the cloth and found that it was a long yellow robe.

"Put it on," the man said. "Quickly, will you?"

Rhian threw the robe over his shoulders. "If this is a trick, conjurer—"

"It is no trick," the man said, moving nearer. "And I am no conjurer. I am a wizard."

"A sorcerer, rather!" Rhian said. "Your spells cannot fool me. I know who you really are. You are Enrhi the Dark!"

The man chuckled. "You are mistaken. Enrhi the Dark? Fates forbid! I am no more my brother than you are your brother!"

Rhian fastened the last button of the robe. "Who are you? You seem to know me, but I do not know you."

"You still cannot recognize me?"

"Have I ever seen you before?"

"Not that you remember," the man said. "But hasn't Pinwy told you about me? I am Rhi the Bright. Now, we have no time to waste. Enrhion's dread hand is falling. Already we may be too late to stop it."

Rhian considered for only a moment. "Very well, Rhi the Bright," he said. He started forward, but his knees buckled under him. Rhi observed Rhian's limp and the streaks of blood on his knees. "Can you walk?" he asked. "If you cannot, I can start alone. Or we can wait."

Rhian shook his head. "I can run," he said.

5

"I still don't see," Marin said, "why Rhian is in such a hurry."

"I don't see why he is in a hurry, either," Pinwy said. "But I don't argue with Rhian. Not when he is in the kind of mood he is in this morning." Pinwy pulled his cloak around his arms. "If I were you, Marin, I would get up. Now. I complained to Rhian when he woke me up, and he gave me a good lashing with his tongue. I don't think he slept well."

Marin pressed her lips. "But it's hardly light," she said. "And I would rather Rhian woke me himself. Why did he send you?"

Pinwy shrugged. "I have no idea." As he went away, Marin stood up. "I suppose this early start is my own fault," she said.

"I'm the one who wanted to leave early. I shouldn't be angry with Rhian. I'm sure he wanted to wait here for sign of Oenan until noon, but he knows I hate this place. He must be leaving for me."

Seeing that Pinwy had gone to awaken Ianwyn and that Rhian was busy with the saddlebags, she turned toward the road, brought out a small iron comb and took it at once to the snarls in her hair.

"Marin! What are you doing?"

Startled, she dropped her comb. Turning around, she snatched it up and found herself face to face with Rhian, who had come up noiselessly behind her. His eyes were on the comb, not on her.

Though surprised by this, she wanted to run to him and throw her arms around him, as she often did in the morning. But before she took a step, he put up his hands. "Not now, Marin," he said. "We have no time for that sort of thing this morning. Nor do we have time for you to admire the sunrise and preen yourself. If you must worry about your hair, do so after we have started."

"But I thought you wanted me to comb my hair so I wouldn't look like a savage," she said.

"Does it matter what you *thought?*" Rhian said, glaring at her. "It doesn't matter what we have done before. We are doing it differently this morning. We will be doing things differently for some time to come. We have been wasting far too much time. The important thing, I have decided, is to reach Fingonlain as soon as possible. The sooner we get to Heithernheda, the sooner we will have the help of the High King of Fingonlain, and the sooner I can regain my throne." Rhian glanced at her, tentatively. "Well, that is all there is to it, isn't it? I am in no mood to argue, so I will hear nothing more—"

"But what about Oenan?" Marin asked in a broken voice. "Has there been any sign of him?"

Turning toward the horses, Rhian frowned. Marin took a sudden breath, for the odd light made his eyes seem almost crimson. "I think Oenan is not here." He hooked his fingers in his belt and gazed down the Old Realm Road. "In fact, I am not sure he ever was."

Rhian started away toward the horses, but he stopped. "Marin," he said over his shoulder. "I hope you will be understanding about our hurry. Do come and help me with the saddlebags when you get a chance. I can't pack them all myself."

He must not have slept well, Marin thought as she went to where they had slept to gather up their belongings. But he was right, underneath his curtness: the sooner they reached Fingonlain, the better.

Pinwy, meanwhile, was kicking earth into the ashes of the fire. "I told you Rhian was in an ugly mood," he said, glancing sidelong at Marin. "I suppose the strain is getting to him. I knew it would eventually, but I didn't think it would happen so suddenly! If you're looking at those bags and thinking of breakfast, you'd better think about lunch instead. I mentioned casually having a bit to eat before we started off, and Rhian went into a rage. He said we shouldn't waste time!" He kicked a dirt clod.

Marin took her eyes from Pinwy and looked into the glen. "Where is Ianwyn?" she asked.

"Ianwyn isn't in a good mood, either, if you want comfort," Pinwy said. "She's not as upset as Rhian is, naturally, but it's bad enough. I've seen her in a lot of moods, but I've never seen her as she was earlier this morning. She seemed on the verge of tears when I woke her up, but moments later she gave me a hug. I haven't seen her since—"

Pinwy was interrupted by a horse's scream, a yell, and the sound of hooves crashing on stone. Marin turned to see that the white mare had reared. Rhian dropped a saddle and stumbled backwards. The mare shook her head and struck at him with her hooves. Her eyes were wide, her teeth thrust out in a prolonged scream.

"Rhian!" Marin shrieked. Pinwy brushed past her before she could move. She saw Rhian fall and throw his hands up in front of his face. The mare reared again, throwing her weight sideways. Then she bore down on Rhian.

A moment later Marin heard her name. She saw that Rhian lay motionless, and that Pinwy, who had called her, held the mare's halter with one hand and was pulling her away from Rhian.

She dashed to him, reaching him just as Pinwy had dragged the horse, which had now stopped whickering and thrashing, to the far side of the road.

Her fear for Rhian ebbed only slightly when she saw no blood. His face had gone white. His eyes were closed. He moaned softly between his teeth and clutched at his chest. She took his head under her arm and laid a hand on his ribs. "Rhian," she said. "Rhian, can you hear me?"

Although he continued to moan, he opened his eyes. Marin expected them to be clouded with anguish, but they were sharp with anger.

"Rhian!" She paused. "Are you all right?"

He snapped his head to one side. "I am *not* all right!" he said, glaring in the direction of the horse. "A step more and that beast would have broken my ribs!" He pushed himself to a sitting position and, ignoring, her, brushed the dust from his shoulders as he drew his legs under him. "Blast!" he growled. "Curse that beast's hooves. They knocked the wind from me. I will pay it back!"

Ignoring Marin, Rhian started toward Pinwy, who had finally managed to calm the mare.

"Rhian!" Marin shouted. "Rhian! What are you doing?"

He sneered over his shoulder. "A wild horse must be tamed," he said. "Or destroyed."

"Now, Rhian," Pinwy said, curling one arm around the mare's neck. "Don't you let your anger get the better of you. It won't help a bit to vent your fury on the horse now. See? She's as calm as ever. By Canrhion, I don't know what got into her. Maybe thorns or bee stings have made her skittish—"

"Skittish?" Rhian bellowed. "You call that madness being skittish?"

Pinwy shrugged. "All the same, I don't think you ought to come near her. She might get upset again. And . . . aren't you hurt? By Canrhion, I thought she had killed you!"

Rhian's cheeks flushed as he approached Pinwy. "Give me the bridle."

Pinwy collected the reins in his other hand and pushed them behind his back.

"I don't want foolishness from you," Rhian snapped. "Give me the reins!"

"I don't think I should," Pinwy said.

Rhian went livid, but before he could speak or act, a voice rang out from the rocks near where the other horse was tied. "I don't think Pinwy should give you the reins, either."

When she saw Ianwyn coming down from the ridge, Marin sighed. Ianwyn seemed to have a good effect on Rhian. He stepped back from Pinwy and watched her scramble down the final stretch of the incline then start toward him. She stopped a pace away.

"Pinwy, tie the mare with the other horse," she said. "I think you should leave the horse alone for the time being," she said to Rhian. "Are you sure you're all right? I ought to have a look at you. And we really ought to have breakfast before we start off."

"But we must reach Fingonlain soon," Rhian muttered.

"True," she said, "but I doubt if half a day will make much difference. And if you're hurt..."

"I suppose we can wait a little longer," Rhian said. He glanced at Ianwyn. "But we must be gone before noon."

"We will see about that," Ianwyn said. "Now come with me and let me have a look at you. You seem bruised, no matter how unscathed you think you are. When a person is trampled by a horse, he cannot come away without marks of it."

Ianwyn held out her arm to Rhian. He seemed to flinch when her hand neared his, but he touched his hand lightly to her wrist, as if it were something very brittle.

They all moved toward the fire, and while Ianwyn spread blankets on the rocks, Pinwy returned from tying the horse. He rounded Rhian at a good distance and joined Marin near one of the saddlebags, where they looked for something for breakfast.

Ianwyn's best efforts, meanwhile, were met with repeated resistance. When she tucked a rolled cloak under Rhian's head, he avoided her touch. When she loosed his collar, he wriggled away. When she offered him some dried fruit, he snatched it from her gingerly. At the beginning of this Ianwyn was doing her best to smile. But her face began to change. Tautness crept across her cheeks and forced her smile to narrow. The gray flame in her eyes faded to a vague silver flicker that reminded Marin of sputtering ashes. Suddenly Marin could not swallow the dried apricot between her teeth, for her throat had gone dry with fear.

Ianwyn's eyes had gone wide, so wide that Marin could see all three of them mirrored there. Her features froze in an expression of surprise; her only movement was a sideways twitch of her head, a feeble denial, a nod of disbelief that made Marin catch a shrill breath.

Pushing himself up abruptly, Rhian went ashen. His features

seemed to melt away until all Marin could distinguish were his eyes, two rims of scarlet fire that lingered on Ianwyn's until they assumed flecks of silver like two falling stars.

"Ianwyn!" Rhian cried out. "Ianwyn! No!" Rhian threw his hands in front of his face. "Ianwyn! Don't do it!"

Still Ianwyn did not move. But her eyes, slowly and deliberately, focused on Rhian's hand, on something on his fourth finger. On Rhian's hand, the ring was unmistakable.

6

Bitter-smelling wind threw Marin's hair into her eyes. The wind screamed in her ears like an enraged ghost; shrouding her senses with smoke, it robbed her for a moment of all knowledge and warmth.

When she tore the hair from her eyes, the world had changed.

Long, low clouds, the color of cold embers, raced in from the east to block off the sun; they cast vast brown shadows over the rocks of Enrhimonte. She saw flickers of lightning in the foothills. Above the roar of the wind, she heard peals of thunder. Sheaths of fog along the mountains spun away into the gloom. A thick-looking vapor began to send dark fingers across the road; it advanced upon them in an instant, like a flood of water. No more than knee deep, it hissed across the ground and splashed around the outcroppings of rock and against Marin's knees. The vapor rushed to Ianwyn and circled her; it seemed to rear up and envelope her.

When the wind scattered it, Ianwyn had collapsed.

Pinwy reached her first. "Ianwyn?" he said. He knelt beside her. "Ianwyn? What's wrong?"

Marin was too stunned to speak. Ianwyn's salt-white lips did not move.

Rhian crept toward her on all fours, with the white fog snarling in his fingers and eddying around his knees. His face twisted. His lips quivered as he neared Ianwyn. His fingers, too, trembled as he reached out toward her. But they did not touch her, nor did his eyes, which were dull and shallow. He seemed, in fact, to be seeing something remote and bright and fading, something beautiful enough to lend a soft glow to his face, but something sad and forlorn and far enough away that its light upon his face was only momentary. As he crouched near Ianwyn, the shimmer faded.

Only shadow remained, deeper and blacker than the shadows from the clouds. Darkness spread from his face to his ears, from his ears to his throat, from his throat to his limbs. And when it colored his last finger, his eyes began to smolder with scarlet fire.

He exploded to his feet. His glare seemed to push away the mist and part the clouds. And he shouted a word so thick and horrible Marin could scarcely bear hearing it.

"Enrhi!"

He searched the rocks with terrible eyes. "Enrhi," he shouted again. "Enrhi the Dark! I summon you!"

He plucked from his coat a long knife, which glinted against the wild sky. "Enrhi!" he shouted. "By the Dark Fate I call you! Come from your hiding in the rocks, or I will batter the whole cursed mountain down to find you! Enrhi! Obey me!"

Marin dared not take her eyes from Rhian; she did not even dare look at Pinwy or try to help Ianwyn. For Enrhi came.

She knew it was Enrhi the Dark simply because there was nothing else he could be. Like the first storm of winter he came, rising slowly from the rocks on the north, looming like a great bat as he descended toward the man Marin had thought was Rhian. The man waited for the wizard with his dagger poised, with flames of fury washing crimson in his eyes. He did not flinch or falter when the shadow reached across the valley. He did not shun the blazing eyes, nor did he wince when threads of malice fell like nets over him. But the sorcerer did not hesitate, either. He hovered closer, his cape dragging across the rocks. His eyes fixed themselves on the man; his lips rounded in delight.

He laughed like thunder. "Fool! Vile and feckless fool! Why have you summoned me? You have summoned your doom!"

The man stood his ground. "You are the fool, Enrhi! You will die a fool! You killed . . . you killed Ianwyn!"

The sorcerer stopped a few paces away from the man. Darkness whirled outward from his cloak. "You are flawed," his dark voice rang out. "You are flawed more than ever I dreamed. But you will not live imperfected for long!"

Velvet darkness poured from the cloak. The vapor wrappe

itself around the man, tightening as if to squeeze the life from
his body. But with two swift strokes of the knife, the man
peeled the darkness away. It melted into the earth. The man
faced the necromancer, his eyes lidded with pain. His teeth
clenched wearily, and his knife arm swayed in the sorcerer's
wind. Only his eyes remained bright.

The man brought the dagger to bear by bracing it against
his ribs. With a grimace of surprise, the sorcerer withdrew into
his cloak, but before he could retreat, the dagger fell upon him.
Plunging forward, the man thrust the weapon up, inward into
the cape. The man's head rolled back in anguish; his golden
hair sifted backward like fire as the sorcerer began to strain
away from the force of the knife. For a moment there was only
the locked confusion of two blurred shapes.

Then the cloaked shape began to retreat with heavy steps,
hunching forward as he went. The man who had been Rhian
fell to his knees and drove his blade upward; his face darkened
and strained. A groan began that at first might be mistaken for
wind; but when the hood fell back, Marin saw that the necromancer himself was crying out. The moan sharpened to a
shriek, but although caught on the dagger, the sorcerer did not
fall further toward the earth. He merely bellowed with pain.
Marin saw then that the man's lips were twitching, that he was
saying something to the sorcerer.

The shriek, like a nightmare at dawn, vanished, and the
dark cloak settled, empty, into the dust. A wind stirred the
falling folds. Silence came, then the robe, too, melted away
like a dream. And the gloom began to lift, the gale to die, the
fog to sink soundlessly into the earth. Red fingers of morning
broke the clouds and pushed into the valley. Marin's terror
faded away. The man stood, doubled over where the cloak had
been. He dropped the dagger and slowly straightened.

Pinwy's hand, cold as snow, folded around Marin's wrist.
"Talwy," he said to her. "That is Talwy!"

"Talwy!" Marin said. It was half Pinwy's echo, half an
appeal to Talwy himself. Not a call for Talwy to come. Not
an offer of hope or comfort. Merely a plea for explanation,
even a single word.

But Talwy said nothing.

He turned his face slowly toward them; Marin read torment
in it. The face, wracked with shadow, was utterly destitute. It
was pleading, but to no one, for Talwy saw neither Marin nor

Pinwy; instead his eyes looked past them. Then he swung his face away and began to stumble toward the thorns.

Once Talwy started off, Pinwy slipped from Marin's hold. He bounded over the embers of the fire to Ianwyn's side again; she lay as still as before. "Forget Talwy!" he cried to Marin. "Come here. Ianwyn—"

Marin hesitated, her eyes lingering on the quiet form near the ashes. She glanced at Talwy, who was scrambling over the stones, toward the thorns. Quickly she stood up.

"Stay with Ianwyn," she said. "I am going to bring your brother back."

"Never mind him, Marin," Pinwy said. "Ianwyn—"

"I will be back. See to Ianwyn."

Marin started off, her legs wobbly with fear. Talwy, it seemed, was bound for the gray wall of thorns. At his approach ravens clouded from the thicket; Marin had never imagined there were so many. They flocked into the sky in droves, cawing noisily. Then instead of circling or descending again, they formed together overhead and disappeared northward over the mountain's arm.

The diminishing calls of the ravens were soon replaced by shouts, thin and strained. Marin halted and looked to the ridge. Two men ran down the slope, but toward Talwy, not toward her. The first of the two men, a version of the dark wizard in less threatening form, ran with the flutter of a white cape trailing behind him. The second man was Rhian. Looking at him now, she could not understand how she had been bewitched by Talwy's ruse, for it seemed that the two of them could not be even remotely related. Rhian's strides down the hill were strong. His face shone. His body was lightning. Talwy, on the other hand, did not seem to be human at all; he was only a shadow, a wretched, starved creature, wounded now, hobbling back toward the margins of night.

Talwy, by this time, had reached the edge of the thorn. Rhian and the other man galloped down the decline, shouting as they leaped from the ledges and over crevices. But if Talwy heard them or saw them, he gave no sign of it. He only moved on, at barely a shuffle, his gray head bent. Though it might have been her imagination, Marin thought a clot of darkness formed around him; it was as if he were blurring, fading, even as the wizard had, into the wind.

"Talwy!" she called to him. "Don't!" She was not sure what

she hoped to prevent him from doing.

Rhian, outstripping the other man, had nearly reached Talwy when he disappeared. A moment later, a thin wail, like a wisp of smoke, lifted from the earth, hung pitifully in the grip of the thorns, then, as the shadow had done before it, vanished.

A curious silence followed, a hush like the quiet of a winter morning indoors or a summer afternoon out. Sunlight flooded through a widening rift in the clouds; it drenched the valley, pouring out light that made Marin blink.

She soon reached Rhian. In spite of the sunshine, a bitter light shone in his eyes. An ugly splash of blood stained his cheek. He stood staring at something at his feet, with the man in white at his side.

He did not notice her approach, and she dared not speak to him or touch him. Instead she moved beside him. Finding that he still had not noticed her, she followed his eyes downward.

She found herself on the edge of a circle of stones. The well pit, which had always been filled with gloom, brimmed now with light from the high sun. Peering into its depths, she saw the stonework of its walls leading downward to a circular stone floor, now bathed in amber light. There, in a bright circle rimmed by shadow, lay the ragged shape of Talwy's cloak. It had fallen into a shape something like one Marin had seen in a king's hall.

"Rhian," she said, touching his elbow. "Look. In a circle."

He nodded.

"One very rarely sees the mark of the Dread Fate," she said.

The stranger looked at her. "You have no trouble identifying the sign, Marin Mont Cant," he said. "Of them all, Enrhion's sign is easiest to recognize. But Enrhion's sign can be obtained only when Enrhion is overcome, so it is won at the greatest cost." Silence followed, during which Marin heard the dry caves deep in the thorn hedge stirred by a freshening breeze. And Rhian, perhaps you will pay more for this sign than for any other. Perhaps you will pay for the seventh sign as long as you live. For each sign someone else paid almost as much as you did—Pinwy for Serron's, Marin for Fing's. But Ianwyn, who lived to pay for everything, most dearly paid for this sign. Rhian, your sister is dead."

Rhian took Marin under his arm and closed his eyes.

Epilogue

Rhian felt rain speckle his cheeks, but he did not mind, for it was gentle and fresh. It smelled of new things growing.

He might have thought moisture would make the rocks of Enrhimonte seem even blacker, but this shower seemed to be doing the opposite: the thunderclouds had rolled across the charred face of Mont Enrhi, hiding the grim cliffs, and along the foothills were places that looked almost green, as if new blades of grass, thousands of them, were pushing up among the stones. The damp earth around Rhian's feet seemed now to be loam rather than ash. It reminded Rhian of the fine farming dirt he had plowed earlier that spring.

The rain persisted, dotting his forehead. But he faced it; the sky made this moment easier for him. A week had passed, and there had been long labor during it. But still, time had not comforted his sorrow with forgetfulness. His thoughts continually drifted back to the graves at his feet.

None of the others would be able to tell, he realized, whether rain or tears had dampened his cheeks. The others. He looked back toward them. They waited patiently, faces dull and red. Oenan squeezed in each hand the rein of a horse. Their saddle were empty, ready. Though Oenan's eyes were distant, Marin' were sharp on him. He sensed her eagerness to leave this place

Turning back to the graves, he decided he was restless, too They had all been here for a long time. Every day since Ian wyn's death had stretched into an eon, until he felt he knew each detail of this place: each pebble, each thorn, each wis of mist. It seemed an age since he and Rhi had climbed to th mountain to free Oenan. It seemed years since they had du

194

these graves, since they had wrapped Ianwyn in a shroud and placed her, and Talwy's cloak beside her, in the ground. It seemed ages since earth had closed over her. It seemed ages, too, since Rhi the Bright had left them for a northward road. And that had been only this morning, just as the rain began.

A touch at his elbow startled him.

"Pinwy," he said, turning. "I didn't see you coming."

Pinwy smiled. "I didn't mean to surprise you. I . . . I don't want to hurry you, Rhian, but I do think you ought to know the horses are getting touchy. They know that their strappings mean exercise, and they have been saddled almost since dawn."

"I will come in a moment," Rhian said. He closed his eyes.

"I've had my turn here at the graves," Pinwy said. "You've been too busy for yours. I don't want to hurry you."

"I understand," Rhian said. "Miles, as you said this morning, will leave memories behind. But miles will also leave Ianwyn behind. Pinwy. Maybe you haven't realized this as I have, but when we leave this place, we may never return to it. How can we know where we will go? Even if fortune takes us back to Canys, we will be far from here. None of our errands will bring us to Enrhimonte."

Pinwy nodded slowly, gazing at the graves. "You can't be sure of that. And even if so, what good will it do to delay now? 'Tears are for the living, not the dead, and once all true tears have been shed, the rest are bled.' A great bard said that. Don't make yourself wretched for Ianwyn's sake. It has taken me time to realize it, but that isn't what she would have wanted."

Rhian found Pinwy's eyes and looked at him keenly. "If I grieve," he said, "I do not grieve for Ianwyn."

"What do you mean?"

Rhian lifted his chin. "We cannot sorrow for Ianwyn," he said in a voice near a whisper. "Ianwyn has not really died. For Ianwyn lived outside herself. She lives on in you and me. She became part of almost everyone she knew: Marin, Oenan, the servants at Fach-ne-Canys. As long as I live, I will hear her voice in the wind and see her face in the stars. No, I do not mourn for Ianwyn, though I will miss her."

Pinwy looked down. "Can you mourn for Talwy, then?"

"He is dead," Rhian said. "He lived inside himself, so his passing is final. In time, no one may remember him."

"Will you?"

"Perhaps," Rhian said, sighing. "I will remember him longer

than most. But we must pity him, just as we love Ianwyn. At least I must pity him and mourn him, for he and I were one. Do you remember how identical we were, up until the very last? Not just how we looked. How we were inside: both of us wanted to be king more than anything else—I no less than Talwy. I simply had the right to it. You remember how I prized Canys, and even put it before you and Ianwyn? Was I really any different from Talwy? Or was I only more fortunate? It was almost as if he were I on another path, as if Talwy Mont Cant was only Rhian Mont Cant in a separate body . . ."

Rhian's voice trailed off; Pinwy paled, then frowned. "I'm afraid I don't understand what you mean," he said. "That was almost as confusing as the reason Rhi gave us for leaving this morning. I've heard that explanation twice, but I still haven't gotten it straight. Living in the future and the past! I'm beginning to suspect that they are fond of being as little help as possible. Rhi did little more than break a few chains with his spells. We might as well have had no wizard at all. It would have been lovely to have him go to Fingonlain with us, though. I suppose I have gotten used to him."

"He has gone all the same," Rhian said.

"But not forever. We shall see him again, both older and younger than he is now."

Rhian sighed, then put his hand on Pinwy's shoulder and said, "Maybe we should go now. Marin will love me better for it."

Soon he helped her into the saddle, then hoisted himself up in front of her. She clasped her hands around him, and when he felt the familiar surge of muscles in the horse below him, he at last turned his eyes away from the graves.

"Sire!" Oenan said. "It feels marvelous to be on a horse again." The chestnut cantered up beside Rhian's horse then pivoted as Oenan reined her. "I can tell you that it would be a long walk to Fingonlain."

"It's a long ride as well," Marin said.

"I am not so sure of that," Pinwy said from behind Oenan. "I don't think Heithernheda is as far off as all of you keep saying." Noticing Marin's expression, he went on. "I was up before any of you this morning, and I talked with Rhi. He told me one of the reasons he was leaving us was that we would be safe before nightfall; safe, I believe he said, in linen sheets with guards at our doors—"

"If your wizard said that, he must have still been dreaming," Marin said. "We could no more reach Heithernheda by tonight than we could reach the moon by next week. *I* know, Pinwy. From Armei Nanth, Heithernheda is a good fortnight's journey. So from here, it is *at least* half that far."

"I don't think," Pinwy said, a gleam coming to his eye, "that Rhi was talking about Heithernheda at all."

An ominous silence followed; the rain slackened, then stopped. "We will find no villages in Enrhimonte, if that's what you mean," Rhian said.

"Canrhion's rise," Pinwy said. "That isn't what I mean at all. You know it. All of you should stop pretending to be ignorant. Rhian has received the last sign, the Brand of Enrhion. He has now been chosen by all the Fates!"

Oenan twisted around in the saddle to face Pinwy. "Now, stay calm, Prince Pinwy. Certainly it's an honor that your brother has earned the approval of all Seven Fates of the West. Though, if you are referring to the old prophecy, I'm afraid what you are thinking is wrong. The Fates of the West, as powerful as they are, will not hand Rhian a crown. Instead they will help him, in quiet ways, to regain the throne of Canys through the help of the High King of Fingonlain."

Pinwy threw back his head. "If you're right, Oenan," he said fiercely, "what's the use of having Fates in the first place? All we would need would be the High King of Fingonlain. I suppose it isn't your fault you can't see it. You are not, after all, a student of legend—"

"Pinwy," Rhian cautioned.

"Let me finish," Pinwy said. "Let me finish what I was going to say. Do any of you remember the prophecy?"

Oenan rolled his eyes.

"*I* remember it, no matter who else does," Pinwy said. "Let me refresh your memories!"

> "*In Rhewar of the seven thrones,*
> *The greatest king, of dust and bones,*
> *Has left an empty winter crown:*
> *With blood one shall find it,*
> *With honor shall bind it;*
> *Signs of the Seven he must win*
> *Before the Fates will set him in*
> *The Highest Throne.*"

"I still don't see how that makes any difference," Oenan muttered.

Pinwy's eyes shone. "I am not finished yet," he said. "There is another part to the prophecy that even the best minstrels often leave out."

> *"And after death of dim and bright,*
> *The Fates will weakness turn to might;*
> *Who never has sought it*
> *From cloudbanks has brought it.*
> *Deeds for Fates he will have done,*
> *A thousand simple triumphs won.*
> *The Fates will fight his battles, then."*

Rhian turned the words over and over again in his mind. *The Fates will fight his battles, then.* He had never really thought about the Fates, their signs, or the possible results of their approval. And now that he contemplated, a silver note of anticipation sounded inside him. It was something like the feeling that had come to him when he had first realized he was king of Canys, when he had taken a horse and rode into the heaths. He had looked from a barren knob over his land, into the rain, and thought of how he would make himself a good king. But the feeling now was clearer, purer; and rather than being eager for it, he was almost afraid of it. Taken off guard by a hope he did not dare quench, he held the reins more tightly in his fists. Looking along the foggy road ahead and then back at the glen, he had the sudden impression that the graves would not be as far away as he had supposed.

"Now, you have to be reasonable," Marin told Pinwy. "You shouldn't let your love of lore cloud your sense. We all understand what you mean. And, of course, it would be wonderful if all the old prophecies came true, if we traveled down the road to find the lost city of Enfach Fawr returned by the Fates. It would be wonderful if the linens your wizard talked about were sheets in the grand palace of the Adracans, and if the guards he mentioned were those from the hosts of the Adracan Legion City—"

"Stop making me seem childish!" Pinwy said. "You should not make light of prophecies, Marin, especially prophecies that are about to come true. Or already have. Have you noticed how warm it is becoming? Things are growing in Enrhimonte,

Marin. Can you feel them? I can. I think the curse the Fates placed here five hundred years ago has been lifted, that the Legion City Enfach Fawr is waiting over a few hills, waiting for the arrival of Rhian, the Fate-chosen Great King."

Marin frowned. "You're trying to make things too simple, Pinwy Mont Cant. But life, as you should have learned by now, isn't simple. Do you know what you're saying? With the hosts of Enfach Fawr, Rhian could regain the throne of Canys within a month, for all the realms of Rhewar put together could not stand against him."

"What is the throne of Canys?" Pinwy countered. "I am not talking about that at all. Have you forgotten the prophecy already? I am talking about Enfach Fawr, about the Great Throne of Rhewar!"

Rhian interrupted before Marin could reply. "Let's stop arguing and start riding," he said. He flicked the rein against the horse's neck. "If the prophecy has come true, we will find out soon enough." They urged their horses into a walk.

But Rhian could not help noticing, as the horses broke into a canter, that the morning mist above the hills ahead was tinted with a familiar color of gold.

Appendices

Appendix I • PLACES

See also the map in the front of the book.

ARMAD *see* FACH-NE-ARMAD
ARMEI southern coast realm; fifth kingdom of Rhewar
ARMEI FIRTH capital and great city of Armei; seat of the House
  Arma-ne-Ithy

BELLAIN, RIVER great river of Oerth
BELLAIN, MONTE mountains dividing Oerth
BELLAIN PASS pass between Canys and Oerth
BELLAIN VALE Bellain river valley; heartland of Oerth
BELLONBAIN capital of Oerth; seat of the House Bellyr
BRAN northernmost realm; second kingdom of Rhewar
BRANFACH great fortress of Bran; seat of the House Branmawr
BRANN, RIVER great river of Bran

CAE IENRHEWAR Gray Sea island belonging to Serhaur
CAE TAL island lost by Canys to Bran
CAE TAUR-NE-ARMA sacred island of the High Kings of Fin-
  gonlain

CAER ONE   islands off the Armei coast
CAER RHEWAR   islands in the west of Ynysandra
CANT, MONT   highest peak of Canys
CANYS   moorland realm; first kingdom of Rhewar
CAVANCAER   island of the Silver Arts

DIMMER LANDS   land of the afterlife
DREADED REALM   Enrhimonte

ENCANT, MONT   second highest peak of Canys
ENFACH FAWR   great city of Rhewar; ancestral home of the
    House Adracan and the ancient great kings of Rhewar; the
    Legion City
ENNEWAR   (ENEWAR) south
ENRHI, MONT   the Dark Mountain; highest peak in Enrhimonte
ENRHIR, MONTE   mountains of Enrhimonte
ERDA   *see* YNYSANDRA
ESERATH, MONT   mountain in southern Canys

FACH-NE-ARMAD   port city of Canys
FACH-NE-CANYS   fortress of Canys; seat of the House Mont
    Cant
FACH-NE-RHOANITH   port and great city of Serhaur; seat of the
    House Esteran
FACH WENATH   ancient port city of Canys
FINGON, MONTE   mountains dividing Armei from Fingonlain

GONOTH   province disputed between Oerth and Fingonlain
GRAY SEA   the sea east of Rhewar

HEITHERNHEDA   capital and great city of Fingonlain; seat of
    the House Tanrhiar
HEITHWR, RIVER   great river of northwest Fingonlain

IMPERIA ISLANDIUM   island confederation in southern Ynysan-
    dra

KING'S HALL   throne room of Fach-ne-Canys

MONT CANT   *see* CANT, MONT
MONT ENCANT   *see* ENCANT, MONT
MONT ENRHI   *see* ENRHI, MONT
MONT ESERATH   *see* ESERATH, MONT
MONTE BELLAIN   *see* BELLAIN, MONTE
MONTE FINGON   *see* FINGON, MONTE
MONTE SERHAUR   *see* SERHAUR, MONTE
MOUTHS OF BELLAIN   delta of the River Bellain

NEWAR   north

OERTH   central realm; sixth kingdom of Rhewar
OLD REALM ROAD   one of several ancient roadways in Rhewar

RHEWAR   west
RHEWAR   great island of the Caer Rhewar
RIVER BELLAIN   *see* BELLAIN, RIVER
RIVER BRANN   *see* BRANN, RIVER
RIVER HEITHWR   *see* HEITHWR, RIVER
ROCK OF STARS   cliff with windowlike opening near Armei
    Firth

SERHAUR   woodland realm; third kingdom of Rhewar
SERHAUR, MONTE   mountains dividing Canys and Bran from
    Serhaur
SERHAUR PASS   pass between Canys and Serhaur
SILENT SEA   sea to the south of Rhewar
SOUTH RIVER MARCH   disputed land along the Armei-Oerth
    border

THORNRAVEN HEATH   glen near Mont Enrhi

WEST, THE   home of the Fates beyond the sea
WESTERN SEA   sea to the west of Rhewar
WESTERREALM   home of the Fates beyond the sea

YNYSANDRA   the world

Appendix II • PEOPLE AND THINGS

See also Appendix III

ADRACAN House of the Great Kings of Rhewar

AMNEWYN MONT CANT wife of Elevorne Mont Cant; mother of Rhian, Talwy, Ianwyn and Pinwy

ANDER War Lord of Canys

ARADYN MONT ENCANT Mont Cant relation

ARAWYN servant at Fach-ne-Canys

ARMADON the Fifth Fate; Fate of the sea

ARMA-NE-ITHY House of the Kings of Armei

ATLANTAN THE TALL ARMA-NE-ITHY one-time King of Armei; father of Marin

AVERAN MONT ENCANT fabricated name

BELLYR House of the Kings of Oerth

BRAN the Second Fate; Fate of the moon

BRANMAWR House of the Kings of Bran

CALDWY BRANMAWR King of Bran

CANHAWR THE ELDER MONT CANT fifth King of Canys

CANHAWR THE YOUNGER MONT CANT   sixth King of Canys
CANRHION   the First Fate; Fate of the sun
CANWYN   wife of Dorhwy-ne-Fach
CANWYN MONT CANT   mother of Canhawr the Elder daughter of Dorhan the Golden
CERICAN ARMA-NE-ITHY   King of Armei
CORBIN I   son of Canhawr the Elder
CORBIN II MONT VENDRA   son of Corbin I; founder of the House Mont Encant
CRESCENT KNIGHTS   the personal guard of the king of Bran

DORAN OERGANT   lord of Bran
DORHAN I THE GOLDEN MONT CANT   second King of Canys
DORHAN II MONT CANT   third King of Canys
DORHAN III ELEVORNE   fourth King of Canys
DORHAN HAMMERHAND   *see* DORHAN I
DORHWY-NE-FACH   founder of the House Mont Cant

ELEVORNE MONT CANT   eighth King of Canys; father of Rhian, Talwy, Ianwyn, and Pinwy
EMRHIN SEAMAN   husband of Canwyn Mont Cant
ENFATH   servant at Fach-ne-Canys
ENGOTH OF THE GUARD   Armein warrior
ENRHI THE DARK   sorcerer
ENRHION   the Seventh Fate; Fate of death and darkness
ERD   the Sixth Fate; Fate of earth and stone
ERIEL   servant at Fach-ne-Canys
ESPAN   War Lord of Bran
ESTERAN   House of the Kings of Serhaur

FATES   guardians of Ynysandra
FATES OF THE WEST   seven immortal guardians of Rhewar
FING   the Fourth Fate; Fate of fire and love

GENEVER MONT CANT   wife of Canhawr the Elder

HOUSE   *see* ADRACAN, ARMA-NE-ITHY, BELLYR, BRANMAWR ESTERAN, MONT CANT, MONT ENCANT, OERGANT, TANRHIAR

IANBRIN BRANMAWR   brother of Caldwy Branmawr; lord of the
   Crescent Knights
IANWY MONT CANT   seventh King of Canys
IANWY MONT CANT   son of King Rhian
IANWYN MONT CANT   princess of Canys
IENAN   groom at Fach-ne-Canys

LAST FATE   *see* ENRHION
LETH MONT CANT   wife of Canhawr the Younger
LYRWYN MONT CANT   wife of Dorhan II

MAERON   the Windfate
MAGIC-SON   *see* TALWY MONT CANT
MARIN ARMA-NE-ITHY   heir princess of Armei
MARMADAN ESTERAN   King of Serhaur
MEB OF OERTH   wife of Ianwy Mont Cant
MERICAN ARMA-NE-ITHY   son of Cerican Arma-ne-Ithy; Prince
   of Armei
MERTA   servant at Fach-ne-Canys
MIRIEL   servant at Fach-ne-Canys
MONT CANT   House of the Kings of Canys
MONT ENCANT   noble House of North Canys

OENAN-NE-FACH   counselor to Rhian Mont Cant
OERGANT   noble House of North Bran
OLYDYN OF FINGONLAIN   wife of Dorhan I the Golden

PINWY MONT CANT   Prince of Canys
PRIEST OF THE SEVENTH FATE   *see* ENRHI THE DARK

RHAN   servant at Fach-ne-Canys
RHI THE BRIGHT   enchanter
RHIAN MONT CANT   ninth King of Canys

SEER OF DARKNESS   *see* ENRHI THE DARK
SERENIEL BRANMAWR   heir princess of Bran
SERRON   the Third Fate; Fate of stars and knowledge
SEVEN FATES   *see* FATES OF THE WEST

TALANWYN ESTERAN   ancient King of Serhaur
TANRHIAR   House of the High Kings of Fingonlain
TORAN   counselor to Elevorne and Rhian Mont Cant

VENDRA   wife of Corbin I Mont Cant

WAR LORD   *see* ANDER
WINTER WARS   the great wars that followed the death of the
    last Adracan king

APPENDIX III • THE HOUSE MONT CANT

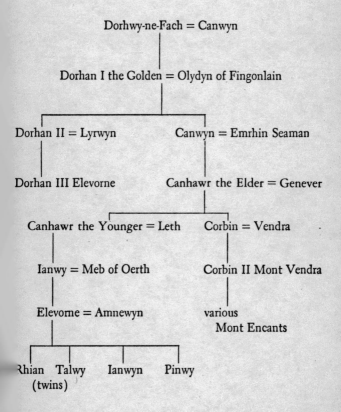

Dorhwy-ne-Fach = Canwyn

Dorhan I the Golden = Olydyn of Fingonlain

Dorhan II = Lyrwyn   Canwyn = Emrhin Seaman

Dorhan III Elevorne   Canhawr the Elder = Genever

Canhawr the Younger = Leth   Corbin = Vendra

Ianwy = Meb of Oerth   Corbin II Mont Vendra

Elevorne = Amnewyn   various
                                   Mont Encants

Rhian Talwy   Ianwyn   Pinwy
(twins)

Do you dream of dragons? Would you like to work magic?
Or travel between worlds in the blink of an eye?
Would you like to see faeries dance,
or the place where baby unicorns are born?

COME ON A

MAGICQUEST™

*In these magical adventures
for kids from eight to eighty from
Tempo MagicQuest Books:*

____	82630-X	**TULKU #5** *Peter Dickinson*	$2.25
____	16621-0	**THE DRAGON HOARD #6** *Tanith Lee*	$2.25
____	31906-8	**THE HAWKS OF FELLHEATH #7** *Paul R. Fisher*	$2.25
____	51562-2	**THE MAGIC THREE OF SOLATIA #8** *Jane Yolen*	$2.25
____	67630-8	**POWER OF THREE #9** *Diana Wynne Jones*	$2.25
____	67918-8	**THE PRINCESS AND THE THORN #10** *Paul R. Fisher*	$2.25
____	81205-8	**TIME PIPER #11** *Delia Huddy*	$2.25
____	51556-8	**MAGICIANS OF CAPRONA #12** *Diana Wynne Jones*	$2.25
____	79591-9	**TALKING TO DRAGONS #13** *Patricia C. Wrede*	$2.25

Prices may be slightly higher in Canada.